I0585990

CELINE L. A. SIMPSON

Convincing Florence

Copyright © 2023 by Celine L. A. Simpson

All rights reserved. No part of this publication may be reproduced, stored or transmitted in any form or by any means, electronic, mechanical, photocopying, recording, scanning, or otherwise without written permission from the publisher. It is illegal to copy this book, post it to a website, or distribute it by any other means without permission.

This novel is entirely a work of fiction. The names, characters and incidents portrayed in it are the work of the author's imagination. Any resemblance to actual persons, living or dead, events or localities is entirely coincidental.

Celine L. A. Simpson asserts the moral right to be identified as the author of this work.

Celine L. A. Simpson has no responsibility for the persistence or accuracy of URLs for external or third-party Internet Websites referred to in this publication and does not guarantee that any content on such Websites is, or will remain, accurate or appropriate.

Designations used by companies to distinguish their products are often claimed as trademarks. All brand names and product names used in this book and on its cover are trade names, service marks, trademarks and registered trademarks of their respective owners. The publishers and the book are not associated with any product or vendor mentioned in this book. None of the companies referenced within the book have endorsed the book.

First edition

ISBN: 978-0-6451611-3-7

Editing by Joeli Woodrow
Illustration by Ashley Quick
Cover art by Murphy Rae

This book was professionally typeset on Reedsy.
Find out more at reedsy.com

For Lara.

To find a light that shines brighter than you would be a task impossible to accomplish.
May you always know how brilliantly you shine, and how lovely you are.

Acknowledgement

Wow, alright.

You'd think I would be somewhat proficient at writing these by now; but alas, I am not.

I love this story, and it wouldn't be what it is without my editor, Joeli. You constantly battle my waves of overthinking, anxiety, and most of all, you make me a better storyteller. This time around was different from MTME (Music to my Ears), you are a mother (an incredible one. Hey Buff, it's me! Your Fauntie! (friend-auntie/fun-auntie take your pick)), a business owner of a shop that continues to grow and flourish (www.bookofthewick.com, check it out), and still you make time for me, for this, for our daily messages. I hope I never have to do this without you.

Brad. The last time I published a book you were my partner, but now you're my fiancé! No matter the years that pass, you're still as excited for me as you were when I published my first book. Thank you for never complaining while you're trying to sleep beside me and I'm typing away, refusing to turn off the light, and for buying copies of my books to support me even though we already have a stack of them at home.

And to you, the person reading this. It's still mind blowing to know that there are, in fact, people reading this. You make my dreams come true with every word your eyes scan. Thank you, thank you, thank you.

1

Chapter 1

I had spent the last ten minutes not doing any work at all. To the untrained eye – and the untrained ear – you wouldn't have been able to tell that.

What I had been doing was, in fact, tapping out the tune of a song I'd been listening to on the way into work, with only the clicker of my computer mouse. Not many people would know this, but it's not the easiest task to undertake, especially when I had set the difficulty level of this exercise to *extreme*. It was like my own version of *Tap Tap Revenge*, and I was consistently number one on the charts.

I'd just completed a faultless rendition of the newest hit by my favourite band *Lady Luck* when I was pulled from my victory.

"Florence." Melissa practically yelled at me from where she lingered in the doorway behind my desk.

"Sorry," I mumbled. She merely frowned, clearly put off by the need to repeat herself.

"I said, the read-along for the children finished up five minutes ago at the back. Their book cart should be ready

1

to go back on the shelves."

"Oh, yep. On it!" I jumped up with so much enthusiasm that Melissa had all but forgotten my previous (minor) offence and walked back into her cluttered little office with a satisfied smile on her face.

I blew out a breath with a little more force than necessary in an effort to dissolve some of the irritation that had bubbled to the surface from the brief interaction. I loved my job, but sometimes Melissa and I clashed and it was all I could do not to scream into my purse.

The short walk from the front desk – my desk – to the back of the library where the reading corner lived, was all it took to forget Melissa; although I obviously wouldn't forget her for long. Most of the time we got on with our days in a comfortable silence, she would usually keep her office door shut, and I would pretend I couldn't hear her own personal renditions of every song from *The Greatest Showman* soundtrack.

Sure, it was a system with flaws, but didn't every system, no matter what for, or where it applied in one's life, have flaws?

The best part about the 4 p.m. reading session was that they were tidy and thoughtful. They always put their pillows back in the pillow corner, beanbags in the beanbag corner, and books on the book cart.

I smiled to myself and pushed the cart towards the direction of the children's picture books. The reading session was for littlies between the darling ages of four and six years old. They were still at the age where their mischief was cute and their taunts were funny. They were also shockingly and scarily insightful, and full of that childhood wisdom we all lose at some time in our tweens.

Don't act like you don't know what I'm talking about. You know, those conversations where they would give you some very simple, yet incredibly on point advice, you'd look at them, ruffle their hair, and say 'Don't worry, you'll learn when you get older', and then you spend the rest of the day thinking on their little words and how right they actually were.

I started to place the books back in their rightful homes on the shelf. For the most part, the books would come back in the same condition as when they were picked up. I was a stickler for any person, who, regardless of their reading level, respected their literature.

"Oh, my god." I was already dry heaving, "Oh, my." Another one.

I had picked up a copy of *The Jungle Book* and placed my hand in what I could only identify as a fluro green booger. It was in moments like this that I actually thought I was going to die.

I started to furiously wipe my hand on the carpet beneath me, having fallen to it in a dramatic, completely unflattering weakening of the knees thanks to my pencil skirt. I mumbled to myself in a sort of calm hysteria, "Please just let it be slime. *Please just let it be slime.*"

It wasn't slime.

I had worked in this library for the last three years, and I had placed my hand directly into a puddle of boogers at least twice a year without fail. But my last incident had only been a month ago, and thankfully there had been no one around that time either to witness what I honestly thought was a perfectly reasonable amount of *eugh*.

I just hadn't expected it to happen again so soon. I was giving myself at least another few months; right before

Christmas was when I'd mentally scheduled to prepare myself for round two of 'Florence versus baby-boogers'.

I had just caught the way the slime-booger had spider-webbed over the carpet where I'd furiously eradicated its presence from my skin, causing another dry heave – that was probably just a little too close to the real thing for my comfort levels – when I heard Melissa call me back to the front of the library by using the oh-so-infuriating *ding* of the reception bell.

I mumbled a frustrated string of curses under my breath as I tried to get up (without tearing the seam in the back of my pencil skirt) in the most lady-like way. Needless to say, the journey back to my feet was not flattering at all, regardless of how good I looked in the just-below-the-knee length, navy ensemble. Just picture someone trying to keep their lower half as straight as possible to the point where they were in a sort of downward facing dog position and had to caterpillar-walk their hands towards their feet. If you could do that, then you could visualise what had just happened, though any mostly sane person may choose to avoid that particular image.

I quickly put the rest of the books away, grabbing the spines in a pinching motion and checking the covers front and back before sliding them back into their places on the shelves. Thankfully, there wasn't that much to put back and I didn't come across any more boogers.

Melissa was hovering by the customer side of the front desk, waiting for me to get back. I swear, she never left the protective cubicle that was the reception and office space area of the library. Every time she was faced with speaking to anyone other than me, the whites of her eyes became uncomfortably visible and she scurried off like she had forgotten how badly she needed the toilet, or the copier machine, or to be literally anywhere else in the library. That might be the only time she left the reception space, and even then, I had a theory that she pretended to be a visitor when she was on the floor to avoid having to do any real work.

I sort of got it though, I also avoided people at all costs. Everyone except for my Grandmother Dorothy. My Dot.

"Florence, you need to stay back and dust today," Melissa said without meeting my eyes and smoothing out the wrinkles of her peplum top.

She always insisted that we took turns. She would dust one week, I would dust another. Huge shocker to know that Melissa didn't dust at all.

I tried to keep my face as placid as possible, so as to not let my scowl show. "Sorry, I can't today Melissa, I'm cooking dinner for my grandmother," I finished the sentence off with a smile.

"Your grandmother?" Her tone was borderline incredulous, like Dot had suddenly appeared out of nowhere. Melissa knew Dot existed because she constantly took advantage of the tray of cookies I brought in weekly, courtesy of the most generous woman to have ever lived.

"Yes, Melissa. You know Dot." I started to move around the desk to begin packing up my things. The library would still be open for a couple more hours, but I wasn't closing today. "I'll do it tomorrow, after I close up for the day."

"Alright, I suppose that would be fine," she nodded to herself with a frown.

And just because I couldn't help myself, I shimmied a toe just over the line of smartass. "You could always dust after you close up today?"

Melissa snapped her head in my direction with a disbelieving look on her face.

I let out a small sigh before I could stop it's escape, "I'll do it tomorrow."

"Tomorrow is good, I'm pretty sure I dusted last, anyway." She shrugged.

I just nodded my head even though I knew that was a big fat lie. My day to day with Melissa was honestly the most human interaction I had in my life with someone other than my grandmother and it was exhausting. It was a reminder of why I was really better off only just sharing my time with my Dot. It just took *so much energy* and it was never really worth it.

I was a firm believer that energy was something that comes with a bit of a give and take. However, something happened along the timeline of my life that I realised I seemed to be giving more than I was getting. When I had that realisation, it sucked big *big* balls.

Anyone I had ever met was always in the business of taking. Taking my time, my money, my love - even taking my lunch - all without a 'thank you, Florence' or an 'I owe you one, Florence', or even a 'next time we will focus on you Floss, I promise!'

You might be thinking that maybe I've just chosen the wrong crowds? That's exactly what Dot said, and Dot was full of a multitude of life lessons that she was passing on to me daily, but I found it hard to believe that there really was such a thing as the 'wrong crowd'. My working theory was that I was born a little too early. Maybe three or four years, that's all. But it was enough to throw a spanner in the works. That 'spanner' being that the minutes of my life consistently collided with the bad minutes of someone else's. Okay, maybe not 'bad'... but perhaps inconvenient?

Those pockets in your day, your week, your month, your *life* that your vibe had dropped or you'd gotten bad news, or you missed your train, or you were working through something that wasn't a quick fix. You had plans and dreams and all your energy needed to go towards *that*, no one and nothing else.

That was when I seemed to form friendships, bump into random strangers, or take a leap of faith and strike up a conversation with someone in the baking aisle of my local corner store, or - and this could totally be dramatic - that was when I'd even made my grand appearance into this world. I was *born* in one of those pockets of time, and every moment since has forced me to believe something that I couldn't forget.

That people just simply weren't worth my time for the simple reason that they'd always let me down. Who sanely subjected themselves to that kind of constant heartache? Who woke up every morning and thought, 'Bring on the pain of disappointment, day, I'm ready for my remaining nugget of hope to fizzle away like a fart on the wind'.

But what about Dot, Florence? I'm glad you asked. Dot was a giver, a free loving, gift to the earth. The only conclusion I came to on why she was so different to everyone else, was that she had lived her life, and lived it to the fullest. So she never felt the need to be anything but kind, and she was the only person who'd never let me down. I had a whole lifetime of actions from Dot that spoke louder than any words. Even though her words were awesome too.

My system of approaching life was that I was better off alone. It was a good system, a system with no holes, probably the only system in existence to be without flaws. It was perfect.

I collected my things from my desk and dumped them unceremoniously into my handbag. My body curled in on itself a little as the library door flung open like its hinges were no longer meant for this world, the wind that trailed in after the fact brought a loud, baritone laugh that immediately soaked up the silence of the library.

Why do I even spend time printing out the rules of the library and sticking them all over the place if people won't bother to read them? *Probably because you have a bit of a stick up your ass, Florence.*

I rolled my eyes at myself - not an uncommon occurrence - and mumbled goodbye to Melissa. I was just glad that at least I avoided the confrontation of letting that man-child (because who even bangs doors open like that?) know that he was in violation of a butt-load of library rules. I was off to the best part of my week; dinner with Dot.

Chapter 2

Dot's house was my favourite place in the entire world.

It was baby yellow on the outside, with a white arch you needed to walk under to move through the front gate. Dot mentioned that a lot of her friends said it looked dated and uncared for, but it was cared for so much that Dot couldn't even fathom changing the colour.

Dot had bought the inner city dwelling before I was even born. When it was just her and my mother, and she was still just a kid. The block was big but the house was small and cosy. Most of the space was taken by the gardens that bordered it. Dot loved to garden, and her garden showed its love back by flourishing.

I kicked my shoes off on the porch before letting myself into the unlocked house.

"Just me, Dot," I called out, making my way to the small kitchen to unpack the bag of groceries I had picked up for us after I'd finished work.

A shuffling noise that got gradually louder as it entered the kitchen was the only notice I got that Dot was home and well.

I pulled myself out of the fridge after putting away the ingredients for a salad and closed the door to take in the sight of my grandmother. She wore some flowy grey linen pants with a pair of Crocs that were lined with wool, and a white shirt she had paired with one of her many Hawaiian patterned button-downs that she picked up from the thrift store. Her hair was grey, but tipped with bright blue bits, and she wore a pair of mismatched earrings; a surfboard on one side, and a palm tree on the other.

Believe it or not, Dot had toned it down today on the outfit. This was her 'causal, not going anywhere, just staying around the house' get up, and I loved it.

"Oh, Flossy. Hello, my darling girl." She continued to shuffle towards me with her arms spread open in the most inviting fashion.

I felt my face immediately soften. Every hard exterior and protective mask I donned for the day melted away as Dot wound her arms around me and pulled me close. She smelt like citrus and freshly cut grass.

"Hey, Dotty. How was your day?" I planted a kiss on the top of her head. "Is frozen lasagna okay?" I reached to take it out of the freezer before she had answered because I knew—

"Of course, my favourite!" She interrupted my thought before it had even finished forming, not to mention it was what we had every week.

I felt a smile automatically move into place at her enthusiasm. There was nothing like the energy that exuded from my grandmother. She tackled most things in life with the energy felt in a football stadium after a winning goal.

Turning around and out of my embrace, she shuffled back to where she had been in the house before I'd arrived. I would like to point out that the shuffling was completely unnecessary. Dot walked everywhere and when people weren't watching, I would wager that she secretly ran from destination to destination. She was more than capable, Dot was probably the most capable person I had ever met.

Standing at a petite 5'2", her blue tipped hair was fashioned in a pixie cut. For Dot, blue was the colour of the moment, but her hair had been orange and purple and green. She was fun but serious, loud but mindful, gentle but fierce. She was my best and only friend.

It had always been Dot and I, and I had never cared to know more about why that was exactly. Sure, I went through periods in my adolescence where I had wondered about dear old mum and dad, where they were, and why they weren't here with me. But everything I needed to know, I already did.

I knew that they had me young, but how young I wasn't too sure. Young enough that it would have impacted their plans and life and dreams. Which is why they often left me here, with Dot.

The house used to be covered, and I mean *covered* in photos of them. They were everywhere. Constantly being forced to stare at the people who knew enough about life to do the deed that brought me into existence, but clearly didn't know quite enough to understand that the repercussions of those thrusts and fab-feels resulted in a chubby, brown eyed, brown haired baby that would need love, attention, and time.

I decided enough was enough. I didn't need the constant reminder of my accidental arrival at the wrong time of their lives, so I took every photo out of every frame and replaced them with photos of Dot and me. She hadn't been mad when she realised what I'd done, the look on her face had been more sad than anything. She never put the photos back up and I hadn't seen a snapshot since.

I was an accident they followed through with. But whatever responsibility they felt they had didn't continue on into my life. There were places they would rather have been than with me, and those actions spoke thousands.

Dot had always said, "When you want the answers to your questions, Flossy, I will be happy to give them."

Every time she said that, I said I already knew what I needed to know.

"You've twisted those words, Florence Valentine, and you know it." Dot would say after I listed out all the things I already knew. But I didn't twist anything. I just took off the rose coloured glasses that Dot laid over the very same words when she told them to me. I spoke them without the sugar and the sparkle that was often sprinkled over the top of sad stories about young parents and accidental pregnancies.

There had been a few times over the years as I grew that I seriously thought about asking Dot more about them, about trying to fill whatever gaps I had. To see if filling those gaps with the information she had would somehow make me feel better about it all.

It made me think a lot about what the answers would do for me if I did know. Would they make me sad or happy? Would they make me feel loved or lost? I felt both happy *and* loved in my life with Dot, I couldn't imagine anyone else I'd rather have as my true north other than her.

Whatever.

It didn't really matter, anyway.

Growing up with someone like Dot as your parental figure could only be summed up in a single word: exciting. It was a kaleidoscope of colours, trying new things all the time, and let's not forget the dancing. There was one week when I was twelve where she insisted we begin every meal with an adjective from a different language. I now know how to say 'enjoy' in seven different languages.

The words 'exciting' and 'colourful' didn't just apply to the good times though. Every lesson that Dot taught me came with an experience of the consequences of the act I was committing.

I will let that sink in for a moment. Actually, let me just paint a clear picture for you: The first and last time I ever smoked pot was in my bedroom, only to have Dot sniff it out from what I was sure was a mile away because I had been so positive she wasn't in the house when I had lit the thing up. Then, when I had finished coughing my way through the first exhale, there she was; a face of shock and horror standing in the threshold of my bedroom. It turned out she *had* been home, and I had just been a massive idiot. Anyway, that little escapade saw me spending the better part of a school night sitting in a little holding cell of the local police station.

Dot knew absolutely everyone, so when she had dragged a sobbing sixteen year old Florence into the police station, wearing nothing more than my Mickey Mouse summer pyjamas and announced that I was to be locked up for a 'crime', not a single person questioned her.

Did I mention that whilst Dot dragged me from my room to the car, she had snatched the poorly rolled joint from my hand and proceeded to smoke it herself?

So yes, life with Dot was 'exciting' to put it mildly.

As the years moved on, Dot mellowed out, and I simply settled on the realisation that not everyone was like my grandmother.

The tender teenage years of my life seemed to come and go faster than they felt at the time, and then one day, boom; I was twenty-one and every year up to that point had reaffirmed the lesson my parents taught me as their parting gift. People were always going to let you down, and I'd be better off keeping to myself.

It's been seven years since that day and still, nothing's changed.

To avoid the inevitable moment when I would eventually need something back from a friend, a boyfriend, just *anyone*. When my giving would run out, my cup would be empty, and I'd need the reassuring words back. The time I had given freely and without an agenda. I'd need to feel special to someone else, to feel wanted and loved only to trust-fall back and have no one to catch me. I've left a sprawling mess on the ground, watching them walk away from me with nothing but a heart full of disappointment, shrivelled hope, and a sore ass from the graceless landing. That if I could just find a way to avoid it all together, I'd be better off.

Dot had always said to me, "Where you invest your love, Floss, you invest your life." She was constantly throwing these ingenious nuggets of Dotty-wisdom at me, and for some reason, this one was one of the ones that stuck. Burrowing deep and staying put.

I invested my love into Dot, and into my job. I invested it into dinners together in my childhood home, and in going for runs before the sun had come up just so I could see the sky change colour before I headed to work. I did *not* invest it into people. People would always let you down in the end, and in my books, that painted everyone with a pretty sucky brush.

You're probably wondering why that is? Probably thinking 'that Florence seems like a bit of a bitch'? Yeah, well, I wish it wasn't the case. And look, I'm not totally inept that I can't accept there would be other people who would be equal in Dot's kindness, and love, and general ability to give; but my experience has been that they're hard to find. So, by painting everyone with the same aforementioned sucky brush, I was just covering all my bases. It was a shitty way to live when I thought about it too much, so I didn't. I got on with my days and let down all my walls behind closed doors.

Dot had then piped up and asked me the tough question, "What if it's you, Florence? And not them?"

I had thought about that for a long time, I really and truly did, and I'd decided that if it *was* me, if I was the reason for all the bad luck, that the poor timing of my arrival earthside had somehow cursed me, then I was still better off; and perhaps, so were they.

Cue the mini violin now, eugh. How did we even get onto this subject? I'd lived this way for a very long time and I was happy.

As if she was summoned, Dot walked back into the kitchen (walked, not shuffled…See? I told you) just as the timer *dinged* letting us know the lasagna had been cooked.

The little salad I had thrown together was already placed on the table, and after a joint 'enjoy' in French, or what I was sure by now was a very loose transition and most definitely not articulated correctly, we tucked in.

"So," I started, "top three things that happened to you today?"

"I planted tulips in the garden, rearranged the furniture in

15

my bedroom, and had you over for dinner."

"You rearranged the furniture again? What was wrong with the last setup?"

"I kept hitting my hip on the corner of the vanity." She made a face for which I reciprocated because we all knew that feeling and, to put it lightly, it fucking stunk.

"You?" she asked around a very large bite of food.

"I had a good run this morning, dinner with you, and when I left work today I avoided needing to reprimand another civilian for breaking about a zillion library rules."

Dot tipped her head back in a laugh that screamed 'I love you despite the stick up your ass' and all I could do was grin back at her.

"Oh, something super gross happened today," I said, scrunching my nose up and shovelling more lasagna into my mouth.

Dot's raised eyebrows were my only prompt to continue, so I told her all about the booger from the children's book to which the most realistic *gag* sound I'd ever heard escaped my grandmother. It made me laugh so much I inhaled a bit of lettuce and then ended up coughing for the better part of five minutes to which Dot insisted on performing the Heimlich. It was only when I threatened I'd piss myself from laughing did she stop.

The night ended as it always did, with a bit of extremely uncoordinated dancing (only on my part though, Dot could bust a move). Growing up, it sort of just became a thing. Another Dotty-wisdom passed onto me was that, "There isn't a situation that couldn't be made better with a shimmy." How true that was I couldn't say, but it never let us down.

I got up and turned on the speakers, pressing play on

whatever CD she had in and *Brown Eyed Girl* by Van Morrison filled the air. Dot shuffled into the living room (obviously she had forgotten about this act when she'd rushed towards the smell of lasagna) and once in position, she grabbed my hand and spun me. It was my suspicion that she shuffled so people wouldn't ask her to do anything, because she could shake her hips, that was for sure. We continued to spin and twirl, singing as loud as we could.

When the song came to an end, Dot walked up to me and took my face in her hands, "You have such a beautiful smile, Flossy. I wish you would do it more outside of the house."

My smile faltered a little at that, but I planted a kiss on her cheek before she could notice, "I think you're the only one who thinks that, Dot," I joked back to her.

"I don't think that's true, there is someone out there for you and I know it." She patted my cheek gently.

"I agree, and that person is standing right here." I poked her side.

She swatted at me as I made my way back to the kitchen to start packing up.

"Florence," Dot called in warning, but I waved her off.

"You're all I need, Dot." I gave her another smile over my shoulder, knowing she wanted to say something else, but held off.

Eventually we swapped places and I moved to tidy the rest of the house. Dot dried the dishes and put them away, all whilst singing a song she had loved growing up. one of many in her repertoire that she had long since forgotten the name of.

I left my grandmother dozing on the couch as I made my way to leave, the lure of my own home and my very big bathtub calling my name.

Just as I had finished tugging on my sneakers Dot called out from her spot in the living room, "I love you more than yesterday, Floss!"

The very same thing she had said to me every day since forever.

"Not nearly as much as I'll love you tomorrow," I called back, before locking up the house and heading to the train station.

3

Chapter 3

Fridays were usually sublime for a number of reasons. There was, of course, the standard TGIF and the endless possibilities of two whole days spent in pasta stained sweats and lounging on the couch. Then there was also the fact that on Fridays, I had the library all to myself.

For all the crap I tossed at Melissa, I knew she wasn't so bad and that she was likely a different person outside of work. Regardless, it didn't change the stone cold truth that Fridays were better because it was just me, alone with all the books.

The last day of the week was usually a bit of a bustling day, people in and out, grabbing books for the weekend, or dropping off stacks from the week that just passed. Today? Well, today was...uninspired? Bland? Shit? It took forever for the clock hand to make its way from start to finish, and due to the lack of any real work I had to do today, as well as the abysmal amount of motivation I embodied to try and tackle another song in my computer mouse rendition of *Tap Tap Revenge,* everything just dragged.

The moment the minute hand ticked over to 5:30 p.m. I

stood up with far too much enthusiasm. My chair rolled away as if glad to be rid of my ass, if only for a moment. I moved around the desk to head to the supply closet where we kept all the cleaning supplies in preparation for the dusting that honestly could have been done at any time of the day, considering how quiet it was.

I moved through the library in a routine known to me as well as I knew my way around my grandmother's house. Setting books back in their rightful places and tucking chairs back under desks, dusting as I went. I stopped when I got back to my desk which lived right in the middle of the library. It sat in front of the entry doors, all open, modern, and welcoming. Half of the library spanned to the left of it, and the other half to the right.

I could tell by some quiet whispers and keyboard tapping that we still had a few occupants in the part of the library that stretched out in front of my desk. So, in the meantime, I decided to put together some last minute stacks people had sent through to request for pick up in the next twenty minutes before the library closed at 6 p.m.

There was something far too entertaining about prepping people's library pick up orders. I felt like sometimes they forgot that there was a person who ran around and collected their books before they came in. If I had to put a number to it, I would say it was probably four times better than people watching, if you were intrigued by that sort of thing. The things that you learnt about someone simply by their library click-and-collect was fascinating.

Some people were incredibly boring, others were very, very horny, and then there were the middle-dwellers. Those who had a good mixture of all things across the board of whatever genres they were occupying their time reading or studying with.

I smiled a polite goodbye to the group of students that had packed up and were on their way out, gathering up my cleaning supplies to head for the other side of the library. At this rate, I could give myself an early mark if the last minute pickups were on time.

As per my usual routine, I had just started at the beginning of the section which stretched out in front of my desk when my entire body jerked with an odd mixture of fright and surprise that had my heart rate pick up twice its normal speed, and I was honestly pretty confident I peed myself a little.

A booming laugh cut through the thick heaviness that had set in around my thoughts of taking off my shoes and ordering in Thai food to celebrate the end of the week. It wasn't all too familiar, but I was *sure* I had heard it before.

Clutching the dirty rag to my chest, I peeked through the shelf in front of me. I'd genuinely thought there was no one left in the library and took a moment to count my small blessing that I hadn't started blurting out a melody as I often did. Not that I was concerned about offending the ears of my could-be murderer.

Florence, you need to have bigger ovaries than this.

Straightening up my blouse, I dropped the rag to the floor and made my way around the shelves, following the sound of the invasive laughter that had dribbled off into breathy huffs.

He sat on one of the study tables that lived in between some of the shelves, leaning back on one hand whilst he held an open book in the other. A smirk of entertainment cast over his face as he read the floppy paperback. *This* was the man-child from yesterday. The one whose library rule violation reprimanding I had gloated to Dot about avoiding.

This is what you get, Florence. Next time, have a little humility.

I opened my mouth to inform him that we were closing very, very soon, but just as the first syllable left my tongue he let out another unrestrained cackle, throwing his head back in the process. The whole ordeal made me jump, again. (Thankfully, no pee this time.)

I watched on as he attempted to compose himself before clearing my throat.

His eyes flicked up to meet mine as he moved the hand he had been leaning on to hold up his pointer finger to me in a motion that clearly requested me to 'give him one minute'.

Is he really holding up his finger in my face? It wasn't the worst of the five digits to receive but I would say it was a runner up.

Not only was today already not at its usual standard of Friday-Goodness but this late-dweller hooligan *knew* I had been standing there, and he was purposely ignoring me.

Lovely. Way to make a girl feel real special.

I really shouldn't be surprised, he was a clear representation of yet another person who reaffirmed the need for my system. I didn't even know him and he'd let me down in the most basic of librarian-to-library-member relationships.

It took a good portion of my willpower not to stomp my foot and throw my shoe at the guy. Instead, I opted to clear my throat again, because even though I expected disappointment, I hoped for the opposite, and I wasn't beyond giving him the benefit of the doubt.

He snapped the book shut with what I would say was a little too much force to be respectful of the literature that was clearly giving him so much joy. He then proceeded to drop it on the table (that he was still sitting on, mind you) from a distance that I would absolutely deem far too high to be appropriate. Not to mention the *noise*.

Of all the things to be concerned about I quickly made a mental note to add '*do not drop books from any height onto any surface, simply place them down once you have finished reading*' to the library rules.

Oh yes, that's why he dropped the book, Florence. He didn't read it as a rule! Of course. That all makes so much sense now.

The worst part though, is that he did both of those things *after* doggy earring a page ever so slightly, in a move I didn't even think he knew I saw. This stranger was breaking my heart, but *why?*

You might be thinking, '*Florence, there's no one in the library, the sound is of no consequence.*' Yes, well he doesn't know that, does he? *And* he totally manhandled a book under my care. I couldn't let him just get away with that. What sort of librarian would I be if I did?

It was moments like these when I felt it would be powerful for me to have a badge of some kind. To be able to thrust that sort of thing right into his personal space bubble. He would quake, I knew he would.

Folding his arms across his broad chest, he looked at me expectantly.

"Sir, you cannot sit on the tables, it's against the rules of this library. We are also," I moved to look at my watch, "about twelve minutes away from closing, so if you wouldn't mind…"

I didn't finish my sentence entirely, but the implication was clear. I also desperately wished I hadn't taken off my blue light glasses before leaving my desk. This guy could use a little grounding that came from a sneer delivered over the top of glasses. It would also have been ideal to have had a little more of an authoritative presence. As he stood to his full height, it became increasingly clear that I was far smaller than he was.

Really wish I had that badge right about now.

Had he been that big when he was sitting down? I dragged my eyes back up to his face.

"The rules? I don't see them written anywhere," he said, glancing around as though he was looking for a sign.

I looked around too, seeing about three posters from where we were standing that had '*Library Rules*' in big, bold letters across the top. I looked back to him then gestured to the walls around us with a bewildered expression. He just shrugged.

He shrugged! And he did it with this little smile on his face that made my lady bits do a few things they hadn't been given permission to do.

We'll be having a talk about this later.

I rubbed my hand down my face to help myself recover from the fact that this person had made me scared enough to pee, mad enough to want to stomp my feet like an overgrown toddler, and now made me question the good sense of my own vagina.

I met his eyes again, "I can get you a pamphlet from the front on your way out if you'd like?" It came out snappier than intended, but this guy had weaselled under my skin and I could feel the flush creeping onto my face as the seconds ticked on.

"That won't be necessary, thank you," he leaned in to peer at my name tag, "Florence. I will refrain from sitting on your tables during my future reading sessions."

I knew he was trying to get a response from me by his reference to them being *my* tables, but I was rise above it. I would rise so far above it that he would be forced to look me in the eye instead of peering down at me like a child.

The gleam in his eyes told me he was clearly enjoying this interaction so I did what any practical jokester hated, I wouldn't give him the satisfaction of knowing he was making an impact.

I decided to turn around and cast my final words over my shoulder (the only power move I had in my arsenal). "We're closed, so if I could please ask you to leave, it would be most appreciated."

One point to Florence. Zero points to book man-handler-rule-breaker.

"Of course you can ask, Florence." The humour in his voice was evident and it stopped me in my tracks, causing me to turn back to face him as he continued, "But, there is still another five minutes left on the clock before 6 p.m.," he pointed to a clock on the wall to the left, clearly having no issue seeing things hung about on the library walls now, "and I would like to spend that time speaking to you." He moved that accusatory finger he had used to not only shush me, but to enforce the time that I still had to technically be open to the public, back towards me.

Oh, he was good. Two can tango, man-child-hooligan-man!

"You what?" I could physically feel the colour of my face changing from the light pink flush of before to a bright, beetroot red. I didn't know whether to be turned on or enraged.

I could be both, right? Definitely both.

He completely ignored my poorly formed question and walked right up to me giving what I assumed was his most charming smile. But he was making fun of me, I knew that, and it caused my chest to tighten, and not in the good way.

"My name is Nathaniel Connors, but you can call me Nate."

I just stared at him with my most accurate 'you've got to be kidding me' face. This guy couldn't be serious. Where in the world did he use a strategy like this to get a girl, and did it ever work?

Judging by the confidence leaking out of him like an overfilled burrito, my guess would be yes. Yes, it worked quite a bit.

My middle finger twitched with a yearning to tell him to fuck off in the hopes of holding onto my remaining dignity, but I was still at work, and this guy was still a member of the public entitled to the use of the library.

"Florence Valentine, librarian." I nodded back my introduction.

"Ah."

"'Ah' what?"

"Oh, nothing." He walked past me, heading back in the direction of my desk.

"No, why did you say that?" I caught up to him quickly and swivelled in front to stop him in his tracks, hands on hips and eyes expectant.

He stared for a moment, the glint in his eyes still very much present, and shrugged, "I thought librarians were, you know, all rainbows and butterflies."

Oh, you have *got* to be kidding me. He wasn't done, either.

I could also totally be rainbows and butterflies if the moment called for it.

"Not that you're not. I'm sure you are, you just seem more of the 'don't doggy ear the page or crack the spines' sort of person."

My eyes felt like they were going to pop out of my face. He

26

knew I saw him doggy ear that page. "Of course I'm that sort of person! Do you have no respect for the written word or its binding?" I asked, incredulous.

"It's *binding?*" he replied, lips clamped shut in what I am sure was an honest effort to stop his laughter. He was still making fun of me, and he either didn't know, or he did, and he just didn't care. I'd bet the latter, though my traitorous heart never learnt not to hope for the former. *Sigh.*

Grinding my teeth together and with an undeniably forced smile, I exhaled dramatically, "We're closed."

I pointed toward the door and turned to leave, heading back into another part of the library I didn't even need to be in if only to get farther away from Nathaniel Connors. I don't think I'd ever seen him before today, and in the twelve minutes I had met and spoken to him, he'd managed not only to insult my disposition, but also my job. My job that I loved.

The whole encounter was only made worse by the echoing laughter that trailed behind him as he left the library. I honestly did wish that my heart didn't thump in that rather painful way that was all too familiar with the aftershocks of embarrassment and of course, the response to others that followed me everywhere, disappointment. Mostly because I didn't mind his laugh, even though he made me want to grab two fistfuls of grapes and squeeze, it almost made me want to laugh too.

Bummer.

4

Chapter 4

I ditched my plans for Thai food and opted for cereal in an attempt not to tarnish my favourite cuisine with the stench of how my day had ended. I'd never felt like an adjective was so well put to use. The day was a stinker.

There had been some real doozies in the library in the past. I had a kid rip a page from a book and stuff it in his pocket, a ratty teen who wouldn't listen to a word I said about the library rules, and I'd been followed by an unaware audiobook listener who'd completely foregone their right to use headphones. For the record, I am totally on board with audiobook lovers. I, myself, dabble quite frequently. Who *doesn't* love a husky voice narrating the most detailed and intimate parts of a carnal embrace between two wolf-shifters into your ear whilst you're browsing the aisle of the grocery store during your weekly shop? But I digress.

Those library-doozy-wrong-doers were going straight to hell. Probably. I felt it.

In the three years I'd worked there, I'd accumulated enough

stories to write a book, but Nathaniel Connors took the cake.

I wasn't sure if I was more upset with him or with myself for allowing him to get to me.

So, why was I so surprised? I had come to expect that sort of behaviour day in and day out, that would result in me specifically feeling like *this.* Like my jeans were too tight and I really needed to undo the button.

I ran through those twelve minutes as I piled Cheerios into my mouth and chewed with such intensity it was practically a soup before it made its way down my throat. I ran through those twelve minutes still, as I poured myself a glass of wine that was likely the equivalent to two glasses considering how close the liquid sat to the rim, and I thought on those minutes even more as I soaked in the tub, which I'd run just shy of scalding.

I allowed myself the evening to wallow. I didn't know what it was that had me so riled, maybe it was because that had been my first encounter in a while with a sub-par human being, or maybe I'd thought that his face seemed too kind for his actions, and that he would apologise. Surely no one who had a laugh like that could be a total toad?

Why was I even *thinking* of his face? Likely because I wanted to flick his forehead.

"Ha!" The sound stained the silence around me whilst I swigged my wine from the warm embrace of the bubble bath. "Good one, Florence."

The wine was doing its job well. And if I was being totally honest, a little too well, so I vowed to pour the rest down the sink after just one more gulp.

I could admit it here, in the safety of my own bathroom, cocooned in lavender scented bubbles, that despite my understanding of the people on this planet, I didn't have it in me to reprimand my heart on the hope it held.

Looking down at my chest, the gentle rise and fall had me mesmerised. "I told you, don't get your hopes up. It hurts." But my heart didn't change its rhythm, even though I knew that it knew I was right. Every time I thought someone might prove me wrong, the joke was on me. I blamed it on all the books.

The saving grace was that it was the first time I'd ever met Nathaniel Connors, and thankfully, it would likely be the last.

5

Chapter 5

F uck, I loved Mondays.

To many people, Mondays meant there was a full five days between them and their pasta stained sweatpants. Though this obviously was true, to me, Mondays were the blank canvas that was my entire week. A fresh start, an unblemished page. I could go on for hours about the poetic beauty that was the start of the work week, but the fact of the matter was that Monday was here, it was a good day to be alive, and nothing could come to mind that had me fearing for the integrity of the day. *Nada.*

The weekend had been exactly what I needed.

After wasting my Friday night wallowing with myself on the short-comings of people and the reasons my system of strategised avoidance was a must, I realised I wasn't ever going to see Nathaniel Connors again. So there was no need to think of all the witty and impressive comebacks to his comments on my lack of rainbows and absence of butterflies.

Come Saturday morning, I was a different person.

My entire weekend was so full of self-care, I still had face mask residue seeping from my pores.

Flash forward to this morning, when I had woken up four entire minutes before my 5 a.m. alarm, and although work wasn't until 10 a.m, taking in the colours of the sunrise during my morning run was two shakes shy of a religious experience.

Shower, breakfast, and a few pages of my newest book lent themselves to the best mood I'd been in since dinner with Dot last Thursday. I had even made my train with such perfect timing that as I descended the stairs to my platform, the train arrived and the doors opened without me even having to change my walking tempo. I mean, *come on.*

I surprised myself by greeting Melissa with a bright smile and a casual wave as I opened the door to the library, catching her attention as she stood at the printer just next to my desk.

She looked confused and maybe even a little scared, but she smiled back before grabbing whatever she had copied and scurried back to her office.

My mental list of how I planned to spend my working day was already forming, itemised in terms of priority and relevance, of course. My mood was technicolour radiance, and there was about a 63% chance I could break out into dance at any moment and it would be, without a doubt, situationally appropriate.

So, because of this high-on-life vibe I was on, it was almost comical how I was stopped in my tracks, mouth agape, as I rounded the corner of the reception to sit at my desk. If it had been anyone else I probably would have laughed. My head whipped around checking for any loitering bodies, before checking to see if there was anyone hiding under my desk.

The soundtrack of my life screeched to a halt right in the

middle of the best song.

I stared at the takeaway cup on my desk like it was going to produce a fairytale creature; a little excited, but also, would I scream? Perhaps it was someone playing a prank on the librarian? I knew how people felt about my passion for the library rules, and I really gave it to the kid last week who ripped that page out of that book I mentioned.

Can you blame me though?

Not to mention that I had a total of one friend, that friend being my grandmother, and she had never sent me a coffee before. If you asked her what 'UberEats' was, she'd tell you it was probably the name of a German themed diner. So, the takeaway cup on my desk couldn't mean anything good.

I approached the situation as one might approach a live explosive: with caution and muscles tensed for the worst. Peering around the side of the cup there was a small note, written in surprisingly neat all capitalised letters, it read, *'It was lovely to have met you Florence Valentine - NC'.*

Oh, no.

My stomach twisted up into forty different types of knots that would flabbergast even the most experienced of sailors. The knots seemed to proceed to fall out my ass, along with the rest of my organs. Talk about adding insult to injury. It wasn't enough to be the cause of his entertainment heading into what I'm sure was an absolute bender of a weekend - a guy like that didn't sit at home doing sweet F.A. - but he'd decided to drag out whatever little back-and-forth this was, into my sparkling Monday morning.

"Melissa?" I called out, my voice sounding calmer than the turmoil that was currently ravaging my internal organs which were now sitting at my feet.

Her head popped out around the side of the open doorway to her office, "Hmm?" she said by way of answering.

I pointed to the cup, "What's that?" I cast my eyes at her.

"Oh! Bugger, sorry. I totally forgot. A very tall, very handsome, fairly large man, he looked very...you know," she was gesturing to her own shoulders and upper arms like I was supposed to understand what it meant, "buff."

"Buff?" It sounded like I was bewildered. I was not, and I was also *very* aware of who she was talking about.

"Yes. Very, very, *very, very,* buff. He dropped it off as soon as we opened, but I told him you wouldn't be in 'til ten." She shrugged it off as if she hadn't just verbally groped the man before returning to her own desk. Melissa's little recap of Nathaniel's physical appearance was somewhat reminiscent of what I had seen with my own eyes, but given I was focused on trying to give off some pretty Big Dick Energy for about eleven of our twelve minute exchange I was still trying to place three of the four 'very's' she used when talking about his buffness. Even so, it did little to dissuade my irritation that he was continuing on with his joke, or whatever little one-sided game it was he was playing.

Perhaps he thought his charmed smile really did the trick and the glint in his eyes that screamed 'mischief' somehow matched the glint in mine that screamed, 'Oh no, you've damaged my book! And get your ass off that table please'.

I picked up the cold coffee and chucked it in the bin next to my desk.

It was a little weird, wasn't it? I was pretty sure he had insulted me for the better part of our conversation, and now he'd decided to deliver a coffee to my desk, letting me know how much he enjoyed doing so. Nice try, Nathaniel Connors, you and your very, very, *very, very,* buff buffness can forget all about me and move right along. I wasn't interested in participating in the volley of words and cold coffee. I had things to do, a library to run, and I would not, I repeat, I would *not,* let him get to me.

Chapter 6

"Good morning my darling Flossy girl, how are you today?" Dot shuffled around the side of the reception counter to pop a plate of freshly home-made cookies on my desk.

Melissa was the human equivalent of a bloodhound that could only smell out cookies. She was a *cookiehound*, and right on cue she casually strolled out of her office and greeted my grandmother with the energy of a firecracker - the very same grandmother whose existence she questioned not just last week when it was clearly life or death to dust the library - before unceremoniously ripping into the neatly wrapped cling film and taking half the plate in one swipe. She moved back into her office so fast she was a blur.

Tuesday had always been cookie days, and when I moved out, Dot would always bring a plate over to my house, and now that I was at work, this was where they were delivered. My favourite part wasn't even the cookies, it was the little sticky note she put on top that said *'Floss and Mel'*. Like give me a break, did I mention she was the best? Absolutely the best of the best.

I started to stand just as Dot leaned in, gripping me in a hug that smelled like spring, and rocked me from side to side.

"Oop, Florence, you have a customer," she said abruptly, letting go of me and smoothing out the long sleeves of my silk top.

I rolled my eyes and swatted away her fussing. "Dot, they're not customers. We don't sell anything here, they're just mem—".

The rest of the sentence shrivelled up and died right there in my mouth as I turned to see Nathaniel walk into the library with a young girl in tow. She had short blond hair and a backpack that looked a little too big. I quickly averted my eyes, sitting back down far more aggressively than I needed to. But I was making a point. What point, you might ask? That was undecided. But the reception desk was massive, and for some weird reason, in my head, *that* translated to 'super cool' and 'badass' and about four other things that made me feel like I was absolutely at the top of the food chain in this situation.

"Does that sound good, Florence?" Dot's gentle voice pulled me from my own mind.

"Hmm? Oh, yeah of course." I gave her a small smile to cover my lack of understanding about what I'd just agreed to, to which she nodded eagerly in response.

"Alright, Flossy, I hope you have a wonderful day."

I reached for her hand and squeezed.

"Thank you Dot, I hope you do too." I looped my arm around her waist as she leaned in to plant a kiss on top of my head.

I had resigned myself to completely ignoring Nathaniel. From the way he entered the library (his young companion aside), it seemed like he had some kind of plan to speak to me, or maybe even talk about the coffee he had brought in the day before. I really, *really* hoped not.

He was after a reaction, so I would give him none. My stomach was doing the worm and I wanted to immediately become invisible to him, just so he'd stop looking at me.

Dot was just moving past him on her way back outside when I heard a quiet "excuse me" fall from his lips and into the direction of my grandmother, followed by a string of other words I couldn't pick up. I watched in horror as he gestured towards me, only for Dot to cast her eyes in my direction and see them light up like the Fourth of July before she turned back to him and continued to have a very animated, and very hushed conversation. I'm talking hand gestures you could see from *space.*

I knew what I was watching. I was watching that so-called 'charm' he had flung my way in what I was sure now was an attempt to lighten the words he'd spoken, the ones that left me feeling a little bruised. He was working his magic on my grandmother. Believe me, I knew that she could hold her own, but she was a romantic at heart, there were no two ways about it. And since Melissa had mentioned just how buff he was... I could, from a third party, totally uninterested perspective, see why someone who *wasn't* in the midst of printing out more 'library rules' posters to place in the empty wall spaces around the library because this man had not seen the ones already hung up and proceeded to break a number of them, *potentially,* see him as scrum-diddly-umptious. And that third party perspective was, in this case, Dot.

The thing was, Dot didn't just strike up conversations with strangers. Nathaniel had to be feeding her lies, surely, to have her turn into putty in his hands. As soon as he walked over, the moment he even opened his mouth to speak to me, I was going to tell him that he and his ass-on-table sitting, lack of concern for community rules, and cold coffee supply could go ahead and remove themselves from my library. I would say it right to his face. I would.

Big Dick Energy, Florence.

I *knew* Nathaniel Connors. Maybe we only had twelve minutes under our belts plus a questionable gesture with the coffee, but he was just one of many just like him. He clearly didn't think about the consequences of his actions or what it would mean for the people around him after he did whatever he decided to do before he went on his merry way.

I was busy punishing my keyboard and responding to emails I would no doubt have to revise once I splashed some cold water on my face, when a new email landed in my inbox that made the book lover in me want to break out in song.

It was a list of some of the latest releases we would be receiving into the library and their corresponding bar codes. I was immediately swept away in entering all the details into the system and organising a printed sheet of said barcodes, ready to stick onto the books whenever they arrived in the week ahead.

For all of my forced focus, I did actually get so caught up in my work that when Dot reappeared in front of me as I stood to grab the sheet of stickers I had just printed, I had to stifle a yelp.

"You scared the bejesus out of me!" I scowled at her, "I thought you left?" It would've been a stretch to see all of her face over the receptionist counter if I sat, so I stayed standing and leaned my forearms on the counter.

"Yes, yes. I just came back to tell you not to worry about what I asked, it's all sorted now," she beamed at me.

Fuck, what was I supposed to know?

"Oh, alright, sure. No worries," I nodded back at her. Whatever she'd said to me when Nathaniel walked in had gone in one ear and out the other. The only saving grace was that now, I no longer needed to do whatever she needed me to do.

Very bad granddaughter, very good luck.

"I just met Nathaniel, did you see?" She looked absolutely smitten.

I scrunched my nose up in distaste, "He's rude, Dot, ignore him."

"He doesn't seem rude, Floss," she threw back at me, completely unfazed.

"No, he's very rude, I assure you" I sat down and made peace with only being able to see half of my grandmother's head for the rest of the conversation.

"I'm standing right here, you know," Nathaniel chimed in as he came to lean on the counter next to my grandmother.

"Yes, I'm painfully aware of that reality, believe me," I mumbled.

"Florence Valentine, *that* was rude," my grandmother chided, her lips thinning in an obvious show of displeasure at my remark. You knew it was serious when she used my whole name. Whipping out that card when she disapproved of something I did or said, or when she had something important to say, good or bad.

"No, Dot. It's true, he's not very nice." I flicked my eyes across to him briefly, but the expression he wore was, surprisingly, unreadable.

"Well, I think you're lovely, Nate. Don't mind Florence." She reached up to pinch his cheek. "Thank you, again!" Dot called back to him as she left, to which he threw back, "Don't mention it!"

Nathaniel had turned back to me just before Dot left. I cast my gaze upon her long enough to see the suggestive eyebrow wiggle she gave me before mouthing 'I love you' and scurrying away.

I rolled my eyes, even if she couldn't see it, and then, there was just him and I. My heart hammered as that realisation settled in and I crossed my toes in hopes of more of the good, sparkly energy I'd started this week with to come in and whisk him away.

Nathaniel's entire focus was now on me and I would be lying if I said it didn't make my whole body tingle. His gaze was intense, and now that I was sitting down and *he* was standing up, I felt even smaller than I did the last time we had this sort of stand off. He was clearly trying to hold in a smile, a small frown was forming under the pressure of his efforts just between his eyes, and his attempt to feign seriousness only added fuel to the fire.

It may be hard to accept this tidbit of information about me now, but I'm actually a very patient person, *he* just seemed to develop a keen sense of enjoyment from pushing my buttons.

The worst part was he knew it - he knew it and he *liked* it.

I didn't react when he pushed off the counter and made his way to peek around into my work space, only to see the plate of cookies and take one without being offered. This theft became the first thing on my *list* for him. The *list* was not something anyone wanted to have, let me tell you.

"Would you like to hang out after you finish work, Florence?" he said after he had consumed an entire cookie.

I looked at him incredulously. "Absolutely not."

"Why not, Flossy?"

"Don't call me that." If he had no idea why I didn't want to hang out with him then he was even more oblivious than I'd thought.

"Why? It's your name, isn't it?"

"No, it's a nickname, and you don't have permission to call me that."

"That's a fair call, I understand nicknames need to be earned," he said thoughtfully, as if of all the things to take seriously, *this* is where he finally made a start.

I continued focusing on my computer. At this stage I was just opening up folders and going through files of things but not really seeing anything. I was, however, very aware of Nathaniel's continuing focus on me, like he knew I wasn't really doing anything either.

"I think you look lovely today, Florence."

I scoffed, "Don't lie to me, Nathaniel." If I had a dollar for every time someone had said that to me, I would have exactly one dollar.

"Nate," he said simply as I finally turned to face him, "and I never lie."

With that, he turned on his heels and moved deeper into the library until he became lost to me between the stacks.

It felt like whiplash because I'd been so sure that I had mountains of irritation built up thanks to him and his careless words. I felt stunned, if not a little speechless, and I certainly had no idea what to think about Nathaniel Connors except for that I had never met anyone like him in my entire life. If you'd asked me a minute ago whether that was good or bad, I would have said outright bad, so what on earth had just happened to make me doubt that even a little?

I'd blame it on the books (again), and maybe even the romantic premonitions of my grandmother, because if there was anything I felt now, it wasn't *irritation*. It was simply, *unsure.*

7

Chapter 7

It's crazy how much you can enjoy your day without buckets of irritation and other less appealing emotions circulating your mind. I wouldn't go as far as to admit that the morsel of a compliment that Nathaniel had palmed off to me ever so casually was the reason for my new found clarity and general enjoyment of the hours in my day, but I could say for certain that there was no excess goopy feelings that were dragging me down either.

All in all, it was unnerving. I'd like to believe I'm a more complex creature than that, but alas, I'm not.

The days of the week flew rather quickly actually, which was equally as unnerving as the compliment.

I'd mastered another three songs on what I was now referring to as *'Mouse Click-Click Revenge',* and moved through my standard weekly tasks with no hiccups, no worries, and no interruptions from certain members of the library.

Reading session clean ups, cart returns, and book pickups came in constant rotation. It felt *good,* like I was on top of the day rather than beneath it. Getting a jump start on the week ahead thanks to that standard TGIF energy, I began auditing and cataloguing the books of the library. Yes, I know. *Riveting,* Florence. But hold your tongue. The process of categorically sifting through every book on every shelf and placing little ticks next to the ones we had and crosses next to the ones we didn't was like a brain orgasm.

It was something we librarians did relatively often, always making sure that the books we had on file were present and accounted for. I bet it's hard to fathom that anyone who loved books could be a total ass-hat, but allow me to enlighten you with the stone cold truth that every so often, someone thought a book was so good, they'd go right ahead and steal it.

Cue disappointment. Imagine expecting anything else.

Some of the 'outs' were looking a little wonky and some of the 'ins' I hadn't seen in far too long a time that I should have already reported them missing. And so it began, printing out the book lists (oh, yes), segmenting said lists into alphabetical order (I'm so close, don't stop), and seeing what we had and what we were missing (ohhhhh yeah). This sort of task took a long time, especially for just one person and a whole library's worth of books, but who was I to refuse the opportunity of multiple brain-gasms and being able to spend time with books over people? A match made in heaven.

Despite the fast pace of the week, Friday was slow. *Again.* That was two weeks in a row now and it sort of felt like the universe was fucking with me little bit. My assumption of the general public, not that I'd asked, was that Fridays were approached in the same capacity as one would observe a roller-coaster. The sudden and daunting incline that drags. You start the week off excited (Monday), get half way up and wonder what the hell is taking so long (Wednesday) then you reach the top (Friday) and pee a little on the swirly decline which happened all too fast and you totally forgot to look cool for the mid-loop camera shot (Saturday and Sunday). But no, it was like I was still on the incline, no swirly pee-inducing decline to be seen. Not that I was necessarily complaining. There was the glorious fact that I was on my own, so there were no unnecessary tasks I had to complete for Melissa. I'd actually managed to tick off all the books we had up to J that were in the library, and all with enough time left to do the end of week dusting. Melissa, who closed yesterday, had actually left a sticky note on the monitor of my computer that said, 'Don't forget to dust Florence, I did it last week remember!'

I will admit I'd hoped in that moment that she'd bite into a sandwich and have all the filling fall out the other end. There was no way the memory of my dusting could escape me in any case. God forbid we forget the intrusion that was Nathaniel Connors.

As if just thinking his name had summoned him, Nathaniel was the first person to walk through the doors of the library in almost an hour, just as I'd returned to my desk to drop off the first sheet of marked books.

I hadn't even spoken yet and he held up his hands in surrender, "I know, I know, you're closing soon. I won't sit on any tables or man-handle any books, I just came in to…browse." He moved his hands from their raised position and tucked them into the front pockets of his jeans before offering me a small smile and headed deeper into the library.

Get your shit together, Florence. Because honestly, what?

I hadn't seen him since his comment earlier in the week, after he'd all but seduced my grandmother and stole one of my cookies (Dot has insisted she 'still had it' on about three different occasions since that encounter), since he told me he thought I looked lovely (right to my face) and veered off the path of predictability he had, up until that point, been travelling on. He had me confused, and I didn't like being confused. It was like watching those videos that show you an item which clearly looks real, but then it turns out to be a cake. Like, what the fuck is that? No, thanks.

Though he had managed to dissipate my irritation, I wouldn't let my guard down so easily. I'd tolerate him in the library but I wouldn't go out of my way to speak to him.

Solid plan, Florence. Hold your front lines, you strong, albeit small woman.

Nodding to myself, that outrageously original plan of attack was solidified into the stone that encompassed my heart and I continued on with my tasks like nothing had happened.

Grabbing the cleaning supplies from the closet in my usual Friday routine fashion, I went about dusting, waving a casual goodbye to a few of the remaining library goers (some who had proven to be trustworthy within the walls I guarded), until I knew with complete certainty that only Nathaniel was left. I dusted the first half of the library and then the second half. Moving through the shelves, laser focused on my cleaning like it was my literal reason for *being*.

I refused to have my eyes pulled away to look at Nathaniel, even though the words *very, very, very, very buff* kept circulating around my head. If I had to assume why that was, why I was so interested in where he might be, or what he might be doing, the likeliest conclusion was because I was worried his rear was planted on one of the tables again.

Oh you big, fat liar, Florence. You can do better than that.

Turning off the lights for half the library, the silent 'last call' finally drew him out from the spot he'd settled in, which was of course the beanbag corner of the children's reading space. I should have guessed, honestly. But it made my mouth twitch at the corner ever so slightly. Not that I'd let him see that, of course. It would surely shatter my impenetrable force exterior, and if that happened I was doomed.

Doomed, doomed, doomed.

With no book to check out, and no sarcastic remarks, not even anything remotely hurtful or mocking as I sort of half anticipated if only to prove my first impression of him right, Nathaniel just lifted his hand in a half hearted wave before he left the library.

It was sad that I wanted him to be a dick so badly, I knew that. But that's just the thing. That's what I knew. And if he was, I'd be disappointed, but what was new there? The devil you know, and all that.

Shhh.

I shoved the thought to my heart which had picked up pace from the moment he was produced to me from the shelves.

Disappointment was my constant, and Nathaniel Connors had veered off course.

* * *

Melissa had messaged me Sunday afternoon asking if I could open up on Monday morning, and then proceed to open and close every day of the week ahead. Something had come up interstate, she said. It was an emergency.

I mean, I highly doubted it. She sounded chipper as all hell on the phone but hey, I suppose we all handled 'emergencies' differently. If she needed to bring forth all the energy of the baby-sun from the Teletubbies to get through it, then power to her.

Usually, we took turns. Whoever started later would close the library, and whoever started earlier would leave early.

My usual shift on Fridays was different, being the whole day 6 a.m. to 6 p.m., which meant that my Mondays didn't usually start until 10 a.m. That's what it had always been. Melissa had repeatedly said that she would cover closes for the whole week after she got back as a way of saying thank you, but I would look forward to that happening on the same day I'm able to get a wax without cursing out important historical figures. I said yes anyway because really, could I have said no?

"I'm so sorry Dot, I should have called you yesterday. I can't make dinner on Thursday." I called my grandmother first thing Monday morning and broke the bad news. Not being able to see Dot for dinner on Thursday's was akin to not having any names for the days of the week. It threw me off completely, I felt like I'd been blindfolded, spun around a gazillion times and then left in the middle of a forest and told to head east.

I relied on my dinners with Dot.

"Oh honey, it's alright. I am proud of you for stepping up at work and covering those shifts."

I rolled my eyes.

"Don't roll your eyes."

"There's literally no way for you to have known that." The smile in my voice was clear as a bell.

"I know you like I know my own name, Florence Valentine."

My smile was full and unrestrained as she spoke the familiar phrase that had followed me my whole life. It was Dot's 'go-to' for anything that required an added emphasis on just how much she knew about something. Facts, trivia, you name it.

"I have a guest anyway so I'll be fine."

"You have a guest?"

"I do."

"Is it that guy from down the street?"

"Who, Daryl?" She sounded incredulous. "Absolutely not, Florence."

My smile couldn't be shifted because I absolutely knew my grandmother was getting some. Perish the thought that I was aware of that fact.

"Alright, well, maybe we'll have to skip cookies this week too."

"I'll pop a container of them in your letterbox."

"Dot—" But she was having none of that argument.

"Nonsense Florence, I've done it since the week you started solids and I won't stop now."

"Alright, I'm secretly glad anyway."

"It's not a secret if you say it, Floss." Another classic Dotty-Wisdom.

"I'll miss you this week, but have fun with Daryl on Thursday!"

"Florence," she warned, but I could hear the tone of humour in her words.

"Okay, okay, it's not Daryl. Bye!" I hung up the phone and laughed. Happy to find myself in one of those life moments when everything feels light and airy, and the ground rising up to meet you is of absolutely no consequence.

8

Chapter 8

I started to relate closing time at the library to Nathaniel's summons. Was that weird? It felt weird in the same way as dipping your fries into a thick-shake felt. Weird but like, I'll have some more please?

Just the same as he'd done the Friday before, he sauntered into my Tuesday afternoon dressed all in dark denim and a cotton crew neck sweater with the little Sea Shepherd emblem over his heart. I couldn't even be mad at how my stomach clenched and my mouth dried out a little.

Sweet cantaloupes drizzled in honey.

Still feeling a little off at the prospect of not seeing Dot, even just for cookies, and the harsh reality that I wouldn't be seeing her at all this week, chased any semblance of the newfound optimism I had found last Friday from my mind and body. I could even feel my posture sagging with the empty cache of motivation within me.

I knew my forte was firmly grasped within the dramatics, but look at it from my perspective: I was lonely, I could admit that. Just because I didn't get on with the general population of planet Earth didn't mean I enjoyed the lack of company. We've established that as far as I was concerned, the majority of the world sucked, sure, but that in itself also sucked. So, today was just not my day and Nathaniel's presence drove home exactly why that was. He was a person who I could, hypothetically, see myself maybe being able to laugh with, someone I could let it all hang out with (emotionally, not physically), but he'd let me down before I even learnt his name. How do you come back from that?

I approached the situation the only real way I knew how to deal with the impending disappointment that would follow his frequent visits. I fixed a glare into place.

"You know," I started before dragging my gaze back to my computer screen before finishing my sentence, "this feels an awful lot like harassment."

If you even smile a little bit Florence, I will forget to charge your vibrator for a whole week and purposefully leave off your favourite chocolate from the grocery list.

Once he made it to the receptionist counter I levelled a stare at him over the top of my blue light glasses. This is exactly the move I had wanted to serve him that very first day we met and holy guacamole was I pouring it all into that stare now.

You have the power, you do, you do, you do. God, I wished I had a badge.

The thing was, he didn't look affected at all, not like how I'd envisioned him to be anyway. In my mind, his face would drain of colour and he'd have the true fear of the universe thrust into his being. I was putting out some pretty massive alpha-female vibes and I just didn't feel like that was *hitting*. Maybe I needed to growl?

I shook my head, needing only for that thought to evaporate

as quickly as it formed. I was *not* going to growl.

I suppose it could have *felt* sassier than it looked. I'd never actually practised it in a mirror. Not that I'd ever thought to do that, I wasn't exactly attempting to humble many people with an over-the-top-of-glasses look often. I usually went for the head down, eyes-on-shoes look. With the sudden fear that I looked more stupid than I did intimidating, I pushed my glasses back up my nose and continued to do nothing on my computer whilst I felt Nathaniel's gaze trace a path over my features.

He did that for a while, and it made me feel like I had something smeared on my face from lunch, or like I had a booger. As inconspicuous as possible, I attempted to wipe my nose and disguise it by the motion of swivelling in my chair to flick through the files that sat behind my desk. It took me a minute but eventually I was satisfied that there were in fact no bears in the cave, and I turned back to see a grinning Nathaniel looking right at me as if he was completely aware of exactly what I had been doing.

Great. Really hone that authoritative demeanour, Florence.

Though that was quite near impossible, I still felt my face flush with the severe embarrassment that can only be felt when you've been caught picking your nose in public. Or like when you had your dress accidentally tucked into your underwear after walking out of a busy McDonald's bathroom. Oh, that's never happened to you? No, neither.

Okay, I was 12.

I groaned, he was making it impossible for me to work through with my pride in place. "Please leave, Nathaniel." I got up and walked the two steps to the printer to make a copy of something. Not entirely sure *what* I was copying, only knowing that Nathaniel's presence seemed to make me constantly pretend to do work I did not need to be doing and I was going to likely end up with forty copies of a takeaway lunch menu from that Chinese place down the street.

"Nate," he corrected, "and I just came in to say hello."

"Hello," the words tumbled out too quickly; they sounded like a hiccup.

"Hello," he said the word slowly, like he was tasting it rolled off his tongue and trying not to laugh at whatever had burped passed my own lips.

Whatever my face did in response only made him smile wider.

"Alright, you can go now." I tapped the button so many times on the printer it made a weird groaning wheeze and the little screen started to load something.

"I thought I could stay." His voice broke the silence just before the printer decided to do its job. *Thank God.*

I threw my head back in aggravated bewilderment.

"Why? What could possibly possess you to want to stay here?" I whirled on him, trying to make the printer copy faster by pushing more buttons.

"Because I want to get to know you." He said it so simply like it didn't even cross his mind to make up any other reason, almost like I should have known the answer already. The words sounded truthful enough, but the way he passed them to me so freely made me immediately distrust him.

"But you don't know anything about me." I had the whole 'deer in headlights' thing going on, I knew it, "And even I can tell that I've been rude to you, sort of." I mean, true as it was - he had poked the lady bear first, and sat on her table, and ignored the rules of her workplace. I'd sooner swap realities with an ant than go through witnessing that again.

"That's why I want to spend time with you." He still sounded so pleasant. It was infuriating.

"You want to spend time with me because I've been rude to you?" Maybe I should call someone to help this man.

He frowned a bit, seemingly frustrated with me or maybe the way he wasn't able to say what he was trying to say properly. *Feel you there, buddy.*

"Well, no. But because of the other half of what you said, because I don't know anything about you." He kept saying things like they should have been obvious to me. Like I should have already *known* that he wanted to get to know me, because, well, why the hell not? Who wouldn't want the pleasure of hanging around Flossy V.? If you had a spare week of your life you didn't need I would gladly fill you in. I could build you a real nice picture, starting with dear old mum and dad.

I stared at him in what I was sure was an expression of disbelief. It felt an awful lot like he was making fun of me, I could always hope he wasn't, but we'd established what a useless thing hope was. I could feel a pressure building behind my eyes and I wasn't sure *why* that was. Maybe because they were words everyone wanted to hear, because they might lead to making you feel important, and cherished.

They never did though. Sorry to ruin the ending of that story for you.

He just stared back, as pleasant as ever. This felt like a new tactic. His pattern of doing the unpredictable had really caught on and I had *no* idea what his endgame here was. But my stomach felt like it was a canoe up shit creek without a paddle, like I was on a long holiday and forgot to pack all my underwear. I felt fucked, and not in the way I was sure we all deserved to be.

The easiest way to pretend I didn't care was to tell him just that.

"Fine, I don't care." *Oh, boy did I ever.* "If you insist on being here, I can't stop you," *Really, really wish I had a badge.* "It's a public space."

His face lit up. "Fantastic!" His enthusiasm only earned him an eye roll from me but I saw the sly smile creep onto his face as I turned back to sit at my computer.

An idea so bright it hurt my frontal lobes was birthed into existence, followed by a sly smile of my own. If he insisted on being here, I wasn't going to make it easy on him. The sooner he was gone the better.

"But," I said, getting his attention, "if you insist on being hip-to-hip then you will have to help me with my work."

His smile brightened as my mistake became frighteningly clear, and the notion that he might be suddenly thinking something about my hips, *my* hips on *my* body, popped into my head. This had begun to backfire, in a big way. I was now thinking about his brain forming thoughts about my hips and I remembered somewhere amongst that clusterfuck of nonsensical images that involved a lot of skin. That, and he was also very, *very, very, very* buff.

Kill me, now. Lonely and horny, what a way to go.

He saw the moment that the ball dropped. His eyebrows raised in a way that said 'Yes, Florence. I know that you're now thinking about what I'm thinking about. I know you know I know.'

He knew.

Accusatory finger at the ready - to do what, I had no idea, point at him? - I pushed up from my chair so fast it rolled back and hit the very cabinets I was rifling through just moments before, earning a loud cracking sound.

It caught me off guard and threw me off balance as I tried to grab the chair before it could do any more damage.

Nathaniel looked right at me and even had the man-coconuts to lean in and say ever so quietly, "You're being very loud, Florence. I can get you a pamphlet if you don't know the rules of the library?"

I wanted to scream into a pillow. He had gotten under my skin and he knew it.

9

Chapter 9

I tasked him with putting away books.

If I was being honest, I had left this particular task for tomorrow morning. It was an easy task that was enjoyable in the way that you had to move through the library to find the right stack. I found it quite peaceful, so when Nathaniel spoke I jumped a bit, having forgotten I'd insisted he tag along to do this chore. How that was even possible was beyond me, I could feel his body warmth radiating from where I stood at the opposite end of the stack to him.

For a plan that was meant to have deterred him from insisting on wanting to be in my company, we sure were getting cosy. I really should have been somewhere else, doing anything else, but all things considered I couldn't very well trust him to put the books back without supervision. So, here we were, past closing, putting books back in stacks all because of my big, loud mouth, and giant frontal lobes.

"You know, I didn't mean to hurt your feelings."

Well, that was unexpected.

"When?" I challenged, hoping he would pick up on the fact

that there had been more than one occasion, and dreading that I'd been so easy to read.

"When we first met," he gestured behind him, in the direction of the table he had christened with his backside during our first encounter.

I avoided his eyes because I wanted to get the words out and I didn't think I'd be able to under the weight of his stare. "Yes, you did." And I meant it too. *Eugh.*

"No, I didn't," he insisted, igniting the hurt mixed with irritation that still stung from that particular meet cute.

I turned to look at him, a stack of books on my hip, "You laughed at me, even *after* I walked away, Nathaniel." I lifted an eyebrow in request of an explanation of *that.*

Try and nice your way out of that one, buddy.

"Nate," he corrected with a small frown, "and only because I saw you blush." He put forward as if that was a great defence.

"I did *not* blush. And even if I did, why would that have been funny?"

I seriously did not blush, and I really didn't want him to answer that question. My chest echoed with the harsh beating of my heart. I wanted to pass out. I'd really have liked an 'out' of this conversation because I really didn't have the resources for this sort of confrontation.

"Alright," he agreed, but it was obviously only in an effort to let the conflict pass. I knew it and I hated that I was grateful to him for letting it drop. The conversation stopped after that, the only sound was the calming slide of books against one another as they fit perfectly back into their intended place.

"I really didn't mean to, Florence. I was just trying to make you laugh."

It was my turn to frown at him. "You were trying to make

me laugh by insulting me and my job? Not to mention the laundry list of Library Rules you broke." I motioned towards my own ass and then pointed at him.

"I—," he started, then stopped. Clearly thinking about what he wanted to say before letting himself speak. "I didn't mean for it to come out that way." He looked at me, and for all the glistening mischief I had seen so clearly in his bright blue eyes, now all I saw was sincerity.

It was unnerving. I wasn't familiar with that and it made me feel like a total jockstrap for being a class-A dick in return, even if my motives were in favour of self preservation. I was desperately looking for what he could be getting out of this explanation, and there was nothing that immediately came to mind which made it all the more frightening. Let me get this right; loitering in the workplace disrespectfully, disappointment, bad jokes for immediate entertainment, cold takeaway coffee, loitering in the workplace respectfully, kind to my grandmother, compliment, loitering and helpful, apology. I will literally wait here until someone explains to me what part of that made sense. Was this how it was to court someone now?

"I'm sorry, Florence," he said quietly, pulling me from the cross-eyed panic my brain had descended into.

"How could I possibly know you mean that?" I asked just as quietly, surprised by how easy the words came out when I wasn't fighting them tooth and nail. The entire interaction completely stripped me of my walls. I'd known this guy all of two seconds and the reality of that jolted back into me. That, and the fact I *did* want to believe him. My own feelings had my internal compass whirling out of control because who knew if this was real or just his natural charm at play?

He held up his pinky finger, "I'll swear on it."

"You can't be serious," I deadpanned, fighting the smile that threatened like my life depended on it.

"Who do you know that *kids* on a *pinky swear?*" He raised an eyebrow at me in question. He had a point, though. I lifted my pinky finger and hooked it with his before I could think any more on it, making sure to press my thumb against his, locking the gesture. If I was going to do a pinky swear, I was going to do it right.

Nathaniel's eyebrows hiked up his forehead halfway to the north pole before an effortless grin started to spread across his face. "You locked it."

"Of course, is it even binding if it's not locked?" My voice was incredulous and it only spurred on that shadow of a grin to transform into a full fledged, dimpled smile.

Heavens to Betsy. I ignored every single one of the butterflies in my stomach and worked on convincing myself they were spiders, that I was creeped out, and *not* turned on.

"No, you're right." His eyes glittered with a lightness I hadn't seen there before, but only for a moment. It was gone in an instant, replaced with a mask of absolute seriousness. "I'm sorry, Florence," he repeated.

I looked at him, really looked, and if it turned out that he truly didn't mean his apology then he would have to have been the worlds best liar and I would have deserved to have been fooled by him should this come back to bite me.

"Okay," I said to him, both surprised and not at how easy it was to get the next three words out. "I forgive you."

* * *

Nathaniel's assistance was actually incredibly helpful. You'd think he'd worked in a library before, the way he managed to identify the books and place them back in the designated spot. Talk about a way to make a lady swoon.

After his declaration of apology, and bonding over the sanctity of a pinky swear, we'd worked together into the evening surrounded by a silence that felt *good*. Which was fries in your thickshake weird.

The books had all been returned to their homes, and though I should have already been gone and done for the day, I ended up in front of the printer grabbing the sheet I had printed off of the books that I'd been referencing for the cataloguing process. It took a minute considering the stunning little stack of what turned out to be an invoice I'd copied forty times (thanks to my frazzled response to Nathaniel's presence). I handed the page to said lady-frazzler and he diligently read through the list whilst I checked the shelf, and any that weren't there he highlighted so I could look them up later to check if they were out for loan or if they were just plain missing.

By the time Nathaniel looked at his watch and mentioned he had to get going, regardless of the fact the library had already been shut for forty minutes, I all but had to shove the words 'please stay' back into my mouth.

I waved a small goodbye as he left, his face relaxed with an expression that said he was perfectly content with whatever interaction we'd just had. Like his goal of wanting to get to know me more was firmly in motion, regardless of the fact that the last hour and a bit was filled with his apology and then mostly silence.

He seemed perfectly content with that and, call me nuts, so was I.

Woah.

I couldn't help but feel like I was in the eye of the storm. That whatever was happening was okay for now, but surely there was something bad to come. I could feel the dread coil in my stomach because I truly didn't know what to expect. And the hope to be proven wrong had wormed its golden light through the hairline fracture that existed within the fortress I had around me. I was built to be wary of the people who were full of charm and dimples, who dilly-dallied around only to then watch the consequences of their actions curdle someone else's custard. But Nathaniel had veered off the beaten path, he wasn't fitting the mould, and what was more dangerous than that?

I stared after him as I mentally flipped through my internal handbook, the one I'd called *Beware of People* that outlined the dos and don'ts. The warning signs that I was about to be the butt of the joke or left behind in the dust.

The worst part was that not only could I not *find* a warning sign, but now that Nathaniel was gone, I wondered when I might see him again.

No, I didn't *wonder.* I *hoped.*

10

Chapter 10

I knew the moment I felt the breeze flitter in through the open door of the library the very next day that it was Nathaniel. I was developing this weird, seventh sense.

I already had six, my first extra sense being that I could, at any moment, put something in the microwave and go about my business all whilst being able to come back to it and open the door with only a second to spare before the infuriating beep. I could do this every time, without fail.

Now I had the same pleasure, it seemed, of being able to note the presence of Nathaniel before I really *knew* it was him.

My breath caught in my throat at the absurd feeling that stirred in my stomach. If I didn't know any better I'd say it was indigestion. But unfortunately, I did seem to know better, and his early evening presence in the library just the day before had made quite the impression on those walls I'd built around myself. Like he'd thrown himself at them again, and again, until there was a Nathaniel-sized dent clearly visible from the inside.

These were, of course, the very same mental shields that

were a crucial part of my system in keeping people at arm's length. It was necessary, an absolute must have. I'd learnt why that was many times before, and had no interest in relearning why I had a system in the first place. Even though there had been moments when the fortress had glitched, and the power to it had seemed to fail, leaving me open and defenceless. That was why there was a backup generator.

This analogy is stupid.

The corners of my mouth lifted into a small smile before I realised what I was doing. But he'd seen it already, I knew by the look of amusement on his face, even though the blank expression I had swapped it out with should've caused him to tinkle in his pants just a little.

Stupid, Florence. Honestly.

That's what I was. I was stupid. Stupid, and confused, and a little bit titillated.

What a trio.

This was amounting to something. I knew that the moment he dropped off the take away coffee the day after he assaulted one of my books, and I knew it even more when he pinky swore he hadn't meant to hurt me that very same day.

I'd never been a fool before.

I'd always managed to side step the charm. I had my own metaphoric red flag for the bulls of the world, and I'd always managed to adjust my eyes and see the real reasons for their interaction that loitered just beneath the surface.

So why did my mind betray me ever so slightly as I saw him approach the reception counter, and think I would want to be just a little bit foolish? Just this once?

"Nathaniel." I couldn't have sounded any more detached and it was truly a real testament to the control I had on my (tumultuous) emotions. I was enduring it like a champ, and in that moment I knew that no one would have noticed.

"It's Nate," he corrected me as he normally did before following on. "Hello, Flossy." He said it so naturally, like he'd always said it that way, and I can admit I melted a little right before the firm slap I gave myself.

Backup generator. Backup generator. Backup generator.

I needed it tattooed on my forehead and this point, if only to remind myself why I didn't dilly-dally around.

This was precisely his intended impact on me. I mean, my own grandmother all but fell apart before him. Sure, I'd wondered what it might be like to be a fool for Nathaniel, even for a bit. That didn't mean I actually *would* be. That was like wondering what it would be like to stick a metal knife in the toaster while your crumpets were crusting over. You could wonder, but you knew for certain you'd be fried like a tofu square if you even attempted it.

I would *not* become a tofu square.

I cleared my throat. "Don't call me that." The words lacked their usual bite, but I got them out just the same and I felt like that was the important part.

Fried tofu square, Florence. God dammit, FRIED TOFU.

Sweet marmalade. I was giving myself motion sickness. I took my glasses off and allowed my head to flop into my hands in silent defeat. Even though Nathaniel was right there, I just needed some peace and quiet from it all, just for a second.

I peeked up at him through my fingers only to find him beaming down at me with his chin resting in the palm of his hand.

"What are you looking at?" I scrunched up my face as I set my glasses back in their usual place on the bridge of my nose.

Completely evading my question, he asked me one of his own, "Am I helping you with the cataloguing today?"

That got my attention. "You've come in, to do more work? More *free* work?"

"That's what I said." He still continued to smile at me in what I was coming to realise was a very *Nathaniel* way, and also, you'd have to be an idiot to refuse free labour. That was precisely what I told myself when I stood up from my desk and gathered the list and highlighters, the phrases of 'back-up generator' and 'fried tofu' dancing around in the back of my mind.

I cleared my throat. "Great, let's get to it then." At this rate I was going to have the catalogue completed before the end of the week.

"But," he spoke the single word that had me stopping in my tracks. I looked back at him.

"But what?" Dreading this was the moment I'd become a deep fried soy-based meat replacement, and wishing for just a solid tit-punch instead.

"You have to ask me a question." He rounded the counter and stood before me, just a little too close to be casual.

"What?" Was that worse or better...I really needed to get a grip, or take a step back.

I did neither.

"A question, Florence. I'd like you to ask me a question." The corner of his mouth lifted in a way that told me he knew exactly what he was doing, and he knew that he was in fact standing a little too close to be casual.

I frowned slightly and cleared my throat, finally taking a small step back so I wasn't breaking my own neck just to look at him. An act I considered a victory.

"What kind of question?"

What did it really say about me that any question I seemed to come up with was somehow irrevocably linked to something sexual?

Sweetcorn on a Sunday, Florence. You need to get laid.

I mean...

Not by him, you animal.

"Any kind." Nathaniel shrugged in response, seemingly oblivious to the nature of my thoughts, though I was sure the words 'sex deprived and willing' were tattooed on my forehead now instead of 'backup generator'.

I gave it some considerable thought. I had a number of very safe options all to do with colours, and animals, and days of the week. And then my mouth was possessed by someone that was *not me*, and the question was out before I could stop it. "What size shoe are you?"

I swear to God. Just give me the toaster, fuck the crumpets.

His eyebrows flew up and all I wanted to do was hide under my desk and rock like a toddler.

"You want to know my shoe size?" I could hear the laughter in his question, but I'd be damned if I was going to let him see this get to me. Clearing my throat for the third time I took another small step away from him, thinking of all the things I could say to back out of requiring his help for the cataloguing. It was most definitely a one person job after all. It wasn't *that* big of a library.

I jerked a nod, not in the business of trusting my own voice, especially at a time like that.

"Twelve."

"Wonderful. Shall we get going?" I pushed past him before he'd even replied, but I knew it was coming. I could feel his eyes burning into the back of my head as he followed me to where we had left things the previous evening. And really, I deserved whatever he conjured up.

"Hey, Floss." Nathaniel leaned in much closer to my ear than I had thought he would, and his closeness made me jump. "You know what they say about big feet, don't you?" He wagged his eyebrows at me.

"You could easily get a job as a part-time clown?" I asked over my shoulder.

"Florence, it means—"

"Shhh*hhhh!*" I smacked my hand over his mouth faster than you could say 'man-hood'. "You are breaking the library rules, Nathaniel." He lifted an eyebrow at me before casting his eyes over the hand I still had clamped over his mouth, desperately glad I hadn't eaten an aromatic tuna sandwich for lunch. I dropped it immediately and wiped my hand on my skirt for added measure.

"What rules?" Nathaniel dragged his thumb over his bottom lip.

I spun away so fast I gave myself vertigo, mumbling under my breath, "As far as I'm concerned, you're breaking them all."

Nathaniel and his very, *very* big feet only laughed and followed me deeper into the library.

Fried tofu, indeed.

* * *

Thursday afternoon would have arrived faster if it were tied to a snail.

When the news of my week of work alone had made itself known, sure, I was bummed. I'd enjoyed my later starts every other day and yes, even I could admit that sometimes I found myself humming along to Melissa's movie soundtracks she often belted without restraint, but then the prospect excited me.

What did I love more than the library and my grandmother?

To be alone and unbothered, of course. Like every other gal in her late twenties. So really, the dream had become my reality and I was thrilled. At least I was for the first couple days of the week.

But for the last two I'd found myself tirelessly waiting for the end of the day to come, all for the purpose that I knew it would likely bring *him* into the library for whatever reason he deemed appropriate.

I didn't even know what Nathaniel did for a living. Now *that* would have been a better question to ask him instead of the size of his shoes. *The size of his shoes.* I felt my cheeks flame as I recalled the memory and clamped my lips shut tight at the smile wanting to burst free.

My attention snapped to the library door, as the very man himself burst through, completely disregarding the library rule of sound levels. I felt my body relax in relief at his arrival, and immediately noted the feeling as something to dive deeper into later. Dive into and dispel.

Nathaniel didn't halt his stride at all as he walked right by my desk and pointed deeper into the library. "To the stacks!" he called out somewhat valiantly, not even waiting to see if I would follow. I didn't give a moments thought to the excitement that fluttered in my stomach at his timely return. A habit that he seemed to be making, and one, it was becoming clear, that I was making too.

I also didn't think about the tiny part of me that yelled about the system, about meat-alternative foods, and backup generators. About how I knew people like Nathaniel and how they took what they wanted, did it all in the name of themselves, and then left me alone and hurt. How sometimes they just stopped showing up without a word of warning. I shoved that tiny part of myself to the corner of my mind, threw a sheet over her for good measure, and stood from my desk to follow.

Three strides towards the direction he had taken off in I remembered what I had packed that morning, not wanting to register that it could have been hope which motivated me to do what I did. *The emotion that shall not be named.* I turned back and rummaged through my bag for the little container I had with two cookies in it, thanks to Dot's Tuesday cookie drop off in my mailbox, as promised.

Grabbing a cookie for each of us, I turned on my heels and followed the sound of laughter that echoed through the library. For once, not being concerned in the slightest at the rules he was breaking.

11

Chapter 11

I'd just locked the library doors after the busiest Friday we'd had in a month and turned back around to finish a few extra bits in preparation, not only for the weekend staff, but for Melissa's return.

She'd left a list of things she needed done, usually things that *she* had to do, but in fact never did, then conveniently forgot she didn't do them. I sometimes envied the way her brain worked because it didn't seem like she was putting it on, but like she had honestly believed that if anyone cleaned the toilet, it *must* have been her.

It was a nice distraction from how furious I was with myself for how I waited so impatiently for the afternoon to come around, *again,* just in case Nathaniel showed up to continue with the cataloguing we'd been doing.

I knew better than to fall prey to the infatuation that came with pretty men, and I still didn't try and stop myself.

I'd barely made it five steps when a loud thump came from behind me. I knew before I even looked it was Nathaniel. That new seventh sense of mine. I really wanted to turn around and flip him the bird for doing this to me. For consistently showing up when all I wanted was to be left alone. But amongst the fury, there was a thrill of excitement that spiderwebbed through my body.

I took in the massive, black clad figure with the bright, dimpled grin mouthing the words 'open up' far too expressively. My feet moved of their own accord and the only defence I had was to be as sour as possible.

I unlocked the door and cracked it open. "What are you doing here?" Cold and clipped was the way my words were intended to be delivered, but their exit had them coated in a pleasant conversational tone, in a voice that was far too demure to be mine when it was directed at anyone other than Dot. In a voice that might have conveyed my run away thoughts about the man before me, should he have had the know-how to sift through the layers my words carried with them.

I added it to my note from the day before, my note that I'd absolutely intentionally forgotten to address last night after I had gotten home. The one about how it felt to see him walk into the library after a day of wondering if he'd show up. I was more than aware that his presence had become routine in the weeks he'd nestled into my life, but just because I was getting used to his badgering didn't mean he had to be brought into the loop on that tidbit.

I didn't need him to be made aware of anything. I didn't need him, period.

Power to you, Floss. You're a total dumbass if you still believe this crap.

Disregarding the lack of invitation to enter the library, Nathaniel shimmied through the cracked door and into the darkened space.

"This isn't allowed, Nathaniel. Also we're strangers, and there is danger in that." I frowned at him, hoping to convey my point in a way that gave it the most impact.

"Firstly, we're not strangers, Florence. I'm even friends with your grandmother."

"Hold on, what?"

"Secondly," he continued without skipping a beat, leaving me floundering at that mental image, "I think you like a little danger."

I was all out of words, not only from the shock that apparently he considered himself in cahoots with Dot, not that she'd shared that with me, not that I had any idea *how* that was possible outside of the single interaction which happened right in the very spot where we both now loitered just inside the library doors. But also, his comment about danger made my whole body erupt into goosebumps and I really didn't feel like I needed to dignify that comment with a response of my own.

"You've met my grandmother once, I would hardly say that makes her your friend." I crossed my arms over my chest and all he did was give me a small smile that looked like it held all the secrets of the world. I was caught between a rock and a hard place, wanting to equally kiss him, and flick him on the forehead.

I take that back. I did *not* want to kiss him.

Perfect, you're going with 'dumbass' then.

Desperate to move away from *that* train of thought, I rolled my eyes and feigned a yawn, hoping that my show of tiredness would make him mosey out of the closed library. Unsurprisingly, he was not fooled and didn't move an inch.

"Wouldn't you say we're acquaintances?" He set his gaze right on me, and boy did I feel the weight of it. I was suddenly very aware that it was only me and him in the dimly lit library. I took a step back, very pleased with the now three small steps that separated us, giving myself the illusion of control over the situation simply by controlling the space between him and I.

It didn't work, let me tell you. But it was better than nothing.

"Barely." I averted my gaze, observing the shelves around us like they all of sudden held the scrolls from the Library of Alexandria.

"Okay," he nodded slowly, "but we're starting to become friends, aren't we?" His left eyebrow lifted in genuine wonder. "I know you aren't nearly as enraged by my presence as you were a few weeks ago."

"That's only because I feel sorry for you." I didn't, I don't even know why I said that. All I knew was that I needed him gone, and gone now. That feeling of something amounting? Yeah, it was strong as heck right now, and I needed to remove myself from the situation or something, I didn't know what, but *something* was going to happen. It felt oddly like experiencing your first orgasm.

Pull your mind from the gutter, you mad woman.

I genuinely couldn't help it. It was like he was doing this to me on purpose.

"No, I think it's because you like me." He wasn't even fazed by my half-formed insult. "And I like you too," he continued, "so I wanted to invite you out for drinks."

"Drinks?"

What was I, a parrot?

"Yes, like, at a bar." He was poking fun, but I had learnt that this wasn't meant to be mean like I had assumed during our first encounter. I think it was meant to be...endearing?

"I know where people have drinks, Nathaniel," I huffed, turning away from him and striding with purpose back to my desk. "And I thank you for your invitation, but I'm not going."

The look on his face said all I needed to know about the confidence he had that I would say yes to his invitation, even though I'd declined his initial one.

How had it just been three weeks?

I wasn't going to go for a number of reasons. I knew what might happen if I did go. Well, actually, let's be honest. I knew what would *definitely* happen because I knew how long it had been that it'd definitely *not* happened and we were in double digits. Let's just leave it at that. Even though it would scratch my itch, so to speak, it would complicate things all the more than they already were, and I couldn't afford to have that happen.

The real reason was that in the weeks that he had started to randomly show up, even though I'd not seen him at all prior to the fateful afternoon - the doggy-eared page still like nails on a chalkboard to the ears of my heart - I had started expecting him to show up.

And what's more, and maybe what's worse, was that I'd begun *looking* for him. This person who'd enraged me slightly, and now I knew his shoe size. I refused to have it continue. I knew better than that. My curiosity over Nathaniel Connors would have me end up in deep shit, I knew it.

"I'm not going anywhere with you." I delivered the words with the right amount of venom.

"What's wrong with me?" If I didn't know better, I would have said he sounded a little hurt, the joking and confident façade slipping for a second, just a second, before a cocky grin split his features. But I did know better. I'd just forgotten.

I gave him a pointed look, hoping my silence would end things faster, and wondering if he'd forgotten the things I told my grandmother about him.

He hadn't, rolling his eyes in remembrance. "Yeah, yeah. You think I'm rude." He gave me a pointed look back that said he thought I was full of crap.

Yeah, well, join the club.

He distracted me then, and I had the sneaking suspicion that I'd been right. That Nathaniel Connors got in the good graces of everyone he met thanks to his dimpled smiles and buckets of charm. It had almost worked for me too. Almost.

"Let's just hang out," he pushed, walking a little farther around my desk whilst I furiously packed up my bag with stupid things like tape, staplers, and the pad for my mouse.

"No, I don't 'hang out.'"

"At all?" He sounded incredulous.

"At all," I confirmed, thinking we were getting somewhere, he was finally getting the point and soon I would be rid of this dimpled, dark haired man who'd messed up my whole system. Who made me want to stick my knife in with my crumpets, even though I knew the jolt of electricity would short circuit my house and stop my heart.

I refused to think of the pang of something unpleasant that shot through me at the thought that this could be it.

"So, it's not just me." He sounded elated.

I levelled him with a bored look. "You're particularly aggravating but no, it's not just you." I didn't know why I was spilling my secrets to this guy, but they were flowing freely now.

"You mean to say that you don't like hanging out with people at all?"

Whatever. What did I have to lose now? Except for hopefully (?) him.

I meant that.

I did.

"People are full of disappointment. So no, Nathaniel, I don't hang out with people *at all.*" I gave particular emphasis to the last two words.

"You can call me Nate, you know."

"No, thank you." I gave up on trying to concentrate on packing things up when I moved to open a drawer and grab a handful of loose paper clips, throwing them in my bag. *Loose paper clips.*

I started to move about the desk to leave, hoping he'd follow. I couldn't very well lock up the library with him still in it, cleaning the toilet be damned.

He didn't, he just stood there and tried again to say something.

"Surely you—"

"Look, Nathaniel," I cut him off, turning to face him as he still leaned against the receptionist counter, staring at me from where I stood, halfway to the door.

"Nate," he interrupted.

I rolled my eyes. "There is really nothing you could possibly do or say to convince me otherwise. People suck. I've seen it first hand, and I'm sure you have too, regardless of your dimples, and your charm." I waved my hand in his general direction. His eyebrows lifted at the compliment but I kept going, "I mean, listen, I'm sure you're probably a great person, with lots of great friends, and not like any of the other many,

many people I've collided with, but I avoid people at all costs because they will drain you dry and give nothing in return but lovely little reusable bags of disappointment, so that when you run into the next sub-par human, you already have something to carry the dregs of your inevitable failed relationships in."

I'd hoped to deliver that evenly, but my chest was heaving by the time I was done. He studied me for a bit before he spoke again.

"Except for Dot." He didn't even ask, he just said it.

I was rendered a bit speechless for a second. That was incredibly perceptive of him. But I knew that he'd met Dot, and spoken to her too.

I blinked my shock at him. "Precisely, you've caught on quick. That's surprising, to be honest."

"I always want you to be honest, Florence, even if I don't like what you have to say."

That made me frown. Nathaniel was now equal parts confusing as he'd been infuriating. But he seemed to have understood what I'd said, better than even Dot had understood it when I tried to explain it to her. He even said so himself, that the only person I had time for was Dot.

Hopefully he'd stop coming into the library now.

Hopefully.

"Alright." He ran a hand through his hair, a mischievous glint in his eyes, "Challenge accepted, Floss."

"Don't call me that," I bit out through clenched teeth. He ignored me completely. "And I didn't challenge you to anything. I want you to leave."

He ignored that.

"You can expect the first round of *Convincing Florence* next week. Bright and early." He turned on his heels and didn't even bother to wait for me to say anything back. Walking right past me without a second glance.

"Do your best, Nathaniel Connors," I called after him anyway, internally cringing at breaking my own rule for volume levels in the library, despite the fact it was closed, "You won't succeed."

Wait, what? Florence stop it, you're—

His hand was poised to push the door to exit the library when he looked back at me, "Nate," the mischief gone, but something else, something darker, and a lot sexier settled over his features, "and we'll see." Then he was gone.

Well, shit.

12

Chapter 12

The smell hit me right in the face as I walked in the doors of the library at 10 a.m. sharp Monday morning. It was potent, and I scrunched my nose up even though it was a favourite scent of mine.

Melissa, for one, had never looked as infuriated and excited as she did just now.

"How on earth did you get *those*, Florence?" Her tone held just enough excitement to cover up her incredulous tones. No 'hi', no 'thanks for covering last week!'. Nope, of course not.

Giving her a tight lipped smile I rounded my desk and dumped my tote bag on my office chair, regarding the bouquet of bright, red roses sitting on the receptionist desk.

'Let this be in place of the Opening Ceremony of what is Convincing Florence Valentine. See you after work - Nate.' I rolled my eyes and balled up the stupid little card in my hand.

"Don't be so envious, Melissa. They're not what you think." I unpacked the stapler and tape that I'd brought home with me the Friday before, all thanks to the nuisance that was Nathaniel Connors. I left the paper clips at the bottom of the bag though.

"What do you mean, how could a bouquet of beautiful roses mean anything *other* than what I think?" Hands on hips, Melissa raised her eyebrows, daring me to insult her intelligence more than I clearly already had.

"I just mean these aren't really for me, Melissa. They're for *him*."

"Him?"

"Yes, *him*." I moved my bag off the chair and sat down, tapping the spacebar on my keyboard for my monitor to light up.

"Who's *him*?" It was the first time in a long time that Melissa had dared to venture outside of the safety of the front desk cubicle that encompassed my desk and her office.

"You've met him already." I tried my best to sound disinterested, wanting her to go away and stop talking to me about this as fast as possible. Mainly so I could dissect exactly why it was that my stomach was turning like I'd just eaten bad sushi.

"You don't mean..." She started gesturing to her shoulders and arms in the same manner she did the first time, "*That* guy?"

"Yes, Melissa. *That* guy."

"But why *you*? That makes no sense." All pretence of excitement had disappeared, all that was left was obvious confusion at why I'd get anyone's attention, let alone very, very, *very, very* buff Nathaniel.

I turned to look at her as she stood a little ways back from the front desk. I hadn't had time to put my glasses on, so there were no frames to peer over to intimidate her like I wished I could have, if only to cover the hurt I tried to hide faster than it had risen up in me, making the back of my neck prickle, and my eyes ache.

"No, Florence, that's not what I meant," she began to back pedal.

I stood up, grabbing a couple of sheets to continue my audit that we hadn't managed to get done last week as I'd hoped.

"I know what you meant, Melissa." I walked around my desk and into the shelves, where I could stand and work amongst my books in silence.

Melissa and I had never really been friends, but we had been friendly enough. I knew that she was a bit off, and sometimes she didn't think before she spoke. There was always an air of respect and understanding that didn't make it feel one sided when I did things like always do the dusting, or the cart put-backs, or cover an entire week of work for her, even though I knew she didn't log in and take the time off officially.

Because when she said she'd pay it back to me, I'd begun making some small plans in my own head about extra time with Dot, and to read my ever growing collection of books.

Melissa had taken, and taken, all whilst it suited her, and then like lightning across the sky; out popped the real person beneath, all with bags, and bags, of disappointment in her hands.

I stood in the stacks all day. Maybe it was childish, but I didn't feel like sitting at my desk and smiling in feigned forgiveness at Melissa whilst I told her 'I understood', and 'Oh yes, of course, I took it the wrong way. Surely you hadn't intended it to be taken that way at all." So I stood in the stacks, away from Melissa, who'd confirmed the person she was, and who I would now have to make peace with working with. Away from the giant, beautiful, heartbreakingly classic bouquet of flowers that I really wished had been given for the pure reason that he might have liked me. And not to mark the start of the silly game he wanted to play, to show me just how *not* like everyone else he really was.

* * *

The little tidbit that I would somehow be seeing Nathaniel after work was something to focus on. I'd tell him I wasn't interested. The entire ordeal with Melissa just confirmed for me, because it seemed that I had gotten slack and lazy in my defences, why it was that I refused to engage with people in this way.

Yes, that's what I was going to do, but still he invaded my mind the whole day.

Melissa had left at 4 p.m., not bothering to find me amongst the books and shelves, and not bothering with her little sticky note apologies that she always reverted to, thinking that come the next day, all would be well.

I locked up the library, clutching my flowers under my arm envisioning a very hot bath, and a very full glass of wine that I didn't notice I'd misstepped so thoroughly that I was heading south until I was coming face-to-face with concrete. It was all I could do to hold onto the glass vase for dear life and pray it didn't smash along with my front teeth when I made contact.

But I didn't. I was pulled up short from what would have been an incredibly terrible situation by the dimpled-cheek charmer who'd been featuring in my mind all bloody day.

Of course.

"Nathaniel," I breathed, not entirely sure if I was relieved or irritated.

Irritated that I was relieved, probably.

The truth was, I *wanted* to like Nathaniel Connors. I wanted to enjoy his company. I knew that I could, too. I could laugh at his jokes and peer at him with his own glass of red submerged in the bubbles at the other end of my bath. But I'd rue the day, I knew it.

"Nate," he corrected. "I didn't realise my presence made you so weak in the knees."

I rolled my eyes and stifled a yawn to cover the stupid smile that broke across my face. He saw it, I knew he did. There were only so many more times I could fake-yawn to cover my tracks.

"What are you doing here, *Nathaniel?*"

"I'm here to walk you to wherever you're going."

"Go home, I'm serious." I started walking, clutching my tote in one arm and my flowers, vase intact thanks to my infuriatingly well timed saviour, in the other. He ignored me and started walking next to me casually. Almost lazily.

I stopped and turned to him, and he copied my movement.

"What if I was walking to my car that was just five metres from the door?"

He frowned and looked around. "Are you?"

"No." I shook my head in annoyance. An emotion I seemed to be feeling in plenty as of the last ten hours. "But if I was, this would be completely pointless."

"Okay," he said the word slowly, "But you're not."

"That's not the point," I huffed, starting to walk again.

"Then what is the point, Floss?" He wasn't even breaking a sweat.

"Don't call me that."

85

I was too busy concentrating on staring at my feet and walking towards my destination as fast as I could, trying desperately to *not* trip over the cracks in the sidewalk and pull another well-timed rescue from the man to my left to note if he'd said anything else to me. I was hoping he would just up and disappear.

I didn't notice at first that Nathaniel stopped to tap a stranger on the shoulder, so when the loss of his presence beside me registered, my eyes flailed more than I would've liked to admit, searching around for him, considering my previous statement. When I did find him, I really could do nothing but look on.

"I'm so sorry to disturb you, but I'm running a survey, and have to ask a handful of strangers a few really easy questions. Would you mind if you were one of those strangers?" He flashed the well dressed business man an award-winning smile to which the man himself could do nothing but smile back and nod happily.

What in the—

"You're a legend, Sir. Thank you for not *disappointing* me." He looked at me pointedly before continuing to speak. "I'll get right into it—"

"Don't you need something to write down my answers?" The man asked with a bit of a frown, like he was sure he was going to be mugged any second.

Nathaniel tapped his temple and grinned again. "I'll save every word up here, all good. It's only three questions."

"Alright, then." The man's face returned to a pleasant smile and I just *really* wanted to know how Nathaniel did it. He'd be able to lead a revolution if he wanted. He didn't know this man from a bar of soap yet he was happy to answer some questions with little to no context.

"You're walking along a frozen river and you hear a crack, you look over and see that a dog, nay, a *puppy*, has fallen into the ice-cold water and is struggling to get out. It's whining, and crying, and scared for its life. What do you do?"

The man looked *horrified*. Like, deeply, *deeply* horrified.

His eyes flicked to mine as I stood there like some random bystander, I could tell the expression on my face was also horrified.

He bumbled around before saying, "I would go and save it, of course. Or if I couldn't, I'd call the fire department straight away and try to help the best I could in the meantime." He pulled at the collar of his dress shirt, still very distraught by the detailed visual given by Nathaniel, who'd looked over at me and grinned like a lunatic.

"Perfect! Question two." He moved his eyes back to the man before him. "You have people over for a dinner party, and you forget to cook. Do you; A: only give them snacks and chips. B: Give them the five day old leftovers in your fridge and hope they don't get sick. Or C: order pizza and have a swell time."

"Option C?" The man was looking very confused, but Nathaniel's smile grew even wider.

"Oh, you're doing very well," he complimented the man before launching straight into the third question. "Last one. You're at your local park that happens to have a water feature at its centre and is home to a waddling of ducks. Do you feed the ducks bread?"

"Do I feed the ducks bread?"

"Yes, sir."

"Uhm, I guess?"

"Oh, no. Well, two out of three isn't bad. Thank you for

your time!" He said in casual dismissal.

"You shouldn't feed ducks bread?" The man asked in confusion, even as Nathaniel had turned to walk back over to me. He stopped and turned back slightly.

"No, you shouldn't. It makes them too reliant on people and stops them from finding their own food," he continued on to me with a "Come on, you'll miss your train." Leaving the man with a contemplative look on his face as he continued in the direction he'd been going down the street. I wondered for a second how he even knew I was catching a train until I realised the sign for the station was just ahead, and that he lived in this city too.

"What in the–," I started, but he beat me to it.

"Two out of three isn't so bad for our first example," he smiled to himself.

"Example of what?"

"I am showing you the *good* in people, Florence. These moments are twofold. They will show you there is no need to expect disappointment when they agree to my questionnaire, and they will also show you they're inherently good when they answer correctly. It will only work if you keep up though. Don't tell me you've forgotten the challenge already?"

How could I?

"This is ridiculous." Surely my face was still horrified from that first question.

"Perhaps, but still, I think that was a bangin' start. I'm feeling very confident."

I held my tongue from saying anything too vulgar as we continued to walk side by side. I'd almost completely forgotten our conversation before running into Nathaniel's first victim of the challenge, that it took me a second to understand the next sentence that came out of his mouth.

"If I really was only walking you five metres from the front door of the library to your car, I would have enjoyed every bit of those few steps." He looked so sincere and I wanted to hate him, simply for making his words sound so believable, especially when I had no way of really knowing how true they were. Thoughts of Melissa moved through my mind, not in a way that had me mull over her hurtful response, but simply as a timely reminder of why I was so sceptical of Nathaniel in the first place.

Nevertheless, a smile ghosted my lips anyway, this one he didn't see.

Nathaniel ended up walking me right to the top steps that descended down to the train station. It turned out to be a ten minute walk, not five metres, and all the while, after our little squabble and his random interview of the stranger we passed by, he started asking *me* questions. What was my favourite food? *Thai.* What was my favourite colour? *Orange.* What was my favourite flower?

"Just so I know for next time," he said, his face an open plan. A sponge, it seemed, for the information I was passing on. It was that very look that lured the truth from my tongue.

"Roses," I said. "I love roses."

His eyes dashed to the bouquet I still clutched tightly in the crook of my arm.

"Lucky guess, then." he said, a smile lighting up his features in a way that made me want to look away. I didn't want to see the way his face lit up when I couldn't even believe his words.

"Lucky," I murmured.

I was the one to break the silence next, "I know you're doing this purely for you to win whatever challenge you've set for yourself. But all you're doing is solidifying the reason my system must exist in the first place."

"That's not true, Florence."

"Don't lie to me, Nathaniel."

"I told you, I don't lie." His voice was devoid of all joking, of all charm, and for the first time since I met him I was 100% confident that the words which had left his mouth were nothing but the truth. No agenda, no scheme, and no challenge.

We stood facing each other at the top of the stairs that descended into the station closest to the library. The one I arrived at twice a day. Heading to work, and then heading home.

"I wanted to know all those things because I find you interesting." His voice sounded softer now, but no less laced with unavoidable truth.

"Interesting just means you find me to be a bit of a puzzle, but all around ugly." I looked him straight in the eye and hoped to convey the same amount of truth he'd given me. What I didn't expect was for him to burst out laughing, clutching his stomach as he wheezed.

He *wheezed.*

It was contagious, to the point that as I watched him fall apart before me, I couldn't help but laugh too. Between giggles of my own that I was failing to suppress, I was whining for him to stop. We were drawing a crowd.

It felt like we'd done this before. Him brought to his knees by my surprising humour (yes, I was funny) and me, unable to help joining in, wishing he'd pull it together.

"I have to go," I said. Nudging his still crouched and laughing figure with my shoe. He finally stood up, wiping tears from his eyes.

"There is no way that anyone could find you ugly, Florence."
His face still relaxed, and made younger by the minutes he'd
spent laughing. Nathaniel bowed slightly before backing away,
sending me a flirty wink and turning on his heels, walking
right back to the library.

There was no funny business. He didn't try to hug or kiss
me. He didn't even shake my hand.

That would've been weird, yes. But I mean, he didn't try
for any physical contact. He'd remained firmly outside of
my personal space bubble, only touching me when I'd almost
kissed the pavement.

He walked with me, asked me only questions that didn't
have anything to do with him at all, called me... *not ugly,* and
then he left.

Nothing Nathaniel did was easy to read, I just needed to
hold out a little longer until his motives became clear and I
could side step them in the way I always did, and hopefully
come out the other side unscathed.

What a load of bullcrap that was.

If there was one thing that Nathaniel Connors had done, it
was get under my skin.

* * *

The smell of garlic, tomatoes, and onion filled my kitchen
with the comforting aroma that was my home-made pasta
sauce. In the oven I was cooking a beautifully marinated piece
of fish to place on top, and in a pot bubbling just behind the

pan of aromatic ingredients, was spaghetti. *Perfecto*.

The TV in my living room was playing *Bridgerton* for the hundredth time, and I watched it intermittently as I nursed a glass of Pinot Noir.

I was stirring a clump of butter into the sauce and majorly reflecting on the day.

There were a few things the day had proved to me, and I was trying to digest them with as much dignity as I could, but in all honesty, I was fucking drowning.

Melissa sucked. There were really no two ways about that one, I hadn't been her biggest fan, but I guess I had gotten complacent. Her efforts with Dot had always been pleasing to me. I mean, if you're in someone's grandmother's good books, surely that's something.

But I don't think Melissa was ever really *in* Dot's good books, I just think Dot thought she was in *my* good books (an optimistic notion), and so she had automatically placed her into hers.

I'd have to deal with her tomorrow, but the plan I had was already in place. I would do exactly what I'd dreaded doing today, I would nod in understanding, and take ownership of misunderstanding her incredibly rude behaviour.

It was lousy, because in another life I thought we might've been friends.

Florence with friends is something you could visualise as easily as a Montarthissle Bug. Are you struggling to visualise it? Well, you should be. Because it doesn't fucking exist, just like my long list of sleep-over buddies.

It took a lot of energy to be mad. To be hurt, and upset, and frustrated. It also took a lot of energy to have so many different words you want to say, but never have the opportunity to say them.

It makes your throat ache and your stomach cramp, and all appetite goes out the window (what a dreadful thing that would be). But do you know what *doesn't* make you feel like that? Not caring. So, I would take ownership, and then I would let it go. It was a lesson I'd learnt so many times.

I took a massive gulp of my wine and moved to fill it back up again before wandering back in front of my simmering sauce.

The other thing the day had proved to me, was that I wanted to be around Nathaniel Connors.

I wanted to know his star sign and his favourite band. I wanted to know what made him walk into the library that day he tortured one of my books and I wanted to know who he got his dimples from, his mum or dad, or were they all him.

"Fucking Antelopes!" I jumped back from the stove as a piece of onion was launched from the pan and onto my arm. I hadn't been paying attention, clearly, and the heat had been too high. I quickly turned everything off and hurriedly mixed it all together, taking the fish out of the oven and placing it on top of the pasta and sauce, then dusting (drenching) everything in cheese.

I sat down at my kitchen counter, a massive bowl of good food in front of me, and a huge glass of wine, with leftovers for days, and for the first time I felt like maybe it would all be that little bit better if I had someone to share it with.

13

Chapter 13

Melissa hadn't been at work on Monday, but come Tuesday she arrived on time, which was of course almost forty-five minutes late, with a box of macarons, and a pitiful look on her face.

The conversation went as expected and I was only glad that Dot had come and gone with her standard plate of cookies before Melissa's arrival.

I hadn't told her about it, only because I knew she would worry, and if I was a different woman I would've seen Melissa and really thought she hadn't meant what her runaway tongue had flapped out.

Now that the cataloguing was finished, a whole week ahead of when I thought it would be thanks to Nathaniel, I began organising the new books to be put into the system. Barcoded and shelved. We already had a list of back orders of people wanting to loan them from the library, and with only a couple of copies of each book, I was bound to put my desk phone to good use explaining that loan times were loan times, and no, I couldn't rush a person's turn.

Sliding the last book on the shelf I hadn't realised until I looked at the clock as it struck 1:10 p.m. that I'd been expecting *him* to show up at lunch time, just like he always did. I wasn't sure what he did on Mondays and Fridays, but Tuesday, Wednesday and Thursday? He was always here. But not today.

It wasn't like he'd promised a visit, or that we'd even made plans. I was at work for crying out loud, and he was, well I didn't even know what he did for work, or whether he even had a job.

Shouldn't I *know* that sort of thing about someone I'd been alone with in dark places a number of times? This entire situation I'd found myself in was getting worse every day, which only made it all the more appealing.

Who even *was* I?

Dot would have a heart attack if she knew. Likely out of pure joy that I'd finally made a 'friend', but a heart attack no less.

So I'd spent my whole day waiting for him to show up at my library, and when he didn't, I had the realisation that maybe I was just like everybody else. That Mr. Dark Hair, Dimples and Buckets of Charm had cast his net and dragged me in.

I couldn't even find it in myself to be mad any more. This was going to ruin me, more than it already had, more than even he knew it would. All thanks to his silly little game.

* * *

Wednesday's were too busy for me to have a wandering mind.

95

I needed to lock that shit down.

Too busy with emails, and calls, and put backs, and organising pickups. The brief glance at my own reflection in the darkened monitor of my desktop told me everything I needed to know about my appearance today.

I looked like I'd been nudged into a pile of twigs and kicked by an elephant.

"Oh, sweet heavens," I muttered, tucking in the strands of hair that had all fallen out of my bun before aggressively ripping the hair tie from my hair, letting the long waves fall down to the middle of my back, and the curtain bangs that usually framed my face blended into the rest of the tangled mess. Flopping back into my desk chair and blowing out a defeated sigh was exactly when Nathaniel thought it was best to make his appearance.

He walked in with two coffee cups in his hands and I didn't care about my pretences of indifference for a second as I reached for his outstretched hand that held the sweet elixir of life.

"Thank you, thank you, *thank you*," I mumbled, completely ignoring his amused expression, aware that I'd never been anything but mildly unpleasant to him upon any of his many arrivals. He probably thought I was having a stroke.

"You're welcome, Florence." He placed his own coffee down on the receptionist counter and simply stared as I tried to drink the scalding hot liquid as fast as I could without burning my tongue. I looked...I'd actually rather not describe it.

Nathaniel had never asked, and I'd never mentioned it, but he'd gotten my coffee order right, by whatever grace was shining upon me today.

No milk, no sugar. Just black.

I cleared my throat in an effort to bring back some of my prior personality. The one that kept him at bay, however poorly.

"What are you doing here? Don't you have a job?" I scowled at him and all he did was laugh like everything once again made sense in the world.

"Yes, Florence. I have a job."

We just stared at each other then. I didn't say anything, thinking the normal and natural continuation of that sentence should come from his mouth, but he didn't speak either.

That got my panties in a twist.

"Why don't you ever elaborate on your answers to my questions more than that?" I snapped.

"Because I want you to ask me."

"What?"

"I want you to ask me," he repeated himself, all traces of amusement gone. "I want you to be interested in knowing things about me without me just telling you because I assume that you want to know."

Sweet home Alabama. He was good.

"Isn't that one of the reasons why you think people are the worst? They talk too much about themselves?"

"Well, not exactly, but—"

"But I'm close?"

"You're not far from the mark, I guess." I sipped my coffee, the direction of this conversation suddenly far too interesting for me to pretend otherwise.

"So," he continued after taking a sip from his own takeaway cup, "I enjoy asking you questions about *you* because I want to know the answers to the things I ask. I just want you to want to know the answers to your own questions about me."

It was quiet for a minute before I spoke, "I think that was the longest sentence I've ever heard you speak."

He grinned broadly at that. "It was an important one to say out loud."

"You mean you say a lot of things in your head then?"

"There are many things I say in my head that would not be appropriate to say out loud, Florence." He did that thing again, like he did the other day when he accepted a challenge I didn't set, when his face set into hard planes, and his eyes became hooded with lust.

I felt my mouth fall open a bit, and had I let it hang any longer I knew some drool would've come dribbling out. Precisely the image I was attempting to cast.

"What do you do then, for a living?" I asked after I collected myself.

"I own a few bars around the city."

"You own *bars?*" Why was I not surprised at that, yet, equally bewildered?

"Yes, three of them."

"You own *three bars?*"

He just grinned again. "I can write it down for you to refer to later if you'd like."

I just rolled my eyes and sipped my coffee trying to take it all in.

"And that girl you walked into the library with a while ago, who was she?" I tried not to make eye contact with him but I could see a little grin make its way onto his mouth.

This is the part he is going to tell me he is married with kids, I know it.

"That was Madeline."

"Madeline?"

"Yes, Madi."

"Ah, of course, Madeline." I nodded my head in feigned understanding, sipping again from my coffee.

"And Madeline is..."

"She's my neighbour's daughter. My neighbour, Jane, she's a single mum, I help her out with Madi when I can."

"Why do you do that?" I asked him seriously. His answer to this question mattered.

He frowned a little at me, not like he was offended by my question, but like he wanted his answer to be the right one.

"Why not? Jane works a pretty demanding job, and Madi's a good kid. If it was my mum, I know she'd have appreciated the help." He looked thoughtful for a minute, like he'd been sucked back into a memory, a pivotal point that shaped a part of who he was today. "I help, because I can."

I don't know why it shocked me, but all of a sudden the way I looked at Nathaniel changed. He had layers, and experiences, and though it seemed stupid of me to assume he didn't, I knew that everyone did, they just didn't factor into anything until this moment.

That was selfless.

I didn't know if I'd been holding my breath wishing that I'd finally become privy to his fatal flaw, or I'd been holding my breath waiting for something that would finally let me fall apart in front of someone that wasn't my own reflection, and not be worried that the pieces would be too many, and too hard to fit back together. But it was like a breath had been let go all the same.

I looked at him a while longer, still rolling the words through my mind, and took the time to take him in.

His dark brown hair that bordered on black was slightly

longer on the top than it was around the sides, but long enough in general that he would push it back from his face, and it would sit without moving. His eyes were a light blue and held a faint dusting of little creases around the corners, that could only be present from a man who spent a lot of his time smiling. Laughing. Living.

He tilted his head to the side, like he was trying to figure out what was going on behind my own eyes.

"I didn't know what you liked."

"You what?"

"The coffee, I didn't know what you liked, so I got black."

"Black is very good. Thank you."

"I want to take you out to dinner, Florence Valentine."

"Why? Because you think you will level up in your challenge?" If he didn't know it was a sore spot before...

"No, because I want to get to know you more." He winked at me, immediately lessening the building tension of the situation.

"You only want to get to know me more because of the challenge, so you can convince me people don't suck."

"The challenge is a bonus, I'm a man of my word, and my word was that I'd convince you, but the challenge in and of itself is just a way to spend more time with you, isn't it?" He asked me like he wondered how I hadn't read between the lines yet, like I should've already understood that.

I was stubborn to a fault, and though every part of me wanted to say yes, I didn't.

I couldn't. Once I did, that would be the end, I knew it.

"No, but thank you."

"That's okay."

"Really?" I asked, eyebrows almost hitting my hairline.

"Sure, it's okay. You're allowed to say no. But I will ask you again, and when I do, you won't be able to help yourself. You'll say yes."

14

Chapter 14

Melissa and I continued on as if we'd never had any sort of tiff. Dot dropped off her cookies shortly after Nathaniel left on Wednesday (a day later than usual but she was helping someone do something), and Thursday was, as always, the highlight of my week with lasagna, salad, and garlic bread with Dot in my childhood home followed by a dance in the living room.

Work was fulfilling, of course. There was always something to do in a library, and as the tasks always had something to do with books, I was always happy to do them. I'd even - finally - downloaded my next audiobook and begun listening to it on my way to and from work. I'd even begun listening to it whilst I ran in the mornings and cleaned the house. Shifter romances were high on my list of interest at the moment and I had all but inhaled the *Shadow Beast Shifter* series by Jaymin Eve. I have one word for you: obsessed. You know when you just can't put a book down? I call them 'weehour reads'. These are the reads that take you all the way into the wee hours of the morning, and the only reason you stop reading is because your body gives out on you.

The weekend came and went too, just like the week before. My routine was the same as always - rehearsed and comfortable.

My days were passing in a familiar way that also felt far too foreign to me now. The start of yet another week saw me sitting at my desk, consumed completely by computer work, emails, and data entry; and before I knew it, it was 6 p.m. and I'd not seen him once.

Not even a glimpse.

Not a wave from the library door just to say 'hi' as he dashed off to do something in that busy life of his - a life I knew was busy, but one where he still made time to see me in the library even when he had no reason to. I shouldn't have expected any of it, but no matter what I threw his way, he caught it all with both hands and without blinking. *That* was why I expected it. Because throw after throw of my bad looks, awful words, half formed insults and date denials, he caught them all. He never tossed them back and always came around again, ready for another round.

It'd been over a month since Nathaniel had walked into my library like some guy straight out of a catalogue for the world's sexiest jeans, and even though my life had fallen back into the pattern it moved in from before he made himself known to me all those weeks ago, it didn't feel as good as I thought it would. It felt lacking, and bland, and boring.

I thought I craved my familiarity. My comfort zone, the walls of my life that I'd built through tears, and hurt, and determination. I'd wanted them all back because they were mine and I'd worked hard to get myself where I was. I had my books, and my job, and my Dot and I had been content with that. I *thought* I'd been content with that.

But Nathaniel had dropped out of my life without a trace for the last week and I'd noticed.

I noticed, and I was all of a sudden very worried that was it, that that was all. Whatever 'it' was, I was incredibly scared that what I'd been determined to keep from happening had happened anyway, and now it was over before I had even given myself permission to give in. To enjoy it. To enjoy *him.*

I'd tried to not let it take over my mind, but I was sure by now you could tell that's not exactly the way my mind worked.

At the end of another week I sat in the bath and went back and forth, furious at the entire situation. This was a common place I'd been bouncing to and from. The other place I'd been dwelling in was that, had I wanted to even message him, I didn't know how I would do that. No number, no email. Nada. Zip. So I resigned to just leave the feelings where they were. The tangled, ugly, and headache inducing mess that they were. Feelings that royally pissed me off. Partially at Nathaniel for instigating the entire ordeal and then half at me, for not even being brave enough to decide how I felt about what I felt.

I was collecting books out of the returns bin near the front entrance on Tuesday morning for the after hours returns from the day before. We had this little mailbox drop-off-thing that emptied into a massive bin inside the library. It was super handy for library members but always a bit of a task to empty, stack, organise, and put back the books. Plus, when the books dropped into the bin sometimes they got a bit damaged, and that made me sad.

I didn't see him until I stood up.

I jumped out of my own skin in a silent but jolting shock,

something Nathaniel picked up on with his ever watching gaze, and something that also amused him, apparently, by the growing smile on his face.

"Did you miss me, Florence?"

"What?"

"Did you miss me?"

"Of course not."

Yes.

"I'm wounded, Flossy."

I turned on a huff, bringing a massive stack of books back to my desk, setting them on the counter next to the book trolley.

"I tell you all the time Nathaniel, I hardly know you."

"All you have to do is ask."

I was coming to learn that Nathaniel's ability to simply *not* beat around the bush was growing on me. He never sugar coated anything and it was alarmingly refreshing.

Well, at first it was alarming. Anyone who was so upfront had to be up to something, and even though I knew he was, it was still nice. That was new.

"Alright. What are you doing here?"

"I've just dropped Madi off at her acting class."

"Madeline is an actress?"

"Aspiring."

"Ahh."

He spun where he stood after following me back to my desk and went to get one of the other stacks of books I had made from the returns bin. The battle to not blurt out what I was about to blurt out had been waging a war of its own in my mind since I saw him pop up in front of me. The Florence of a month ago would have laughed in your face if she saw me now. Walls down and craving this man's company. But she was also happy in her old routine, rules, and life. The Florence of today was not, as we recently discovered.

Something had happened, and so that was why I was as equally relieved as I was mortified that the question flew out of my mouth.

"I don't see how you can convince me that people don't suck if you're never around," I chucked the statement at him like a hot potato, busying myself with alphabetising the books in the book cart so it would be easier to put them back on my way around the library.

"Florence, this is wonderful news."

That got my attention. "What?"

"You basically just said you wanted me around more." His smile was blinding.

And there he goes.

"Sweet grief, Nathaniel." I ran my hands over my face before planting them on my hips.

"Why can't you just admit that's what you said?"

"You're actually infuriating, I'm regretting this entire conversation."

"Come now, Florence," Nathaniel tutted with a mocking expression of disapproval.

"Can you please grab the last stack of books?" I asked him instead, wanting to shift the conversation away from his request to admit what he wanted. Of course it was true, but I had my limits.

I watched him bring the stack back and he watched as I put them into the cart. He trailed me lazily, biding his time before he was ready to say whatever it was he'd been thinking about the entire time.

"Alright," he broke the silence which had turned quite

comfortable.

"Yes?"

"I've decided it doesn't matter if you don't say that you want me around in those exact words."

"Oh?"

"It's written all over your face."

That stopped me in my tracks. I always worked hard to control my expression, my features. "It is not."

"Oh yes, it is. Florence, you have one of the easiest faces to read ever."

"That's a lie." I scowled at him fiercely.

"We've talked about lies already."

Well, he had me there.

"You cannot possibly read my face, no one can read my face."

"Perhaps I'm just special?" He lifted his eyebrows slightly.

I barked a laugh that certainly broke the rules of the library, which only caused Nathaniel to break out into what I could only describe as a shit eating grin.

The silence stretched between us like a rubber band on a catapult before I decided that I'd let go a little more. This was what I'd fought myself so hard on, so why not make the decision without thinking about it? Fly by the seat of my pants and all that jazz.

"Okay," I whispered into the quiet of the library.

"Okay, what?" His voice was just as quiet.

"You can think that."

He took in a big breath, no doubt in preparation to pepper me with more things he'd read from my apparently incredibly open expression, but I was faster. Turning around without a note of warning, I had both my hands on either side of Nathaniel's face - his cheeks squished a little, puckering his lips, my palms tickled by the slight shadow on his jaw. It was all I could think to get him to stop. To hold him off a bit longer on spilling secrets I hadn't even been ready to think to myself yet.

His eyes widened in clear shock at a move he definitely had not anticipated, he had been so careful *not* to touch me. But it morphed quickly into humour, as he attempted to smile with his face still squished between my hands. I was grateful that he doused the situation in cold water, reducing it down into something digestible, not leaving it to overheat like it could have done.

"You're incorrigible," I whispered to him.

"Hank hew," he whispered, words that were supposed to sound like a 'thank you' left his still squished and puckered lips before I dropped my hands back to the books on my cart and we continued putting them away. Nathaniel continued roaming around behind me, comfortable as we were in one another's company, and all whilst my hands glided over the covers and pages of books, they still felt oddly cold after no longer feeling his skin beneath them.

Chapter 15

Silence can be amicable. It can be comfortable and safe, and it can also hold a *buttload* of sexual tension.

That was where we were at.

It became increasingly clear about halfway through putting the books back. After I'd touched his face with my hands.

I was thinking about something, it was actually funny, not that I remember what it was now, and I'd turned to look at Nathaniel to tell him (completely out of my nature mind you but beating a new rhythm and dancing to a new drum and all that) and *boom*.

He was looking at me with hooded, hungry eyes. I even looked behind me, like there was maybe someone else, and I was accidentally in his line of sight. But no, his eyes were all sex and all for me. So, naturally I just stared right back. I wasn't about to take that lying down.

Ha!

I could give sexy eyes. Well, they *felt* sexy, but there was every possibility that it was reminiscent of my intimidation stare swirled with the face of constipation, not at all conveying the emotion I'd wanted it to. Either way, It was certainly not in my nature to be coy and blush, so stare I did.

So then, we were in this dark, electrifying, sexy staring competition, and it didn't break until some teen cleared their throat to get to a book from behind me.

I turned on my heels as soon as the trance was broken, my cart still littered with a few books, and legged it back to my desk. My nice, safe desk with a high counter. Where my glasses lived, and provided a protective shield to peer over.

Nathaniel didn't break a sweat following me back to the reception desk, and what's more is I felt his gaze travel over me that held a promise of things unsaid, and actions yet to be acted upon.

Holy pink flamingos.

The moment the desk was between us, the buzzing in the air quieted down. My pulse dropped from likely the high one-fifties to a normal pace, and Nathaniel took up residence with his chin resting in the palms of his hands, elbows anchored to the counter. His face had also lost all the heat, replaced with a look of contentment that unnerved me a little.

He'd done this before, looked like he was happy to be here, like he didn't want to be anywhere else.

Melissa had gone out for lunch, so she was just coming back as Nathaniel and I situated ourselves after quite the excursion of putting books back. Make no mistake, I noted exactly how her eyes roamed all over his black-clad figure. I chose to ignore the flare of jealous rage that zapped through my whole body, being caught off guard by the feeling entirely, and unsure if I was even *allowed* to feel that way at all.

Nathaniel had begun to change in my eyes, he didn't know that though.

My gaze flicked from Melissa's approaching form, to Nathaniel's face, then back to Melissa. I may have chosen to ignore the emotions that raced through me, but Nathaniel, I knew, was painfully aware of them.

"Excuse me, Miss?" he called out to Melissa, his eyes not moving from mine.

"Me?"

He dragged his gaze from my face like it was the greatest task of his life. "Are you in charge? You look like you're the boss around here." He broke out one of his side smiles that could make angels cry.

Nathaniel was turning on his charm, but for what, I didn't know. It was odd being on the outside looking in, I was enthralled. All I needed was popcorn. He truly was a master of his own allure.

Melissa immediately stood up straighter. "Oh, yes. Yes, I am."

It was all I could do not to roll my eyes. I needed a new move to convey my bafflement.

She walked back the two steps in our direction and shot her hand out to Nathaniel. I could tell you the amount of times I'd ever seen her do that when introducing herself to anyone.

Zero. Literally never.

"Melissa Anne McGinty."

Who on Earth *introduced themselves with their middle name?*

"Nathaniel," he replied, his smile still natural and heartbreaking. "Melissa, I was wondering. Do you have a volunteer program?"

My head snapped to Melissa. Oh my *god.* He had to be joking.

"A volunteer program?" she parroted.

111

"Mmm. I've been spending some time here and would like to know if I could join a volunteer schedule? Maybe be notified when there's an opening?"

Melissa looked like she'd been frozen in time.

"Your colleague here, Florence, is quite apt at what she does. I find it fascinating, and would love the opportunity to learn more."

What a brown-noser.

"You want to learn more? From Florence?" Her voice raised a couple octaves.

Steady on Melissa, we've only just barely recovered from your last quip.

"Oh and you, of course."

"Of course," I chime in. Nathaniel's humour-laced gaze flicked my way and I had to clamp my lips together to stop from grinning.

"Oh, well," Melissa tucked her hair behind her ear and hugged her purse to her chest, "well, we don't really *have* a volunteer program."

"Oh." Nathaniel's eyes dropped downward, his face falling with the sting of rejection. I think, I couldn't be sure, but he was very good at whatever he was doing.

"But," Melissa continued on, her hand outreached towards him slightly, as if the mere thought of upsetting him was beyond her comprehension, "I can make one. I am the boss, like you said."

"Yes, you are," he beamed.

"Alright, that's great. Florence, you will have Nathaniel shadow you through the week."

"Tuesdays through to Thursdays," he added, now fully focused on me again.

"Wonderful," Melissa nodded. "I look forward to having you around more, Nathaniel." And with that, she spirited off to her office and closed the door.

He just stood there, a smile beaming on his face that was nothing short of beautiful. I narrowed my gaze at him in an attempt to do something *other* than roll my eyes (I did that to him a lot and no need to become predictable), and pushed my glasses up my nose, if only to cover the rolling of my stomach. The choking need to reach out and feel his skin beneath mine again.

Honestly, Florence. Get a grip.

"I will see you tomorrow, Flossy," he interrupted my thoughts.

"You'll what?"

"I'll see you tomorrow." His smile was smaller now, but no less magnificent.

"I can't believe you did that. You've been coming here for weeks without creating a fake volunteer program."

"I have," he agreed with a sharp nod.

"So? Why charm *Melissa Anne McGinty* into making you an official volunteer?"

"Because, now you know *officially* when we'll see each other. You'll know the exact days I can convince you that people are not the bane of your existence. You'll be sure of our time together."

He— what?

"That's presumptuous of you to think I'd want that, Nathaniel." I scowled at him, but it didn't match my tone.

"They were the words written all over your face." He shrugged and turned to leave, always ending our conversations the same way. With so much left unsaid that needed to be read between the lines, something I was *not* apt at.

As he was pulling the door open, I shot up from my seat. "Wait." I didn't say it loudly, library rules and all, but he halted his movement immediately, turning back to face me.

I grabbed my phone, heart hammering, and rounded the desk until I was standing right in front of him. I held my phone out between us, and he looked from me, to it, then back to me.

God.

"Would you put your number in my phone? I don't have it. Just in case of a library emergency." I didn't want to look at his face, but I did.

"A library emergency?" His lip twitched.

"Yes, they happen sometimes." I lifted my chin a little higher, determined to get through this with at least 3% of my dignity intact.

He cocked his head to the side, like a puppy eager to play. "Like what?"

"Like boogers on books and doggy-eared pages." My smile was small, and try as I might, there was no keeping it under wraps. It was all for him and he knew it.

A toothy grin finally broke out across his face and I felt a surge of triumph at being responsible for its existence in that moment, even though he was likely remembering the same thing I was the first time we'd met.

"I thought you'd never ask, Florence." He took my phone, punched in his number, and then handed it back, but not before doing something that I would have never guessed.

He leaned in and kissed my cheek. It was feather light and if I had my eyes closed I could have imagined it. But I kept my eyes wide open, probably to the point where I looked insane, and I took in the entire interaction.

"I'll see you tomorrow," he whispered against my skin before leaving, sending a flurry of goosebumps all over my body. *All over.* Their presence had nothing to do with the cold wind tracking in as the door closed slowly.

Well, I guess we moved past the whole 'no touching Florence' rule then, didn't we?

16

Chapter 16

Something had snapped. It would have been my sanity, but I was somewhat sure that was still fine.

Whatever it was that existed between Nathaniel and I had changed shape and started to feel more comforting than worrisome. It was no less consuming than it had been before, but I was just less apprehensive, less stressed about it. I'd felt less stressed in general, like I wasn't always on the defence any more.

Like clockwork, Nathaniel was at the library from noon until 1 p.m. - Tuesday through to Thursday - precisely when Madi was at her acting lessons.

I will admit I was curious about how a kid had acting classes in the middle of a school week, so I asked (gasp?). He smiled when I'd asked and merely said it was like doing a college unit during high school for extra credit. She would come during her lunch break and it would help her get into a drama specific high school. Or something.

Whether or not it was good, or healthy, or conducive to productivity, my entire week revolved around those three hours. I mean, not in an obsessive way, but in a way where I was motivated to get up and get to work, and then when he'd come and gone, I was left content. Satisfied.

He was dutifully and consistently on time, and surprisingly open to the tasks that no one wanted to do, the tasks that didn't have anything to do with books (the man could scrub a toilet). Not to mention his absolute glee at the weekly cookie drop off from Dot earlier on the Tuesday mornings (I had started to put some aside for him).

He still spoke about her as if he saw her all the time, which I had to put down to being a 'Nathaniel thing'.

He emptied the bins around the library, cleaned the single bathroom in the back corner, took the pillowcases off the pillows to be washed - that sort of thing. But then he also helped me, and sometimes we spoke and asked questions of each other. He asked more things, simple things, like he did on our walk to the station, and I started from the beginning.

I wanted to know more about him than his shoe size, why I had all of a sudden seen him in the library when I never had before, the name of his bars, and if he was one of those bartenders that referred to themselves as a 'mixologist' (he wasn't, thank the Lord). When his face dropped at that little jab, I couldn't stop the bubble of laughter that escaped me. The only thing that got me to stop was his threat to doggy-ear random pages of random books around the library, and leave me to worry what books he'd offended.

When he did help me with book things, he didn't complain about those either.

An entire cart of books came back from a reading session of the really little kids, where every page of every book was stuck together, most probably from saliva, or the infamous baby boogers that we were all too familiar with.

"Oh no," I mumbled when I came across the first pages stuck together.

"What is it?" His brow creased with worry, but it was only a matter of time.

"Look away, Nathaniel." I was holding in the gag with everything I had.

"What? Why—." He stopped suddenly from the sound of my dry heave. It looked like someone had slapped him.

"Oh my–." Another dry heave. "This is–." Another one. My eyes were watering.

"Florence, are yo—." He was interrupted again by my gagging before he stole the book from my hand. "Is this—."

"Baby boogers," I finished for him.

"And you?"

"Can't cope." I gagged again and that was the straw that broke the camel's back. Nathaniel cackled. He let out an unrestrained belly laugh that just wouldn't stop. Every time I tried to reprimand him, he would just show me the pages he'd cleaved apart, dotted with the boogers (wet and dry) and I would be set off again.

It took us a very long time to move past that situation, but at the end we both had tears in our eyes and stiff abdominal muscles.

Overall, the first week of Nathaniel raining havoc in the library went smoothly. He even bought us coffee, a different message on every one of my cups.

'Flossy is smart', 'Flossy is lovely', 'Floss, I know you stare at my butt when I'm not looking.'

When his laughter boomed through the library after he heard me throw the last coffee in the bin on Thursday, I didn't scrunch up my nose like I knew past Florence would have done. I should have done it. I should have tried to remember all the reasons why this was a bad idea, and why I had a system for so many years, but I didn't.

Instead, I smiled, and spent the rest of our last hour together for the week explaining to him that I was confident the barista whose Sharpie he constantly stole to write those messages with would think he was absolutely, without a doubt, out of his mind.

Chapter 17

The following Tuesday, Dot decided to drop her cookies off at midday, mentioning that she wanted to see Nathaniel.

Now, a few things struck me as odd here. Firstly, and I cannot be the only one who was confused by this, they met *once* and all of a sudden they were besties forever? Secondly, I hadn't yet told Dot about Nathaniel volunteering at the library and thirdly, they hugged like it had been too long since their last catch up. Like they *hung out.*

Something was going on, but every time I tried to speak or voice the concern, they were too busy finishing one another's sentences. And before I knew it, Dot was blowing a kiss over her shoulder, mumbling about not being late for dinner on Thursday, and then she was out the door.

Nathaniel sent her back an equally enthusiastic wave and smile, before handing me a coffee cup that said *'Flossy is divine',* and heading straight to the back of the library to begin collecting all the bins.

I stood there until Melissa whisper-yelled at me from the

threshold of her office, saying something about scaring the library goers by pretending to be a human statue, so I walked back to my desk and tried to comprehend what had happened. I didn't understand it at all, and I knew I wouldn't until someone, namely the two who just hugged like old time friends, explained it to me. I sat there for a whole twenty minutes until Nathaniel came to get me to put the books away from the reading session at the back, mentioning something about a weird dark patch on the carpet.

If there was anything that was going to make a person forget their questions, it's the prospect of having to try and remove urine from a carpet. But even after he had packed up and left for the day, leaving me with yet another lingering kiss on the cheek that caused me to think of even more questions than realise any answers, I just kept thinking of Nathaniel and Dot, *my* Dot.

How they hugged, and how he smiled back at her like how he smiled at me. Like how *I* smiled at my grandmother. Like she was someone to hold onto.

I loved it.

* * *

Dot texted me on Thursday and reminded me not to bring anything over for dinner. Her freezer was still packed with the frozen lasagne's, and she'd grabbed all the other necessary pieces for the salad and garlic bread that morning from her local farmers market.

Yes, Dot went to a farmers market. No one is surprised.

She mentioned to pass on her hello to Nathaniel, and also to not be late for dinner, *again*. I only passed on the hello part to him, obviously. I did think about how enthralled Dot was with Nate when she came to drop off the cookies. She was utterly bedazzled by him, as almost everyone was (I would consider myself to be the exception there). To have looked upon him for the first time and not been turned into a puddle of goop, rather I had resembled more of the Sahara, peak drought. But Dot, she had been all giggles and light pink blushing cheeks. It was actually sort of wonderful to see her like that. My grandmother was a happy woman, she was content, but it had felt like a very long time since I'd seen colour in her cheeks that wasn't artificially applied with a brush.

It made me think about how I should invite him to one of our dinners, maybe. Maybe in the future, maybe not. It was just a thought.

Thursday was, as it always was now, spent with Nathaniel, at least for an hour. Completing a second audit of the library where we went through every single book on the shelves and noted the ones too damaged to keep in the stacks, the ones that needed replacing. This had actually been part of our daily work all week, but I didn't do it unless Nathaniel was in for his hour of volunteering. He made the job that much faster, and should I move forward without him, it would completely upset the balance and routine we had created. That was the *only* reason.

Shut up.

I knew that even as the words circulated around my own mind I was full of shit. They would speed across the forefront of my mind, closely followed by words that read *'you're in denial'*. Whatever. I was in denial that I was in denial, and I had placed all of that in a box to deal with later.

Incredibly healthy.

As Nathaniel left the library, leaning in for his customary kiss on my cheek, I made the split second decision to evade him, if only to ruffle his feathers. Boy, did that backfire.

I couldn't help the playful grin that pulled at the edge of my mouth, the act only causing his eyes to ignite with an inferno of mischief that made me feel *all* the things.

"Is that how it's going to be?" He cocked his head to the side, looking predatory.

I stepped a little closer to him, "Oh, I suppose I can allow just one kiss." Leaning forward, closing my eyes I presented him with my cheek.

I felt his breath skirt across my skin, but never touching. The path he trailed led all the way to the shell of my ear, pulling an eruption of goosebumps from me just before he whispered, "No, thank you."

My eyes snapped open as a hybrid whine-growl left my lips. I was only in time to see his back shake with laughter as he made his way to the exit. I turned with vigour back to my desk, determined not to give him the satisfaction of having to watch him leave. A plethora of curses after being one-upped by him were flowing pleasantly through my head, acting as a balm to the loss I had suffered in whatever game we'd played, when strong arms wrapped around my waist from behind. My breathing hitched as I was pulled tightly against his broad chest, and a soft, lingering kiss was placed against my cheek. A shiver wracked down my spine, and he said nothing as he pulled away again, leaving for good this time. (It took me a moment to recover from that one.)

I'd decided I was going to message him on the weekend.

Even just to say hello. The idea unnerved me completely and I felt stupidly juvenile. I was pretty forward as it was with almost every interaction. I was a grown-ass woman for crying out loud. Whether it was at the grocery store, a cafe, or a random blind date set up by my grandmother. I was always straight to the point - 'No, I do not want my eggs on the bottom of the grocery bag, they'll break, can you please repack it?' and 'Sorry, this coffee is actually cold, may I have another?' and 'look, we both know this isn't going anywhere, and the food at this restaurant sucks. How about we head back to mine, get a little crazy, and call it a night?' I was good at that sort of thing, but *this?* This felt different. So texting Nathaniel Connors on my weekend to see what he was doing, or even just to say hi, felt like a big deal.

I was running through how I would phrase the text in my head as I packed up the library Thursday evening.

I was on autopilot. Stacking paperwork and tucking in chairs, all whilst deciding if I would start the text with a 'hello', 'hi', or 'hey'. Maybe none of the above, and I'd aim for the stars with a 'howdy'. That's as far as I got when I arrived at Dots, letting myself into her front garden by unlatching the rickety gate. I was a little late, but considering it was summer, and it was still very much day time, I knew Dot wouldn't be too upset with me.

I turned after relatching the gate and stopped in my tracks.

Right there in front of me, was a jean clad, rather firm looking ass, sticking right up skyward. The head that belonged to said firm-buttock was shoved in Dot's flower beds, pulling up weeds and chucking them haphazardly in my direction.

My mouth opened and closed a few times as I stared on,

namely because I had stared at this particular jean clad rump for the last couple of months. There was no mistaking who it belonged to.

Before my voice box returned to working order, a very serious-faced Dot walked out of her home.

"Fanny, dear, remember to get the whole root when you pull the weed out, or else they will come right back with vengeance. And if you're not sure—."

"Pour a little weed killer in the hole, I got it, Ditty, don't worry." He moved onto his knees, smiling up at her and wiping sweat from his brow. It might have been early evening, but oh yeah, she was a warm one.

"I—." There really wasn't actually anything I could say to accurately express what was happening internally. I wasn't given a real chance to process not only the scene before me, but the *nicknames* they just passed back and forth like peas at the dinner table. Just as my mouth opened on what I was sure was a yelp of horror, Dot realised I'd arrived and cut me off.

"Come now, Flossy. You're late and I need you to put the lasagna in the oven, I've had it defrosting on the counter." Dot waved me into my childhood home, but my eyes remained firmly on Nathaniel. He still wore his prized smile, but he could tell. He *knew* my fuse had officially been lit. The one that when it reached the end of the rope, my mind would blow up.

He got up from where he was kneeling and approached me with caution. For all his faults, I would give it to the man. He was smart.

He walked toward me slowly until he stood so close in front of me that I had to crane my neck to look up at him.

"*Fanny?!*" I wasn't sure what my face looked like, but the

humorous exasperation on Nathaniel's face was enough to make me want to laugh until my bladder gave out.

He swiped a hand down his face and proceeded to massage his temples. "Believe me, I've tried to explain to her *why* that's not a good nickname, but she won't listen. She said it was cool 'back in the day'. I'm just going with it now." He just stood there and allowed me to gather my thoughts on his explanation.

I nodded in understanding. That sounded like Dot. "Okay, and *'Ditty'*?" I got a show of both dimples immediately and a wicked delight entered his eyes.

"She doesn't know it yet, but I told *her* that it was a popular nickname for Dorothy. I wanted to see how long it would take for her to realise it's just the word 'titty' with a letter changed over. You know, in payback for calling me Fanny every time she sees me."

I couldn't help but grin, but not for the reasons he thought. "She's going to kill you when she finds out."

"Oh, I know." He slid his hands into his front pockets after dusting off the remaining dirt and kept his eyes on me. But then I realised that he was still, in fact, at Dots house.

My expression turned serious. "Nathaniel, this is my grandmother's house."

"What?!" He looked around in mock surprise. "You're joking, I had no idea. And it's Nate."

"This isn't funny," I said to him. He cocked his head to the side in challenge of that statement.

I rolled my eyes. "What are you doing here? At my grandmother's house?" By the time the sentence had left my mouth I was in this weird, whisper yelling state.

Nathaniel replied in a regular conversational tone which

seemed to irk me all the more, "I've been coming to help Dot with her gardening the same days as I am at the library after I finish up with Madi."

"You're saying you've been in cahoots with Dot for *weeks?!*"

"When I first met her at the library, she commented on how fit I was," he cracked a small smile at that, typical, "and mentioned she had some heavy duty gardening work that she wanted to hire me for. She knew we were friends—"

"We were certainly not," I cut him off.

"Okay, so maybe not totally the friendliest of friends then, but that's beside the point. I told her payment wasn't necessary, and I'd be happy to help. I swing by when I drop off Madi, and usually I'm done by the time you come for dinner. She's asked me to stay every time but I don't becaus—"

"Because you're in cahoots with my grandmother, and neither of you told me?!" Cue the whispered yelling.

"Florence, what does that even mean?" He quirked an eyebrow.

"You know," I said, making a range of hand gestures that I didn't really even fully understand, "*that.*"

"Oh good, that clears everything right up." It was his turn to roll his eyes at me, and the gesture was so foreign on his face that it took immense effort on my behalf not to laugh. He turned to head back to his spot in the flower bed to tidy up his tools and gather his plucked weeds.

"You're saying that she's asked you to come over and garden, and you thought that was a perfectly fine thing to do?" I couldn't, for the life of me, figure out why I was still whisper yelling but it felt circumstantially appropriate.

"Of course I did."

"She asked you to come and garden?"

127

He heaved a sigh, like he knew this conversation would've been as difficult as it was, but still, nothing could've prepared him. "Yes, Florence, even if I hadn't wanted to, which I did, what would I have said to that? A request from an older woman who needed the help of a hot, fit, young man?"

"Oh, I don't know, maybe–" Just as I was about to tear him a new one, not so much for helping Dot which I was actually incredibly grateful for, but for not even bringing me in the loop, Dot appeared on the front porch and, in turn, mildly ripped *me* a new one due to her lasagna still not being in the oven as requested.

Tail between my own legs, I moseyed up the stairs to sort out the still desperately frozen dish and set the table for dinner, leaving the two of them outside in whatever conversation they were having about fertiliser.

Alright, so Nate - *Nathaniel* - was meeting Dot a little earlier than planned, but I could work with that. At least it made sense why Dot and Nathaniel seemed like bosom buddies.

It was clearly because they actually *were* and I was the only one late to the party.

18

Chapter 18

I thought I would spend the entire time making excuses for Nathaniel's quips to Dot, explaining away jokes that held some kind of sexual innuendo, and apologising for his general lack of manners. None of that happened.

Actually, it was exactly like usual, except Nathaniel was present. It was calm, cosy, and laughter travelled between us in the easiest way imaginable.

Dot, as per her usual hostessing capabilities, steered the ship that was our conversation, and kept up a steady stream of her own questions that would have given Nate - *No, Florence. Nathaniel.* Given *Nathaniel* - a run for his money.

She asked him all the questions I'd been hoarding away in my 'need to know' pile since I'd met him, but was in no way going to ask them without a boatload of tequila.

You don't need to tell me, that sentence even felt stupid just thinking it. It made sense at the time to hold that ground firmly though.

Dot asked him all about who he was and what he was like, and though he was speaking with her, his eyes kept flicking to me, like he wanted to make sure I was listening, or check if I was interested at all.

It turned out that he was quite the outdoorsman, though had I had a few guesses, I probably could have gotten to the same conclusion. The man was built for movement. You didn't look like *that* by doing once-off gardening jobs (on the house) for older women, I'll tell you that for free.

He loved to hike, bike ride, and his new favourite thing was indoor rock climbing because he wanted to eventually learn how to free climb. If I knew what that was, I'm sure I'd be clutching my pearls. It had 'reckless recreation' stamped all over it.

"Oh, Flossy would be up for rock climbing." My grand-mother tossed me her most pleasant smile to which I returned to her with a scowl.

"Oh, would she?" I asked, catching the way Nathaniel's lip quirked to the side as he moved some food around on his plate. I'd be up for it, sure, but I didn't need Dot volunteering me for a pity date.

We continued on with our meal in a comfortable silence, but it hit me right towards the end, that even though I had so much new information about this man who'd wandered into my life and lived rent free in my head now, I wished I'd known before Dot. I wished I'd been the one who'd asked him those questions.

The pair of them continued to talk some more about whatever it was they'd done today in the garden. I was ping-ponging my gaze between them, not really taking in anything they were saying. I'll be honest, I don't think you could've paid me to care about what type of poop you're supposed to put on some types of flowers versus others. It's just poop, to me. Poop you buy in a bag.

It was *poop* you *pay for.* No, thank you.

My gaze landed back on Nathaniel as he was explaining something using relatively colourful hand gestures, and my eyes just...went for a wander.

I guess it hadn't been a total priority for me to really notice before, but his body was toned and defined from use, just like he'd explained. He was broad, and tanned, and *solid,* and had anyone else at the table been paying attention to me, they might've noticed the very clear, and very audible swallow I did.

Even as his hands flew around in the air in front of him, his muscles moved fluidly beneath the soft fabric of his shirt. In an effort to see a bit more, I leaned back in my chair.

"Florence?" Dot said my name so loudly, catching me in my visual exploration that I inhaled sharply, causing the piece of lasagna I was chewing lazily to lodge in my throat. What made it all so much better was that Nathaniel was up and out of his seat in a second, and patting me on the back to help.

He was *patting me on the back* because I was *choking on lasagna.* You've got to be kidding me. Once the coughing subsided and Nath - ugh, fuck it. *Nate* - set a fresh glass of water in front of me, Dot levelled me with a stare, not concerned at all that we were not alone.

"If you're going to look at someone like that Florence, make sure you do it discreetly. Don't give them all the cards too early."

That wisdom was delivered as I was covering up my disbelief with a long drink of water, causing me to inhale again, sending me into another coughing fit, Nathaniel into a laughing fit, and Dot to pop on her smuggest of grins before leaving the table.

* * *

Once we'd finished, Nate, ever the gentleman, offered himself as tribute to do the dishes.

I'd learnt something then that I didn't realise before; there is a certain allure to a man wearing bright pink washing gloves, standing by a sink, doing the dishes.

Determined as I was to finish my visual tracking of his form, I appreciated again how his clothes were snug but not overly so. When he moved to rinse a dish in the water and place it on the drying rack, the muscles of his back rippled, dancing beneath his shirt in a way that told me they were not usually used for such mundane tasks.

It was my job to get the dishes from the table and take them to him. The issue with this job arrangement was that when he ran out of dishes, he turned to look for me, and boy did he find me. Open mouthed and wide eyed, checking out his ass.

"Florence," his voice was laced with a smile that I refused to look up and take in.

"Coming." I quickly gathered up the last of the dishes and dumped them unceremoniously in the sink.

"Were you checking me out...again?" he asked me, fully expecting me to blush and cower away.

Ha.

I looked him dead in the eyes. "Yep," popping the P for emphasis.

Dot, as usual, had impeccable timing and saved me from

any further conversation about my eyes and Nathaniel's rear when she called my name from somewhere in the house. I felt his eyes on me as I walked away, and maybe put a bit more swing into my hips than necessary.

"Coming!" I yelled back.

* * *

Once we'd cleaned up, Dot came out to make tea and put out some cookies, only to mention that once she'd done all the above, she no longer felt like either.

I had to roll my eyes at her lack of subtlety.

Never one for letting tea go cold or cookies go stale, we sat down at the table again, quietly making our own teas, and filling our own plates with cookies.

The cup and saucer looked undeniably funny in his hands, like all of a sudden I couldn't stop noticing just how much bigger he was than me. I'd never had to factor it in before. I'd never cared much about it before either, but now I saw it every time my eyes were drawn to him, which seemed like all the time.

Even the way he sat, walked or stood. It was all incredibly sexy.

Ugh.

"Florence?" My name rolled off his tongue like he'd said it more than once.

Dammit, I really needed to stop doing that.

"Sorry, what was that?" I sipped from my tea quickly.

"I asked if you had a good day?" He hid his small smile

behind his own tea cup.

"Oh yes, no, yes I had a good day."

"Yes?"

"Yes." I confirmed. "And yours, Nathaniel? Was it good?"

"Nate," he corrected like always, unaware that calling him by his full name was getting harder and harder to remember to do. "Yes, I did. Thank you."

I decided to take the lead and just ask him the things I'd wanted to know.

We spoke a bit about Madeline, how her acting classes were going (they were good) and then a bit more about his bars, their themes (outdoors, big shocker there) and the different parts of the city they were in (all around). We talked about their trips to the indoor trampoline bounce places, and lunch times at the park where they made friendship bracelets on the odd occasion when her acting classes had been cancelled (they never knew until they arrived because her mum never got the messages).

Friendship bracelets. Have mercy on my soul.

He held his wrist up to me.

"Natty?" I read it out loud.

He gave a small smile. "Mhmm."

It shouldn't have, but at the small sound he made, every part of my body tightened completely. Every word that came out of his mouth, I became increasingly aware of my own. It was definitely presenting itself as an issue. I'd spoken to many handsome men before, gone home with plenty too, and speaking to *them* had never been a problem.

Nathaniel was handsome. So stupidly handsome, and I didn't entirely know why I'd ever thought otherwise. Determined to keep my concentration on the words coming out of said handsome mouth, as opposed to the mouth itself, I pushed the thought...not away, but just to the side, and peppered him with more questions about the things that came up through Dot's earlier rapid fire enquiries.

I learnt that his love for the outdoors came from his own father who lived back in the U.K.. I didn't notice it straight away, but when I listened, especially when he was being particularly cheeky, it was most definitely there; an accent.

Pinch me, this is honestly getting too much.

It took me a second too late to realise the words had escaped out of my mouth when Nathaniel broke out into the biggest smile I'd seen yet, both of his dimples out in full force.

It seemed like absolutely the right time to clean up and hit the road. It was far later than I usually stayed, and I quickly packed things away, swatting away Nate's hands when he tried to help.

I rushed in and kissed a sleeping Dot on the forehead before heading back into the kitchen, turning off the light, and locking the door of the house behind us.

Nathaniel was already on the street just out the front of Dot's house. "I can give you a ride home if you need?" he asked softly, though in the silence of the night as we stood under a street lamp, it seemed like a shout into the void.

The question seemed much harder than it really was.

Realistically, I really didn't want to train home. It was a lot later than usual and even though I could take a man down with a well placed knee to the crotch, I was more than happy not to be placed in that position. But to go home with Nate? That would mean he would know where I lived. Was I really ready for that?

He waited patiently as I digested his offer, thinking my

thoughts as I did. He was quite good at that, actually. Especially when he was asking me his questions. He never rushed an answer from me, always more than happy for me to speak when I was ready.

I guess I didn't speak to enough people to realise it was something I did; take a long time to reply. I really only spoke to Dot and Melissa, and now Nathaniel. I'd always been the sort of person to think before I spoke. I supposed my reply time could take anywhere between a minute to an hour, but I had a feeling that no matter how long it took, he would always be happy to wait for my reply, without complaint. It was that thought which pushed me to say yes, and even Nate couldn't hide the look of utterly gleeful surprise that crossed his features.

With that, he motioned for me to head down the street towards the direction of his car.

Oh, boy.

Chapter 19

I took a minute just to stand and take it in.

I was equally shocked, and also not shocked at all, at the kind of car Nathaniel Connors owned. Now that I knew more about him, it made absolute sense for him to drive a - I walked around to the back of the vehicle to get a better look at the name - a Toyota Tacoma.

He drove a truck.

"You drive a truck."

How insightful, Florence. You're doing great.

"I do." He gave me one of his small smiles and my stomach flip flopped.

"I think I would have been surprised by that had I seen it before tonight."

"You're not surprised any more?"

"No." I turned to look at him.

"Why not?" His head turned on its side slightly, like he couldn't help the motion and it was tied directly to his curiosity. I'd noticed him do it before.

"I feel like I know you now, at least a bit better. I think it suits you to drive a car like this, and the colour too. It's very you."

The car was a dark green. Not a weird, baby booger colour, but more like dark, pine tree-esque. I couldn't say I'd ever seen a car that colour before. From far away, in the daytime, I could see it easily being mistaken for black, and the closer you got to it, the more green it got. I don't think I could ever picture him in any other car now.

I was still standing, facing the car with Nathaniel just to my side, watching me with his hands in the front pockets of his jeans. He moved so quickly that I blinked and he appeared right in front of me, between me and the car.

He was in my bubble.

This might not have been a big deal for many other people, but considering it had been months and the most I'd gotten from him was a kiss on the cheek - the most sensual kiss on the cheek I'd ever experienced in my whole life - he was now as close as he'd ever been to me, without having to catch me from coming face to face with sidewalk.

I wasn't usually quite so dense, but I'd come to realise that how I seemed to react to Nathaniel Connors was not like anything I'd ever experienced before. It took me a second, but then I knew it straight away.

He was going to kiss me.

His chest was rising and falling like he'd run a block to stand in front of me, not just a single step from my right. He opened his mouth to say something, but then shut it immediately, stepping back a bit and pressing his back against his own car. Running his hands through his hair, he pulled it so that it stood up every which way before running them over his face.

After a second, he stepped right back up to me, putting

himself very much within my personal space bubble again, and I did what he'd always done for me. I gave him time to speak.

"I want to kiss you." His voice was rough, like the minutes of silence had turned it husky.

He said it like it was painful. Like the very thought of both wanting to do it, and the possibility that he may not be able to, was too much to bear. His eyes darted around my face in a desperate frenzy, trying to read my reaction like he read everything else off my face.

"Okay." I nodded. Neither of us spoke for a second, both just…taking it in. I took a deep breath. "Why do I get the feeling you're not totally happy with that realisation?" My voice was hardly more than a whisper. Anything else seemed too loud with the quiet street pressing in on us.

He shook his head once but hard, "Didn't you hear me, Florence? I said *I* wanted to kiss *you*."

"Yes, Nathaniel, I'm fairly confident I heard that part."

"It's selfish, isn't it?" His face was just this side of devastated. "To want that? To tell you that I want it, without you wanting it first?"

"No."

"No?"

"No."

He looked even more pained, if that was possible. "Why not?"

"Because I want you to kiss me too."

He stood there for a second before a shudder wracked across his giant frame. His demeanour went from timid, to confident, not quite domineering, but he definitely looked like he owned the space he took up in my bubble, that's for sure.

His hands moved, one to grip my waist and the other curved behind my neck (not going to lie, it was sexy as hell).

He wasted no time bringing his lips to mine. It was tender at first, like he'd built the moment up so much he wasn't sure how to go about it any more, at least that was the case for me. I stood there like a stone statue until his tongue teased my bottom lip, causing me to gasp.

Holy shit.

I melted into him in the most cliché way imaginable, desperate to feel every hard plane of his body against mine. It was electrifying and I began to ache. *Everywhere.*

A small soft sound left my throat as I confirmed the existence of every ripple of muscle I assumed lived beneath his cotton T's. It was all I could do to stay up right, just as a sound of battling restraint came from Nathaniel as he pulled me even closer to him, until there was absolutely no space between us.

Moving to stand on the very tips of my toes, my hands slid up his chest, refusing to break contact, onto wrapping around his neck and into his hair, tugging gently, earning another deep groan from him. Pulling apart only to catch our breath, he rested his forehead on my own, refusing to release me just yet.

When my heart rate settled and his breathing eased we moved apart, barely, the only sound was my heels making contact once again with the pavement. My hands lifted to my lips as what just went on flashed behind my eyes and I had to exercise some serious self control not to fist his shirt in my hands and pull him back to me for another round.

"Goodness," I breathed, hand still tracing my swollen lips.

"Good?" he enquired.

I couldn't help but smile. "Did you want me to detail it for you?" I lifted an eyebrow as I dropped my hand.

He shrugged, "I mean—"

I reached out to shove him gently, only to have him capture my hand in his and run his thumb across my knuckles. It did stupid things to me. Very, very stupid things.

"Was it good for you?" My voice was still quiet, but unmistakably husky in its own right.

"Are you serious?" His face was deadpanned.

"Yes," I nodded, frowning a little.

"Yes, Florence. It was good for me. You are incredibly sexy, and I'm finding it quite hard to stay standing even *this* far from you."

I felt my eyes go wide as his words. It wasn't the words themselves so much as no one, and I mean *no one*, was quite as honest and open as Nathaniel.

"Nathaniel, oh my—"

"What? It's the truth," he said, unfazed.

"Maybe, but you don't have to say it so…outwardly."

"Why not?"

"Because people just *don't*." I tried pulling my hand from his but he wasn't having any of it.

"I'm not *'people'*, Flossy."

And I knew what he meant. He meant he wasn't one of the crowd. He wasn't one of the people that I insisted I didn't like, that let me down, that left me disappointed.

"I told you," he went on, "I don't lie, and when I can tell the truth plain and clear, I will."

He leaned in, pulling me towards him with the hand he still clutched and placed a gentle kiss on my neck before turning and moving to open the car door for me to hop in.

He helped me, given that the car was just a fraction too high to make entry easy. I told him my address and he pulled away from the curb smoothly.

The drive was short, but only because I was consumed with every thought running through my head.

What we did, what he said.

I'd learnt so much more about him tonight, and the need to ask him even more questions was only getting stronger. The more I knew, the more I wanted to know. It was like everything and nothing changed, really the only thing was I was no longer happy to close my eyes on the man sitting beside me. My eyes were open, and I couldn't even bear to blink.

I lived a little farther out than Dot, mostly because I wanted to live alone, and not with a housemate, but I also wanted room. I loved my little town house, and as soon as Nate pulled up outside of it the sense of being home washed through me. I jumped out of the car on my own, realising my mistake immediately as I barely missed rolling my ankle and scarcely managed to hide the issue before Nate rounded the car.

He followed me down the path that led to my house and I wasn't even kidding myself with the decision I knew I'd made from the moment I got into his car.

I was going to invite him in.

Chapter 20

I walked slower than I needed to. A little for Nate's benefit, but also for my own – to collect my thoughts. I shouldn't have worried too much. Turning back to look at him as I stopped just in front of the front door, well, I wasn't expecting what I beheld.

This was not the cheeky, courteous, flirty man that now roamed my library with a returns cart mumbling to himself the last name of the author until he found the book's designated spot.

This man. He looked at me like I was an oasis and he was dying from dehydration.

Dramatic, for sure, but you need to understand the smoulder. He was looking at me with *smouldering eyes.* If that wasn't enough to make all the ladies drop their panties in a five mile radius, then nothing could.

The light of the moon sat behind him perfectly illuminating him in a devilish sort of way. His hands were in the front pockets of his jeans, and he looked at me through long, dark eyelashes, and lowered brows.

You're getting the picture aren't you?

Holy jalapenos.

Except, he was keeping out of my personal space bubble.

It was almost too intense to be standing there, in the quiet night, just outside the threshold of my home. But then thinking of my space, where I stood, and cooked, and drank my wine, and soaked in my bubble bath. To think of him in *there* was baffling, and it sent a flutter of so many different emotions through me that all ended up settling at the base of my stomach. Had you told me this was where Nathaniel Connors would end up, I would've probably bet my collection of first editions on that not being true. And I would've lost.

His lips parted like he was about to say something, but then he didn't. His breath remained hitched, and his lips remained parted, but the words that were swirling in his shadowed eyes remained a secret to me.

I knew what he was doing. He was letting me write this story, letting me make this decision. Surely, he knew I already had. He, who'd been able to read every thought on my face as clear as day from the moment we met.

But still, he waited.

I thought of his not-so-selfish declaration of wanting to kiss me, and I guessed it meant I owed him one, in a way.

I stepped into his bubble, never taking my eyes from his, sliding my hands up his chest, determined to feel every inch of his body before I gripped the dark, messy strands of his hair, and pulled his lips down to meet mine.

As soon as we collided, a sound of anguished relief left me. A sound I'd probably have been embarrassed by if it hadn't been for the similar, deeper sound that left him. His arms wrapped possessively around my waist, pulling me closer to him. The curves of his body that I'd been so resolved to feel beneath my hands were now lining up with the lines and dips of my own body.

"Florence."

I'd never loved my name so much as I had hearing it roll off his tongue.

"Yes." My reply was breathy, and I was panting, but I didn't care.

"I want to take you out first." He said those words as his grip on me loosened ever so slightly, like he was admitting defeat to himself. I'd seen the look in his eyes, felt how he held me and the desperation in his grasp. This completely juxtaposed all of that.

I was, for lack of a better word, perplexed.

"I was going to invite you in." I totally wished my thoughts hadn't just escaped out of my mouth, but as I said; perplexed.

"I know."

And I knew that he did know. I knew it'd been written all over my face, clear as day, in the single step I took into his bubble.

"You don't—"

"Oh, I do," he cut me off before the thought had time to finish, "I really, really do." His mouth lifted slightly into a smirk as the British flare of his accent that I now couldn't stop picking up on surfaced. "I just want to do it properly."

Now that I had picked up on it, I wished it would happen more.

"Do *it* properly, or *me* properly?" I wagged my eyebrows at him in an attempt to smother the slight bite of rejection I felt, even though I knew it wasn't intended.

Now was not the time for joking, Florence.

There was no humour left on his face as his single answer moved from his lips and brushed against my own.

"Both."

Oh, heavenly fire, burn me to a crisp.

He took my face in his hands gently, giving me a kiss that was as soft and tender, as the others had been raw and unforgiving. I wasn't sure if it was heartbreaking or sexy as hell.

I stepped back from him. It was incredibly difficult to do.

Well, shit.

"Good night, Nathaniel."

"Nate," he corrected me as always. "Good night, Florence." His hands dropped from my waist as I turned to unlock the door, but he didn't move. I knew he wouldn't, not until I was safe inside.

I unlocked the door in a familiar motion and pushed it open. The dim glow of the lamps I'd left on illuminating the simple but cosy interior, his eyes wandered a little, taking it in.

If the roles were reversed and I was getting a look into *his* space, I knew my eyes would be furiously looking over his shoulder in an effort to learn whatever I could with a glance, to see what he chose to surround himself with when he was in his own little world.

I paused halfway in, turning back again to face Nathaniel as he waited in the very same place, arms crossed over his chest.

It was Thursday today, which meant it was Friday tomorrow, which meant one very big, specific thing.

"I won't see you tomorrow." I stared at him unflinchingly. My system was blown to smithereens now. You know what they say; if you're gonna get done for knicking a horse, you might as well fuck it.

"You won't," he confirmed coolly.

"Not until next Tuesday." I felt myself frowning at the statement.

"Would you have liked to see me tomorrow, Florence?" he asked in a quiet voice that seemed too soft for the weight of his question.

I should've said no, of course, but it'd been a while since I'd done anything I should've done, so I was honest with him.

"Yes."

Just like every time before, I didn't shy away from his gaze as I gave him my answer. Not that he couldn't have just read the word all over my face anyway.

I turned into my apartment and closed the door gently behind me, only waiting a second before locking it.

I stayed there with my forehead leaning against the cool wood until I heard Nathaniel start his car. I waited while I heard his truck idle on the street out front of my house for longer than necessary, and I stayed there even still, long after I heard him pull away and drive into the night.

21

Chapter 21

I'd decided the moment I woke up that, even though Friday's tended to be slow as of late, I was going to be *uber* busy. I was going to dust the living day-lights out of the stacks, and do everything I needed to. Even the mundane things I usually put on my 'wait until Monday' list. I was keeping to my goal pretty well. In the moments when I did find myself with a handful of minutes to spare, I turned my attention to my computer and tried to master another song in the trusty game of *Click-Click-Revenge*.

Like I said, I was doing *fine*.

The only thing was…you know when you're trying not to look at someone, or stare, or whatever, it could be anything. Just, when you're not supposed to be doing something, that little version of you that sits in your brain, keeps on saying 'look, look, look, look, *look*'. And so, I looked.

I looked every five minutes towards the front door of the library, and even though I knew he wasn't going to show up, I still looked, and I still hoped.

Fickle thing it was.

Was this what liking someone was like? Was I always going to be the rabbit, and Nate the metaphorical carrot, dangled before me. Forever demanding my attention?

'Cause if it was, this freakin' sucked. It sucked, but also, I loved it?

The little flutter in my chest, the pounding of my heart, the coiled warmth in my belly. And I know what you're thinking, and yes, I was well aware of the fact it had been a hot minute since I'd...*gotten some,* but it felt different. More important. It felt like *something.*

There had been a few moments in my life where I'd noticed a behaviour of mine, and actually had an out of body experience where I could see just how *not* normal my behaviour was. Usually I busied myself with something else and forgot about it, then when I did eventually remember, I just didn't care about it as much.

This was one of those moments. Allow me to enlighten you.

I was desperate in my determination to prove to myself that even though Nathaniel Connors lived in my head rent free, I was not being dictated by my hormonal imbalance towards him. Being that all of the hormones in my body had turned into little minions demanding copulation, I'd convinced myself that the very reason Nate didn't show up today was because he knew I had wanted him to.

Ladies and Gentleman: May I present to you, self sabotage.

Now, I knew exactly what that sounded like, but this was where we were at, and it wasn't going to change any time soon as I shoved books back into their spots without concern for catching corners or lining up spines.

I hate myself a little for that, but it's so secondary it's sad.

Somehow in the hours of the day that had passed, his spiel

about his selfish need to kiss me had turned mocking, and I'd turned into a fool.

The more I thought of him, the more I realised how foolish it was of me to think that *he* would be interested in *me* for anything more than a conquest to overcome. That was, after all, how this had started.

Nathaniel had seen a challenge, and without even needing to be prompted, he took it. When I thought of the glint in his eye, the excitement in his stance, when he'd turned back to look at me on that very first day, it made everything that followed seem like something I'd conjured up in my own mind, and the worst part was, I'd believed it.

The *worst* worst part, even now, was I'd become far too good at convincing *myself* to see the worst in people, even beyond the good they'd decided to show, that I was confused at what was real, and what I'd made up.

Exhausted by my own train of thought, I locked up the library later than usual. So caught up in my own head I'd spent about forty minutes dusting the same book in the children's reading corner at the back. Considering both the state of my fragile mind and the darkness of the night around me, I called an Uber to take me home. The car showed up within minutes and got me home in what felt like record time.

Kicking off my shoes, I went to run a bath, but not before letting Dot know that I'd be around tomorrow.

I never thought I'd say it, but I was in desperate need for some Dotty-Wisdom. Stat.

* * *

I got to Dot's early enough to let myself in and make breakfast for when she got up. I'd decided to turn her record player on to diddle in the background quietly, just so she didn't tip-toe out of her room with her emergency golf club in hand. If I was playing music, she'd know it was me.

I'd been right, of course, as I flipped the bacon in the pan in front of me, two gentle arms, decorated in bright coloured bangles and tipped in dark coloured nail polish wrapped around my waist from behind. I'd never turned so fast to capture her in a hug of my own, and even though my squeeze was hard and relentless, Dot's remained soft.

"Oh, I see," she muttered, making soothing circle motions on my back. "You sit, I'll finish."

"No, no, I got it," I said, turning back around.

"I'll make coffee then." She nodded to herself. In that moment, and it didn't happen a lot, I desperately wished to be sixteen again, living back here, in my very first home. It seemed like the world had gotten a bit too big for me lately, like I'd stepped a little too far out of my comfort zone and now I wasn't sure I could go back to how I was before.

That was the thought running through my head when, after we'd eaten in silence and cleaned up, Dot placed my gardening gloves on the empty table in front of me and then held her hand out for mine.

I knew she didn't really need help in the garden, and the flower seeds we were sowing had already been planted in a different spot in the garden, and we were doubling up simply for something to do. We did that until lunch time, Dot had made her way inside and fixed us something to eat without my noticing, only her little tap on my shoulder broke the methodical meditation I'd been in prepping the soil, sowing the seed and watering the little guys in hopes of giving them a bright, blooming future.

We ate with a little conversation about why she'd gone with the flowers she'd picked for this year, and then she handed me a broom and directed me to sweep, then to mop, then to dust, all whilst she popped out to the grocery store.

Nathaniel Connors had been here, in my childhood home, and I wasn't sure if I was glad or sad that he had touched this space too, with his buckets of charm and eagerness for challenges. It put me off balance as much as it centred me, and as all that *sounded* conflicting, imagine *feeling* it. And when he'd roll-on-out of my life like I'd predicted at the very start, he would've still left his mark on this house and the garden around it.

I was sitting on the front porch, the day was still sunny which made the cold wind manageable, when Dot came out bum first, backing onto the porch past the screen door. It closed slowly behind her as she placed the tray she was holding on the table between us. Tea and cookies, and a couple of little sandwiches.

Ugh, she was the best.

"Nathaniel is a nice boy, Florence," she started off softly, making tea for us both, just the way we liked it, and grabbing a cookie for herself before pushing the plate towards me.

I picked up my tea and a cookie, and sat on her statement whilst I felt my sip of the hot, sweet liquid travel all the way down my throat.

"He's fine." He was more than fine, but the very thought of him exhausted me now.

"Just fine?"

"Yes, Dot. Just fine."

It was quiet for a bit. The only sound was the wind blowing through the branches of the tree in the yard before us, and the birds that called it their home.

"He's started volunteering at the library for an hour, three days a week."

"Oh that's lovely, I knew he loved spending time there, so that sounds like a wonderful fit."

"No, Dot." I looked at her, clutching my teacup in both hands. "He is inserting himself into my space." I knew that my grandmother would pick up on the fact that these were the very words that featured heavily in my own internal debate about the situation.

"Is he?" she asked me simply.

This was often how conversations with Dot went. She was very good at starting a conversation, and also very good with helping it along in a way that had you answering your own questions and figuring out your own problems. I'd never spoken to anyone who used so few words as my grandmother did. I mean, not that I ever *spoke* to a lot of people, but you catch my drift.

I thought about her question. It wasn't any different to the questions I'd asked myself, but when they came from her, they just seemed to make more sense, and they led me in the right direction.

So, had Nate actually inserted himself into my space? Literally? Well, apart from that one time when he'd wanted to kiss me, and he stepped in, then back out, the answer was no. And the library was a public space, he hadn't even come into *my* house when he knew I was going to invite him in.

It was harder to admit the truth than it was to hold onto the falsity I'd created myself. The answer was no, he hadn't really.

"No, not really," I told Dot as much.

She reached out her hand, so strong but still so gentle, and placed it on my arm.

"Would it really be so bad, Floss?" she asked me the question earnestly, like she already thought she knew my answer.

I was nothing if not stubborn.

"Yes, it would. I've already told Nathaniel how I feel about people." My grandmother rolled her eyes at me in a way that would put even the sassiest tween to shame. I completely ignored it and continued on, "And you know what he did? He decided he would take it as an invitation to challenge those beliefs. The entire system I lived by, and he decided that he would single handedly convince me that people aren't so bad."

"Well, you like me, don't you?"

"Yes, Dot, but you're *you*," I clarified, honestly baffled that she didn't know how far apart she stood from the majority. She gave me a small smile at that, because really, despite how she felt about my system and my aversion to people, she understood what I meant.

"I'd like to give you some advice." She drew her hand back to her lap, and picked up her tea cup for a sip.

"Okay." I knew this was coming, it was why I had come, but still, I was a bit nervous. Every time she gave me advice it was something new, something different. Dot wasn't a double dipper in the wisdom department. Every kernel was fresh.

"The purpose of life, Florence, is to be happy."

Well, I'd be lying if I didn't say I deflated a little. I'd heard that one before, just not from her. I mean, everyone had. You can buy that on mugs and pillow cases, and I was confident that one in every ten people between the ages of eighteen and thirty had it tattooed somewhere on their person.

Dot saw every thought I had as it crossed my face and it made me think that maybe Nate was right, maybe I really was an open book.

She took another sip of her tea, looking out to the garden in front of her that she loved so much. "When you've lived your days, and you're the one pouring tea instead of the one weeding, the only regrets you'll have will be the chances you didn't take. I do know that it's easier to be alone, Florence, but it's also a lot lonelier. I know that it's *safe* to say no, but to say yes is to be brave. Do you understand?"

She had turned her full attention to me, and just like every time she shared her wisdom with me, I felt like I'd gained another piece to the puzzle that was my grandmother.

I jerked my head in a nod, not fully comprehending everything that she'd said, but I would dissect it word for word later. Most of the life advice that Dot passed on to me was done in every way but direct, mostly it was in riddles, or in a really broad delivery that she would lay over me like a blanket and see which parts of my life I decided it moulded over best.

It was ridiculously annoying because it was so very effective.

I helped her tidy up and left her with a kiss on the cheek before returning to the comforting embrace that was my home, with my soft couch and scented candles. I placed some leftovers in the microwave and kicked off my shoes before I sat at the kitchen bench. The sound of my fork clinking against my plate took me by surprise.

It was a sound I knew existed in my life, but for the first time, literally ever, it seemed to echo back.

It rang in my ears and all I could do was think about just how utterly perfect Nathaniel's booming laughter would sound travelling across the walls of my town house because of something he'd read or seen as I prepared another plate and called him to sit beside me.

* * *

Sunday for me this week meant a very cold shower after a very long run. Speaking with Dot had done a lot of good, but had also sent me spiralling into chaos. The universe demanded balance after all. Now, every time the little inner me said something to sabotage the weeks that Nathaniel had become a part of my every day, there was another voice that yelled *'LIE'* whilst pointing an accusatory finger.

Awesome.

The man was persistent, that much was true. I suppose if you thought of dating as a game of chess, I could be considered a seasoned player. Seasoned enough to know that the kiss he'd delivered to me was top of the line, of the highest quality, and absolutely, utterly, panty melting. A proper check-mate.

These were simple truths. And the fact still remained that the man loved games.

I was woman enough to step up, take one for the team, and tango. The team being myself - party of one. I would volunteer to tango with Nathaniel.

You're going insane, Florence.

Did I mention I was pacing? I was pacing.

My hair was still cold and dripping down the back of my shirt as I paced the floor of my bedroom. It was then that I made a decision.

If I played the game, and accepted his challenge for real,

then I would have to do it with a compromise with myself, because let's be real, old habits die hard. I'd go into this with my head totally out of the sand. I would go into this with open eyes, and a tight grasp on the understanding that if he does cut and run, then I would be ready for it. If I was aware of everything that could happen, all the bad bits (should they come to pass; *hello hope, your presence is welcome*) they wouldn't be as bad.

For such a shitty plan, it really did feel solid.

* * *

Thank God for Mondays.

10 a.m. on the nose, standard Monday vibes, I showed up to work right on time and sat at my desk, clicking my screen alive to check for any emails that had come through over the weekend.

It hadn't even been ten seconds since the aforementioned screen clicking when someone strolled into the library, with zero idea about the volume requirement, and yelled my name like the town crier.

"Uh, yes! *Yes.* Hello, yes. Please stop yelling, yes, I'm Florence." I waved at him awkwardly, unable to remove the cringe from my face. The man set a bag down on the counter and left the same way he came in; loudly, and without any manners.

I mumbled a 'thank you' even though he was long gone, and then thanked my lucky stars that Melissa was too busy singing *From Now On* from *The Greatest Showman* soundtrack to notice the man hollering in front of the reception desk was not for her.

I reached into the bag and pulled out a takeaway coffee cup with a rather comprehensive sticky note on the side.

'*Florence, I really can't wait to see you tomorrow. Also, I think this deserves some points in the people department; hot coffee, delivered straight to your desk. Don't roll your eyes, they'll get stuck. - Nate*'.

I did in fact roll my eyes, and then I smiled. It was big, and it was goofy, and I felt a little stupid.

Perhaps if Nate turned out to be like the crowd that surrounded him, then I could enjoy the time in between. The thought sent a pang of uneasiness through me, but I set it aside in that box in the corner of my mind and took a big sip from my coffee, not entirely sure my day could have started any better.

22

Chapter 22

Practically falling through my front door, I barely made it to my bed before falling asleep with my shoes on, and waking up the same way.

Given the state of things, I was incredibly glad it was Tuesday for a number of reasons. By the time I'd gotten home yesterday, I'd gone through another few stages of being equally pleased with my decision to go with the flow, and down right furious that I'd even deigned to drink the coffee Nate had delivered to me. All I knew was something had to happen, and it had to happen fast, or else I was moving to Alaska and cutting off contact from everyone except for a yearly mail correspondence from Dot.

Opening the library was a mindless action I was grateful for and it required nothing more than muscle memory to get the job done. I'd done this exact thing so many times; moving through the building, turning on lights, making sure that everything was in place after the close yesterday, and then finally wheeling the cart over to the bin to collect the books that had come in after hours last night, ready to be scanned back in and placed back on the shelf.

I'd sent out a notice to all the overdue books in the system, which resulted in a full trolley. I'd have to cross check them with the missing books from the audit Nathaniel and I had done together and see which ones had found their way home, and which ones I'd have to reorder.

I was about to make a note to do exactly that as one of the jobs to accomplish in the hour of Nate's volunteering today, I stopped myself. Was it an issue that I was wanting to wait for his arrival to really start my day?

Lord knows he wouldn't wait for me.

Okay, that was a lie, yes he would.

Of course he would.

This inner turmoil was killing me slowly and making me nauseous. Was this what it was always like when feelings mattered? I hated it.

Hoping that something would happen and my mind would drift far from him I busied myself with scanning all the books back in, if only to make a real point to myself that my day was *not* going to revolve around Nathaniel Connors, when the next group for the reading session rocked up.

I showed the itty bitty humans to the back of the library and made my way back to reception, intent on continuing my task of loading up all the returns into the cart for another round. I made a mental note that, after putting the books back, I'd print out the new returns, cross check them from the list from the audit, and order some replacements. My mood perked up just thinking about spending my day doing that. It was *riveting.*

Look at you go, Florence. You strong, independent woman!

I printed out said list and placed it on my desk with

emphasis, the smack of the wood polluting the air of the quiet library, but I was making a point, and actions spoke louder than words. It was on the tail end of that thought that the library doors opened to present a windswept Nathaniel, dressed head to toe in his classic black skinny jeans and plain black crew neck sweater. It was like he was completely oblivious to the utter turmoil that'd barrelled through my mind like a tornado the last four days.

He gave me a smile that showed both his dimples, and had I been a weaker woman, I would have whimpered. He was so beautiful, it was ridiculous.

Proceeding to walk right up to me, he snatched the list from my hand with an offhanded "Good timing, hey, Floss?" Grabbing hold of the cart filled with books, he pushed it in the direction of the shelves, the original highlighted audit already on top, and got straight to work.

23

Chapter 23

"You're quiet today, Floss," he said, giving me the side eye, like if he were to face me fully something might happen that he wasn't prepared for. He sensed something was up, and he was dipping his toes in.

"Don't call me that," I snapped back. It wasn't at all what I'd wanted to say, but it was sort of like when the doctor hits your knee to test your reflexes.

"Oh, no." His shoulder sagged a bit.

"What?" I whipped my head to him, my tone softening a little.

"We've gone backwards. I was worried this was going to happen." He ran a hand over his face then through his hair, making it stick up a bit.

"We've not gone anywhere. *I've* just come to my senses."

Oh sure, Florence. Just divulge all your deepest, most secret thoughts, that's fine.

"Mmhmm."

I turned to face him completely at that, "What do you mean, '*mmhmm*'"?

"Florence, stop yelling. We're in a library." He didn't even look at me after that one, just began putting the books back again like he'd been doing a minute ago, and I took a very big, very needed calming breath.

Every plan I had developed for going into this whole thing with my eyes wide open and dealing with the aftermath just shattered before me in a billion pieces. Fuck that.

Fuck that. There was a reason I'd lived by the rules I had - it was to avoid, specifically, feeling like *this*.

All that was happening where Nathaniel was concerned, was I was going around in circles. I was 'yes' half the time, then 'no' the other half. I couldn't live like that. Did everyone live like that? For God's sake, all I wanted was to be sure. Just *sure,* one way or the other. Was that really so much to ask?

"Florence."

I ignored him.

"Florence," he tried again, saying my name like a statement, not a question.

I ignored him a second time.

Nathaniel made a motion of sticking his finger into his mouth and letting out a 'pop' sound as he pulled it free. It was mere seconds from that moment until I felt a wet finger enter my ear, and probably another half a second until my glass-shattering shriek pierced the quiet veil of the library around us.

Everything went suddenly completely silent. I looked at Nathaniel, a mask of utter shock on his face, and he looked at me, seeing whatever it was that was on my face (something mixed between horror, fury, and shock). I could feel my eyes getting wider as the milliseconds passed and then I was laughing. Gripping onto the shelf in front of me for dear life as my knees threatened to give out. Like the flood gates had lifted, my body made its unflattering descent to the ground, the only sort of descent I was capable of in my favoured pencil skirts. I was on my hands and knees clearly looking for the marbles I'd lost as I literally *heaved* a breath. Nathaniel was wiping tears from his own eyes, struggling for breath himself.

When the dust settled, I leaned back onto the balls of my heels, feeling like something had snapped. Whether it was my sanity or the stress of assuming to know another's thoughts over the last four days, it was just gone, and when Nate held his hands out to help me up, I took them.

* * *

Nate had strolled into his Thursday hour of volunteering in a determined expression, and I was grateful for the act of trying to puzzle *why* after Dot had to cancel our dinner for a second week in a row (She was going to host a Tupperware party and couldn't get out of it. Understandable). It wasn't until half way through his visit that he turned to me and said, "Let me take you out to dinner, Florence."

"No." I'd said no before, but this time it didn't sound mean or snappy, just soft and unsure.

"Why not? You don't like free food?"

I looked up at him as he leant on the counter of the reception desk, "What sort of question is that?"

"A very good one, considering my offer and your refusal."

I could do nothing but look at him, sometimes he really baffled me. My plans to hate him, plans from way back when, were now non-existent. Then there was the whole 'give and no take', and then the 'just take what's given phases' too. It was like my body was drained of its remaining energy all at once, and I flopped unceremoniously back into my desk chair as it rolled backwards, only to be stopped by the cabinets behind me.

Nate just leaned on the counter, his chin resting in his palms as usual, and watched me. I could only imagine what he was seeing on my face, I couldn't even figure it out. All I knew was this was *exhausting*.

During my deep contemplation, his head swung around as the library doors opened, bringing in a gust of cool air. I peered around Nate to see what had grabbed his attention, but it was nothing more than three boys who looked maybe fifteen. Not uncommon for a public library. I turned my attention back to Nathaniel, intent on finishing my train of thought and finding an answer to give him somewhere in there, but he wasn't looking at me, he was still looking at the group of boys.

"Hey, fellas," he called over to them, all three looking behind their own group to double check he was actually speaking to them.

Oh, no. Surely he's not going to do this again.

"Yes, you three. I'm running a survey on library dwellers and I wanted to see if you could answer a question for me."

For the love of—

The middle kid was the one to answer, pushing his glasses up his nose and hoisting his backpack further on his shoulder. "What's in it for us?"

Classic. Only in it if there's something in it for them.

"Absolutely nothing. What do you say?"

I couldn't see him, but I knew Nate was flashing them his charming smile, and when I told you I was floored by what happened next, I meant it with my whole, damn heart.

"Whatever, sure."

Colour me, without a shadow of a doubt, completely surprised.

"Wonderful. Can you please tell me what your purpose for being at the library is?"

"We're here for a project," the kid to the left of Glasses answered, pulling his baseball cap further down over his eyes.

Nathaniel turned back to me quickly, raising his eyebrows slightly and widening his eyes a little as if to say *'See? Good people; exhibit B.'*

"Alright, so you're all studious. That's perfect."

"Anything else?" Glasses asked, pushing them up his nose for a second time.

"Mmm, actually, yes. Did you beat anyone up today?"

"What sort of question is that? No?" They were all frowning like he'd lost his mind.

"That's awesome, great answers gents, have a good study session." He gave them a two-finger salute before turning back to me.

"Hey?" He lifted his eyebrows and gestured back with a thumb over his shoulder. "That was pretty impressive, right? Example number two, tick." He made a little ticking motion in the air.

"Impressive?"

"Studious and nice to their peers. This is a good variety, different age groups and interests. I expect this is paving a good picture of the general public so far. I still feel very good about it."

"You're hoping I've already got a good idea of the moral

status of the general public after you interviewed an old man and three teenage boys?" I didn't want to smile, I really didn't.

"I will admit, our first example let me down with the whole *I'd feed the ducks thing*, but so far I think I'm pleased with my foundations."

I looked at him a little longer and felt something in my chest tighten at the little grin on his face and it made me pick up the train of thought I'd lost before. I was so tired of thinking about what I should be doing, verses what I was really feeling, verses what I used to do with my whole system thing. There were so many ways to go about this that I felt were right at different moments. It was like I was trying to please someone, or like I was feeling guilty for changing my own rules.

Do you know how much energy it took to consistently and actively maintain a level of constant dislike for everyone, so as to not be pulled in by their agendas? It was *exhausting*. And just like Dot said, it was lonely.

Safe? Yes. But still lonely. So, there was really no other option than to be brave.

"Okay." I stood up from my chair and walked around to face him.

"Okay?" He looked like he'd been slapped.

"Yes, okay."

"Okay?"

"If you say okay one more time, Nathaniel Connors, I will take it back."

"Okay."

I raised a single eyebrow.

"I mean, alright," he said, the side of his mouth lifting ever so slightly in a cheeky, yet triumphant, sort of way. "I'll pick you up after work, right out front."

"I finish work at 6 p.m.," I said to him with a little nod, my heart thundering beneath my chest in a way that was going to make me start sweating profusely.

"I know," he said quietly as he lifted his hand to cup the side of my neck. "I'm going to kiss you now, Florence."

"Okay." I couldn't take my eyes off of his face. For the briefest moments when I allowed myself to really look at him, all sane and reasonable thought left my mind.

"We're not allowed to say okay, Flossy." He was so close now I could feel his breath on my lips and the very real fact that we were standing in front of the reception desk in a library that was currently open to the public didn't seem to bother me one bit.

"Okay," I said again, my brain on autopilot as I tried to remember to breathe through my nose and not my mouth, completely terrified that he would inadvertently know what I'd had for breakfast or something. Then he kissed me, and the magnetic pull that always seemed to surround Nate sucked me in as his arms wrapped around me. He pulled away after a teasing swipe of his tongue over my bottom lip.

"See you at six." He kissed me lightly on the cheek before heading out of the library and I watched him go, standing there clutching the counter. I thought that this could end very, very badly, or maybe, it would go very very well. At that moment, my money was on the latter.

24

Chapter 24

Nate was leaning on his car, arms crossed over his chest, and feet crossed at the ankles.

It was your standard 'hot guy' pose and I wasn't mad one bit, especially not when his face broke out into that dimpled smile and he waved at me like I wasn't only ten feet away.

The moment was cut short however, because I'd found myself suddenly unable to move my feet. My breathing started to come faster. "Oh, no," I choked out.

Nathaniel's exuberant waving ceased immediately. "What?"

"I'm scared." The words still not coming out louder than a breathy whisper. I knew I was looking akin to a deer in headlights, which was why it confused me when Nate's expression lit up again like a Christmas Tree.

"That's fantastic, Florence!"

"Why on earth is this fantastic? Dinner is a big deal, Nate." I eyed him like he was insane for not realising that, because it *was* a big deal. Wasn't it?

He just stood there, his smile getting even bigger.

"You look insane," I muttered as his behaviour snapped me out of my bout of anxiety.

Nathaniel watched me with that same massive smile as I rounded the car to the passenger side. He followed me all the way around, and then just stood there in front of me, still smiling concerningly wide.

"Please explain to me what's going on here. Usually I can pick up on the *why* but not for this one," I motioned towards his face with my hand.

"Honestly, Florence, It's Nate -" He said on instinct, then realised what had just happened. "You called me Nate." His face softened in a way that made me want to hold him.

"I always call you Nate," I countered.

"You don't."

"Of course, I do."

"You only ever call me Nathaniel." He crossed his arms and looked at me pointedly.

"Out loud, yes. Internally though, you're usually Nate." I crossed my own arms.

The side of his mouth quirked. "And what are you doing when you think of my name, Florence?" I could feel the heat flowing off him in waves.

"I'm usually imagining a scenario." I started, heart pounding.

"Yes?" He had leaned towards me a little more and I could see his pupils dilating.

"And I'm usually asking you to be quiet."

"Oh? Because we're being loud? Loud doing what?"

"Well, there's a lot of slapping and—."

"*Slapping?* Florence–." His throat bobbed as he swallowed, moving closer, and closer.

"And then finally," I hedge, feeling his breath against my

face.

"Finally?" he breathed, so close that if I just moved forward, our lips would touch.

"I manage to push your head below the surface of the water and if I can just *hold* you there..."

He straightened so quickly you would have thought there was a string connecting the top of his head to an anchor in the sky above. I doubled over in laughter. "That," he pointed at me with a scowl, "was not funny."

"Oh, it was funny." I grinned at him with unrestrained victory.

His scowl remained in place as he crossed his arms again, now entirely serious for a different reason. "If you say it in your head then you should say it out loud, that's only fair. My name, that is."

I rolled my eyes, "There is entirely no logic behind that statement, but if it gets me in the truck faster, I'll agree."

"Perfect!" He clasped his hands together, "It will. Shall we?" He opened up the door for me and held his hand out to help me hop in. "Are you ready for a night of taste explosion, Florence Valentine?"

I didn't really have a response for that, so I just looked at him, trying to see if a comeback would come naturally. (It didn't.) He nodded to me in a gesture of mild defeat. "Yeah, I'll give you that one, that needed some work."

"Does it ever," I smiled at him playfully as he closed the door and rounded the truck. Sliding in, he started to brief me on the date he'd prepared as he put the truck in drive and pulled out of the parking spot. Apparently, the evening would be a bit of an adventure as he'd looked up a bunch of different places to eat, and picked the ones with the best reviews, making bookings for entrées only. I wasn't even sure that restaurants would let you do that, but if anyone could make it happen, it was the man beside me.

"It would be a bit presumptuous for me to just pick a place and take you, or to even take you to my favourite restaurant and assume you'd like it." He passed off that doozy in a casual conversational tone.

"Well, I mean–." I was glad when he interrupted because I was speechless. He'd thought about this date. Like really, and truly, *thought* about it in the most Nathaniel way ever.

"These are all new places for me and I'm hoping you haven't been to any either, so we can decide if we like any of them and maybe one will become our place."

"*Our* place?" You could *hear* my eyes widening.

"Sounds nice, doesn't it?" He looked over at me with a toothy grin that I matched with my own, because it did sound nice.

It sounded perfect.

* * *

We started with Japanese to kick off the night, and then headed to an Italian restaurant. Up next was some sort of French fusion place that served us something that bubbled in a test tube and you had to stand to eat. From there we hopped to Indian, Nepalese, and this food truck that did tacos. I should've expected it, because Nathaniel had questions planned and ready for all of our waiters and waitresses.

At the Japanese restaurant we were served by a young girl who looked to be maybe in her early twenties. After she'd set down our food, he flashed her his classic smile and she was all but putty for him.

"Would you mind if I asked you a couple questions?"

"No, sure. I mean, of course." She tucked her hair behind her ears and I couldn't even be mad, I knew what it was like to be on the other end of that smile.

"The person in front of you drops some cash and they don't realise. Do you take it for yourself or call out for them?"

"Call out for them," she answered with a small nod.

"Oh, you're right on the money," he said with a wink, which earned him the giggle of all giggles.

Good grief.

"Alright, last question. What's your opinion of wasting food?"

"I think it's awful. I try to just buy what I need and I have a compost bucket for my scraps." She beamed like her answer would win her Nathaniel himself and not just the goofy thumbs up he gave to her.

"Legend, thank you for your time."

She looked a little sad knowing her weird interaction with Nate was over but I forgot all about it when he turned his elated smile back to me.

"And you thought there wouldn't be more variety in my examples! I present to you, a young woman to go right alongside the three teens and the old man."

I challenged him after that, that if he asked the same set of questions to another person they might say something different, and so in standard Nathaniel fashion, he took that challenge and asked every server the same two questions.

At the Italian restaurant we were served by a man who looked to be in his mid-twenties. His answers were, *'I'd pocket* the cash' and 'I don't waste food because I never have any leftovers.'

All Nate could do was stare, his face so clear with the bewilderment he felt that I couldn't help but laugh at his expense. He assured me there were bad eggs in every bunch and it was better to get them out of the way now.

The waitress we had at the French restaurant could have been in her late thirties, and her replies were 'Give it back but if I couldn't catch up I'd donate the money' and 'I've been working on my food waste and have been trying those meal kit services where you only get the right amount for your meal and that's going really well.'

Nate thanked her repeatedly and held his fist out to me for a first bump, to which he yelled, "Back on top, baby!" He also mused that her answers were so good it sort of made up for the shitty answers from our Italian waiter.

"Does not," I said, "The world doesn't work like that, Nathaniel." To which he replied without missing a beat, "Sometimes it does, Florence."

Our waiter at the Indian restaurant was a man around the same age as our waiter for the Italian restaurant. 'Of course, I'd catch up to him and give the money back' and 'There's a use for pretty much every part of the ingredients you buy, so I don't waste much food.'

After the man had walked away from our table, Nathaniel stood up with his arms wide, basking in the glory of a relatively good reply, calling out to the diners around him if he could "Please can I get a round of applause?!" whilst I resisted the urge to crawl under the table. It would shock no one to learn that within seconds, the entire restaurant was applauding this man across from me for reasons completely unknown to any of them.

We didn't have a server at the Nepalese restaurant as it was a buffet style situation, and the taco truck was way too busy to bug the poor man with any questions.

Before I could even blink, or rather breathe, between the laughter and easy joy of the whole entire night, I had a waffle cone in my hand with three scoops of ice cream, each a different flavour. I'd only asked for two, but the older gentleman behind the ice cream bar had added an extra scoop on the house, letting me know it was his favourite flavour, and I'd be missing out if I didn't try it.

"I didn't even have to *ask* him any questions. He was good all on his own," Nathaniel had whispered in my ear as he stood behind me with his arm over my chest, holding me close. There was pure glee in every step he took as we walked over to a bench just out the front of the store, causing the smile on my face to come easily now.

"Except I sort of cheated on this one," Nate said around slurps of his towering ice cream.

"Mmm?" My mouth was also otherwise occupied.

"This is my favourite ice cream shop and he always gives me an extra scoop. I kind of knew he'd give you one too." He sounded almost shy about it, but it really was beautiful.

The store front was lit up like an old fashioned diner, and the people inside wore those little white hats and pin striped aprons.

"I'll let you have that one. I think this is my favourite ice cream shop now, too." I smiled behind my massive cone, a shiver wracking through my body as the evening started to settle in on us. Sure, it was a bit nippy but the evening had been *spectacular*.

"Yeah?" His eyes held this undiluted, pure hope and elation.

The colour of them gave me every insight into his emotions, but I knew it was only because his guard was down for now. It was moments like this that I realised he might have had a wall of his own behind his brilliant blue eyes.

I nodded as we finished our ice cream in comfortable silence, bodies sitting side by side with no room between us to spare. When we were done, an involuntary bubble of laughter erupted from me at the state of Nate's face. It was covered, and I mean *covered,* in ice cream. There was none on his hands or his shirt, but it was all over his dazzling face and I just couldn't stop laughing, to the point where my cheeks hurt. Nate wiped his face with a napkin only to pull it away and find it looked like it'd been finger painted by an infant.

He walked away for a second to put our rubbish in the bin, and in the quiet that surrounded me, I couldn't remember the last time I'd smiled so much. Not just right now, but the whole evening. Nate had waltzed me through meals, restaurants and conversations, like this wasn't the first time we'd done something like this. He held my hand as we dallied from street to street, and not for a single moment did I want to be anywhere else. Not once throughout the entire evening. It was both incredibly frightening and not frightening at all to realise that for all Nate took, he gave back.

"What's wrong?" His face looked pained, I hadn't even realised he'd come back to sit next to me.

"Nothing." I gave him a small smile as I began coming to terms with the emotions swirling around in my head.

"Oh no, we've been doing so well, you didn't make that face once," he pointed right between my eyes.

"What face?" I scrunched my nose.

"The one of deep and contemplative thought."

"I had a wonderful time." I reached out and took his hand in mine, something that now felt as familiar to me as the air in my lungs.

"I knew you would, free food, and such a diverse sample group of moral goodness." He wagged his eyebrows as he turned his hand over mine to hold it properly. I could see the humour didn't reach his eyes though, he was still worried.

"Not just because of the free food, or the sample group."

He waited for me to go on, letting me take the time to organise my thoughts. "I had a good time because of you."

"And you're saying it like it's a bad thing because..."

I wanted to tell him. I wanted to explain to him all the things that he seemed to be forgetting. That this had started off as a challenge for him, and it still was. He only needed to look at the people he was asking questions of to be reminded of why he was here at all, that eventually he would up and leave and I would be back at square one, trying to believe that people just weren't worth it, but that I would inevitably struggle with the reminder of this very night. I wanted to explain to him that my minutes and the minutes of someone else's life never collided as perfectly as they seemed to now, that I never got this lucky even though I wished for it quietly, *constantly,* in the back of my mind. That this was all I'd ever wanted and I was sad, and mad, and heartbroken about getting a taste, but that I knew it wouldn't last. I wanted to tell him everything.

But I'd seen him smile. *Really* smile. With both dimples. I'd seen him laugh, and heard the remaining English curl that still existed beneath the layers of his accent get heavier and heavier as the night got darker and our time together ticked on, and I knew what it meant. What he felt, when it surfaced. I'd learnt the way to get under his skin, the way to stir up the mischievous side of his charming and patient self. I had seen *Nathaniel.* So, instead I pushed it all aside and leaned in to press my lips to his in a kiss that he reacted to straight away.

Slow and lingering, and far too sexy to be doing outside of an ice cream store.

"No," I breathed.

"No, what?" he sounded just as breathless.

"It's not a bad thing, Nate."

And I pulled his lips back to mine, ice cream store be damned.

Chapter 25

N ate lived in the sort of place you would imagine he would, but also *not*.

Realistically, I would place him in a cabin in the woods where he wore an unbuttoned flannel and chopped wood to pass the day. But put the man in a city and you have him situated in a house of exposed brick with black trimmings on the windows and gutters, a fence that looked like he'd made it himself - but in a really put together way - and lots of well maintained bushes out the front offering maximum privacy.

He kept looking at me over his shoulder as I followed him up the path to his house. It was a short walk and he'd left the outdoor light on that illuminated the front entryway.

He looked nervous.

"What?" I arched an eyebrow at him, trying not to let any ounce of a grin grace my lips. I wasn't laughing at him, but this was the first time I'd ever seen him look, without a doubt, unsure. Maybe even out of control.

Even when he seemed to lose control of his well handled facial expressions and the emotions I sometimes saw swirling behind his eyes, he was *always* in control.

"No, nothing." He turned away quickly, his keys clinking together as he unlocked the deadbolt.

"Well, you have to tell me now?" I said it sort of as a question to soften the hard prompt.

He glanced at me again, his shoulder sagging a bit in defeat, like he thought he'd get away without having to say anything at all.

"I don't usually have people over," he muttered.

The door had been unlocked, but we remained standing together under the light at the end of the path we'd walked up.

I gasped, and his eyes widened a bit, "Oh *God,* you have a weird doll collection?"

The crease in his brow disappeared immediately and I could tell he was battling with the nerves he felt.

"Oh, okay, I know. You're obsessed with painting yourself in the nude."

His eyes flicked up to me, the twinkle in them that I'd begun to miss was reappearing, and the small, sly grin was firmly back in place.

Much better.

He laughed, the sound filled the night and settled into the space between us like a tether, pulling us closer. "Close, but no."

"I'm all out of ideas then," I huffed, throwing my hands up in the hair.

He nudged the door open just a little, but not all the way. It sobered my mood a bit, making me worry that it was something *I'd* done.

"What is it?" I asked, and then I waited, as he always did for me.

He scratched the back of his head before pushing his hair off his forehead. "I just don't really have people over. I usually *go* places, you know."

I did, I knew exactly what he was saying. How big of a deal this was for him, and how much it meant to me that he was taking the step of inviting me into his space, because I'm not sure if it was something I'd be able to do, not just yet. Because then it would be just like Dot's house. I'd look around, and all the things that were mine would all of sudden remind me of him.

"I know what you mean." My voice was quiet, but I knew he would hear the understanding in it. The knowing.

"I know you know." His lips tipped up at the side like it was a secret we shared before pushing the door open the rest of the way, and slowly backing into his own home. It was perfect. It fit everything I'd learnt about him, down to the ground.

It was so Nathaniel, it *hurt*.

It was clean, and tidy, and filled with all the most perfect neutral and outdoorsy colours that it was as if he had taken the very forest I'd pictured him living in, and painted the inside of his home in the exact same shades. There was a small kitchen that opened into a cosy living room fit with a well loved couch, and a table with two chairs nestled behind it. The space was full, but not cluttered.

And of course, littered in every available spot were plants of every sort, alive and thriving. Dot would have swooned.

His house wasn't small, but it was one of two on the same block, there was another almost identical just behind his. It was perfect for him, if you asked me. I felt like I could *breathe* in this space. It might've just been all the plants, but I was pretty sure it had something to do with Nate.

A bathroom and laundry off to the side, a room he had converted into his home office and another for his home-gym, and then there was his bedroom.

He took me on a tour of his whole house, leading me from place to place with our hands entwined. We got to his room, and he dropped my hand, stepping back against the door frame and leaning on it casually. The stiffness in his shoulders gave it away though, Nathaniel Connors just couldn't shake the nerves.

"And my room," he nodded to the space I was in.

His bed was massive. Of course it was, the man was a half giant if you asked me, no way he would make do with a double mattress, his feet would hang off the end. The thought made me huff a laugh as I took in the hardwood bed frame that held a king sized mattress donned in dark cotton sheets. I wanted to just belly flop onto it, it was *that* inviting.

Turning on my heels I found him already watching me, his stare held so much weight I felt my knees go a tad wobbly before he broke eye contact and lifted up a hand to rub the back of his neck. I knew he wanted to make a move, but he was waiting. Still, even now, he was letting me decide, he was letting me choose.

I made my choice in a single step back in his direction. I knew he could see it all over my face, the need and want that had been building up since I'd first seen him in my library, whether I had wanted to admit it or not. With that one action, his eyes snapped to meet mine, and his whole demeanour changed. It was like he released the bind on what he was feeling in a single moment, and I felt the reverberations of it wash over me with a shiver. His gaze went from nervous and perhaps *too* self-aware, to heated and heavy. All the layers I'd worn today all of a sudden felt too much to carry.

My bag that I still clutched in my hand - aching now from the grip I had on the handle - dropped to the floor in the same moment that Nate pushed off the door frame and took the two long strides needed to get him standing right in front of me. His hands came up to my face, one to snake around the back of my neck, the other holding the side of my cheek with crippling gentleness.

He was a walking paradox, Nathaniel Connors was. A first glance at him, with his preference of tight denim and dark shirts, his tousled dark hair, and his piercing blue eyes, you might've never known he was able to touch you so gently, in a way that conveyed all the bravest emotions that people usually kept under lock and key.

Our eyes met, clear and focused in a bit of reprieve from the lusty haze we were both being dragged under by, and I'd never been more sure of something in my whole life as I was when my lips crashed into his.

26

Chapter 26

I took a certain amount of pleasure (okay I took a *buttload* of pleasure) in knowing that Nate's hands were grazing every plane of my own body in the same frenzied way mine were gliding over his.

The man was a work of art and it was high time his shirt came right off.

He was too tall for me to do it on my own, so I tugged and pulled at it until he got the hint and removed it in one swift motion, breaking our connection for a millisecond before he reached for my own shirt, but I stepped back just a bit, making him freeze in place.

I had to look for just a moment, because *my god* he was glorious. And what made it better was that he was inherently good. He was *kind*.

Who knew that kind and sexy would be the perfect combination?

"Holy pinto beans, Nathaniel."

"What?" He reached for me but I grabbed his hand, pausing our...*activity* for a bit longer.

I lifted a single accusatory eyebrow at him causing a small and very knowing smirk to suddenly appear on his mouth. It was hard to believe that I'd once believed that exact same look to be mocking. It was simply a Nathaniel smile, and I couldn't get enough of them now.

I felt my face soften, my sassy raised eyebrow no longer offering the invitation for flirty banter it did a second ago. I walked back to him, my fingertips feather-light as I gently traced them across the planes of his chest and all the way down to his navel.

I couldn't help myself, I wanted to do it again and he let me. Standing still and patient, his eyes burning with the emotion I knew he held locked down behind walls of his own, but he was letting me take my time. I moved my hand back up to his neck, lingered maybe a moment too long along his collarbones, and followed the dusting of dark brown hair down his chest until it disappeared below the waistband of his jeans.

I just shook my head. How could this even be happening?

Get a grip Florence, you'll blow this entire moment.

That would be the sane and reasonable side of my brain, but the other side that had sat at table after table across from people, who I'd always known were temporary and fleeting in my life, of all the people that could've even remotely been candidates for permanency, I didn't in a million years think it would be someone like Nathaniel Connors.

My hand moved of its own accord, prepared to trace down the body in front of me until I knew it even better than my own, but then he captured my hand in his and held it still. His eyes roamed my face asking the questions he spoke anyway.

"What's going on? Are you okay?" I could feel his grip tightening on my hand, as if he was readying himself to step back despite the difficulty that decision would present.

I shook my head again, trying to clear the trance I'd fallen into. Shaking the flood of feelings and emotions that lingered. "You're beautiful," I whispered, meeting his gaze and keeping it. Something shifted in his eyes at my words, and he captured my face once more, moving in to claim my lips. This kiss was slower, deeper. It was just *more.*

His hands moved over the buttons of my blouse, deft and sure, whilst I took care of the zip at the back of my skirt. I wasn't usually someone who cared too much about modesty. Once I was in the bedroom there was usually just a single purpose, and it was always easier to be naked, but I thought I would care more in this moment and I certainly surprised myself when I didn't.

I didn't even think about it for more than a breath before the sound of rustling fabric indicated that clothes that covered me had fallen to the floor all at once, and then it was just him and me.

I knew he would, and it both thrilled and terrified me, when he stepped back and took me in unapologetically. I kept my eyes on him, trying to give him the same time he'd given me, but somehow it was harder. He looked at me in a way no one ever had before and now I never wanted to be without it.

He saw the fear of that move across my face. I know, because he saw everything. He swallowed hard as he kept my gaze before he moved back to me, our bodies were as close as they'd ever been. His skin on mine.

"You're— you're *everything,* Florence." His voice was husky and full with the emotion he was finally loosening his hold on. It was painfully sexy, not to mention (that as you'd expect) he knew the exact right words to say that could bring a gal so close to orgasm she might as well have called it a night.

His hands were on me again, knowing where to go, how hard to press, and how quick to move. I was just along for the ride at this point but you'd hear no complaints from me.

No, sir.

I had no experience in this, but I thought this was what it would feel like to be praised, and I knew that my standards had all but shifted up a thousand levels from this moment onwards. This was what it was like to feel beautiful.

His lips replaced his hands as he lifted me from the middle of his room to his bed. The blankets settled around us smelling exactly like him. Clean, and woodsy, and utterly masculine. It was almost unbearable, wanting him even closer though there was no more room left between us.

"Nate." His name slipped out from between my lips, but before the rest of the demand could form into existence, his lips were back on mine, all encompassing.

"It sounds perfect," he said, his lips still on mine.

"Mmm?" Words were almost impossible.

"Always call me Nate," he said as he moved his attention to my neck, my hands curling into his hair.

"Why?" I breathed, determined to pull his attention back up to my lips, or maybe down a little lower - I couldn't make up my mind.

"Because it means you've let me in. I want you to let me in." The gravel of his voice brushed against literally every nerve ending in my body, I was going to shatter then and there.

I might've pulled him back up to me a little harder than necessary, my legs wrapping around him, demanding he let me feel his weight above me but it wasn't nearly enough. In a motion that I knew Nate helped with completely, we rolled until I was straddling him, looking down and taking him in.

Sweet singing canaries, how is this happening? I'm going to lose my mind.

His hands found my hips before they moved to linger down my thighs, the clear effect of the entire situation being made very apparent beneath me, even though - unfortunately - he still had his jeans on.

I took my time taking him in once again, using my lips to trace the planes of his body that had already mesmerised me once tonight, his hands still gripping my hips tightly as a shiver wracked his body.

A yelp escaped me from the surprise of Nate flipping us over again, before settling between my legs.

"This is killing me, Florence," he choked out, so I just nodded.

"Yes," I whispered as my hands moved between us to his jeans, finding and flicking the button, just as he pulled himself off me and did that thing everyone does where you use your feet to take them off a bit at a time, and grabbing a silver packet from the drawer beside his bed.

I was staring.

Of course, I was staring. I was never really one who understood the glorification of the male anatomy. I'd always thought they all looked a little off and I was glad their purpose was for internal use because they weren't awfully pleasant to look at.

That was before Nathaniel Connors.

I'd sooner frame it and pop it on my wall before I let him hide it away again.

Joking, of course. (???)

I couldn't imagine not being aware of him in this way, even

when I thought he was rude, or annoying, or when he was gardening or sitting across from me at Dot's dining table. I'd had to have been beyond oblivious, to not have been aware of him like *this*.

I moved up to my knees, removing the rest of my underwear, until it was just us there.

Floss and Nate.

He moved back into the position he'd been in above me. The perfect weight, though I would have been perfectly happy to be crushed by anything 'Nathaniel', to be fair.

It was all breathy pants and sighs until a blast of cold air shocked me when he took my nipple in his mouth. A yelp escaped me first, followed closely by a moan. Had it been anyone else I might've been embarrassed. I usually took control of these situations, but right now? This was all Nate.

"Florence," he ground out as I reached for him, lips crashing to mine as his fingers made their own journey south, and my sounds - and believe me there were plenty - were absorbed by his mouth on mine. He pressed his forehead to mine. "Are you sure?"

"Absolutely." I'd never been more sure about anything.

God, he was so gentle. I knew he was aware of how I was feeling, any small change of my expression and he would have been all over it like a hawk. He pushed into me, inch by inch unit I thought I was going to die. His mouth parted and his breaths became more rapid until finally *(finally)* he stilled.

It was maddening, and the moment I pulled his lips to mine, mumbling something I hoped had resembled the word "move", any restraint he had left was completely lost. It was skin, and teeth, and pure chaos in some moments, and I'm almost certain he slapped my ass on more than one occasion.

Not complaining at all.

"Nathaniel. *Nath—.*" I couldn't even speak.

"*Fuck*, you're incredible." He took my bottom lip between his teeth and bit just this side of too hard. Every time his hips met with mine, I needed more. Like he wasn't close enough. *Deep* enough.

I felt the first wave of an orgasm bloom in every part of my body when he pulled out completely, no warning at all. An involuntary whimper escaped me, and before I even had time to voice my utter disbelief, he'd flipped me onto my stomach and lifted my hips into the air. My face was pressed into a pillow that smelt like nothing but him and before I could get my bearings he drove into me again with a solid, powerful thrust. I was a goner.

His name fell from my lips almost as much as mine fell from his, so lost in the feel of our bodies pressed together, of him inside me, of our limbs so tangled together that it was near impossible to figure out where he ended and I began.

The man had stamina like I'd never known to exist. He moved us again, into a contortion I wouldn't have been able to dream up (I learnt that Nathaniel was a man who favoured many different positions) and I was once again able to see his bright blue eyes darkened with lust. His body glistened with a sheen of sweat and all I wanted to do was drag my tongue across every single visible surface of it (it was all visible). My hands traced up and down his back as he moved his face to the crook of my neck, kissing sweet nothings.

"Florence, I'm—." His eyes moved up to meet mine as he pulled my wrists from his body and gripped them above my head.

If I died like this, that would be okay.

"Same. *Same*," I panted, not daring to move my gaze away from his, not until he broke our stare to take my nipple in his mouth. He passed over the job of securing my wrists to only one hand, and moved his other down my body until he reached between my thighs. His fingers landed in the exact place I needed them, and then my world shattered, and the only thing I knew was him. The only sound was our ragged breathing as his weight pressed down on me more than before, and I would've loved nothing more than to never move. Ever.

He pulled away though, after a few minutes. "That was–."

"The best date you've ever been on?" I supplied for him, needing to take some of the weight off of what we'd just done. Because it had been... it had been so much more than I thought it would be.

"I was going to say the best sex I've ever had." His face was completely serious, the lusty gaze from before moving over his eyes once again. I gave him a small shove so he landed next to me, suddenly feeling like I was the gazillionth girl he'd said that too and the perfect moment was seconds from collapsing around us.

"Now is not the time to lie, Nathaniel." I started to move off the bed, but his hand curled around my waist, taking none of what I was dishing out. Like he knew me so well now that he also saw those words for what they really were; an effort to make this into something it wasn't. He wouldn't let me. Nathaniel pulled me back so I was laying on top of him, moving my body with ease, just as his body was already showing me that this was going to be a very long, active night. And if I wasn't ready to accept what that meant now, I'd have no choice by the time we were finished.

"It's Nate, and I told you Florence, I never lie."

191

Chapter 27

Things had changed. Obviously.

I wanted to hate it, it felt unnatural *not* to hate it. But I didn't hate it, not at all.

It felt more habitual, the want to hate something just because it was different to how I'd interacted with the people and places around me before. A defence mechanism, if you will. Something I was starting to learn to let go of, and holy cow did it suck to let go.

It sucked and it was hard, yes, but it was a relief too.

A relief to smile rather than to frown, to simply sit and be content, instead of acting like I had a string pulling my body straight and taut, prepared for anything. Always on the defence. It made me cringe to even use the word, but it had been blissful. That night with Nate, and the morning that followed.

There was no waking up before the sun, only coming-to gently and looking over to see his dark hair mussed on the pillow, his arm draped over me like my being there was the most natural thing in the world. Like we'd done it time and time before. He'd stirred, and struggled to open his eyes against the dim light, but only when I had begun to trace the planes of his face; his nose, his jaw, his lips.

He pulled me closer, nuzzling his own head beneath my chin, peppering slow kisses across my collar bones and neck as I ran my hand through his hair.

I don't know how long we stayed that way until he rolled away with a deep breath like it was one of the hardest things he'd ever done.

"Coffee?" he asked, his voice still thick and heavy with sleep.

"Coffee," I confirmed with a smile in my voice, and watched as he stood up, dressed in nothing at all, and strolled out to the kitchen.

* * *

I jumped in the shower, only taking the time to do the basic cleaning needed to be able to start my day with confidence, towelling off quickly and putting on the same clothes from the day before (sans underwear). A quick run of my fingers through my long hair before strolling out to see him and I was as presentable as I'd ever be under the circumstances. He'd magically found some pants in our time apart and set up breakfast whilst he was at it.

It was two bowls of cereal and two black coffees. No frills and no sparkle. Just perfect, peaceful, and very Nathaniel. I couldn't even bring myself to care that I'd be going to work in the same clothes I'd been wearing the day before.

He looked at me over the cup of his coffee as he leaned

against the counter in nothing but the pair of previously mentioned magically appearing pants in a way that had me remembering every single moment from the night before.

"I like your hair down, Florence."

"You don't like it up?"

"I like it up, but I very much like it down. I like that I might also be one of the few to see you with it down."

"That's very alpha-male of you, Nate."

"It was bound to happen again."

"Again?" I looked up at him, a spoonful of cereal in hand and on its way into my mouth.

Ah, again.

More moments flashed across my mind of his hand on my body, his teeth, his tongue.

I cleared my throat, knowing that his gaze only darkened because mine did.

"If you look at me like that, I won't ever get to work," I mumbled, shovelling the cereal into my mouth finally.

"I'd say that would be okay but I know you love your job, and I happen to also love mine, so I'll put a pin in it." He made the action of putting a pin in something just to drive the point home.

I looked at him over the lip of my own coffee cup. "You do that."

The moment the coffee cup was back on the counter and out of my hands, I was hoisted up and into Nathaniel. Chest to chest with my feet nowhere near the floor as he held me at his eye level.

On instinct I wrapped my arms around his neck and my legs around his waist, giving him the freedom to reach up and tuck a piece of hair behind my ear.

"This feels good, Florence."

My head cocked to the side. "Good, how?"

"Just right," he said with a kiss to the corner of my mouth before setting me down and turning toward his bedroom. "Let me grab a shirt then we can kick it. Don't want *Melissa Anne McGinty* to get cranky."

My inhale of surprise sent my coffee spraying out my nose at his recollection of her entire name. When he re-emerged with a crooked smile on his face, he swiped a thumb under my nose with a whispered, "missed some." My face was beetroot red when I slipped my hand into his outstretched one and he led me from his home to his truck.

The drive was quiet but comfortable, and almost like he didn't mean to, his hand remained across the console on my leg for the whole time, only moving to pull up the hand brake once he'd stopped the car.

"Enjoy your day, Florence." He gave me a small smile that I was coming to learn was one that only really appeared when he was at his most content.

"You too," I said while looking at him, but not moving. After a minute I finally said, "Will I see you soon?"

"You will." He reached out in the same manoeuvre as he did this morning, to tuck a piece of my long hair behind my ear.

"Bye, Nate." The words were out of my mouth, and my body was leaning over and into his before it all registered. My lips barely touched his cheek before I pulled away and dashed for the library doors.

It caught me off guard, the way I hadn't thought much about what I was doing, how vulnerable it made me feel, not until I was already in too deep, like I hadn't had control. Even though it terrified me, it eventually floated to the back of my mind, leaving me to bask in the remaining emotion of the last twelve hours.

Chapter 28

I 'd made a point not to be the first person to send a
message. I'd even placed my phone in a drawer in the
kitchen most of the weekend after I stared at it all day at
work on the Friday after my date with Nate. Sort of like how
a predator watched its prey.

It was now Monday and I was going to give myself shingles
from the stress of it all. I refused to sit and *watch* the device.
I was all for pushing my own boundaries, clearly, but I
had pushed them quite substantially when I was naked in
Nathaniel's bed to be quite frank. And to make it all a little
bit worse, the majority of the weekend was spent thinking
about my kiss-and-dash moment. The more time that passed
between that moment and the present made it seem more and
more like a monumentally stupid mistake.

*You kissed him on the cheek, and then you ran away. Who even
does that? Who—.*

My phone was face down next to me on my desk whilst I
stared at my computer, spiralling in my own mind. I'd gotten
to work early, like same-time-as-Melissa early as opposed

to my regular 10 a.m. start because every moment I'd spent at home made me think about how, now that all my deepest desires concerning Nathaniel had come to fruition, now that he'd broken down all my walls thoroughly enough to let what happen last week *happen*, he'd be on his merry way.

I stared at the phone until the little ding went off with the reminder that it had been two minutes since I'd received a message and had yet to open it.

I was acting like a baby, someone who was not in control of their shit. I was most *certainly* in control of my shit.

I grabbed the phone and turned it around.

Nathaniel Connors: I am hoping that I've left enough
time between coitus and now for this
text to not be too soon, or weird, or creepy.

A bubble of laughter escaped from me in both relief and amusement. Who even said *'coitus'*? I looked at his message trying to figure out a reply that would also make me seem not creepy, and like I hadn't had my phone locked in a drawer all weekend in an effort not to message him and tell him how much of an asshole he was after having gotten me into his bed and then move on like it hadn't been some sort of monumental event.

Nathaniel Connors: Fuck, this was too soon wasn't it?
I thought maybe I would just come in
and see you, but that felt even weirder.

Florence: Not too soon.

Nathaniel Connors:
Did you have a nice weekend?

I could see him now, maybe sitting in his car somewhere staring at his phone. Maybe wondering if we were going a few steps backwards from where we'd been last week.

What wasn't going to work was me thinking that every time we hung out and didn't speak, that he'd all of a sudden sprouted horns and a forked tail.

Florence: Did you?

Nathaniel Connors: It was a pretty busy weekend
at the bar. I left my phone at home all 3 nights
so I didn't message you.

Florence:
Why?

This was it. He said he never lied, and I believed him. I didn't think he'd lie now, even if it was to tell me that he didn't want to maybe get a message from me whilst entertaining in the company of another person. A person who he'd also have had naked in his bed.

Were his sheets even clean? That bastard.

Nathaniel Connors: Well, I was worried I would message you too soon and maybe freak you out.

Florence: Freak me out?

Nathaniel Connors: Yes, like I know you're freaking out now. I would imagine you've called me some sort of profanity at least a dozen times since last week.

Florence: I haven't.

My coffee was churning in my stomach, it might've been relief or utter terror that he could possibly know that.

Nathaniel Connors: Florence...

Florence: I have imagined you with horns and a forked tail, and also just called you a bastard with unclean sheets.

I stared at my phone for at least another ten minutes with no reply. No three little dots indicating he was writing, then rewriting his own insult to fling my way.

It was probably for the best. If he could always be honest with me then I owed him the same, even if it was putting my foot in my mouth. I could only assume that his lack of response was because I'd hit the nail on the head. I huffed a breath out and threw my phone in my bag.

My body was instantly full of nervous and angry energy, something that tapping out a song with my mouse would just *not* solve. I usually liked to save putting the books back on their shelves until after lunch if I could help it, something to help pass the afternoon by in a stress free way, but on days like today, it was a before lunch sort of task.

I walked to the cart with more purpose than I needed to, the knots in my stomach and the tingling in my fingertips making every action angry. I was *angry*.

I took a long time putting the books back. I felt every cover and relished in the sound of the books sliding against one another as I placed each back into their home. Something that should have really only taken me ten minutes turned into a thirty minute exercise but as I pushed the empty cart back to the front of the library I felt more grounded. Less angry and more hurt.

I was stopped short as the front desk came into view and a black clad Nathaniel was leaning on the counter facing away from me. He'd heard me of course, but he didn't move to look in my direction.

Fine, if he wanted to do this in person, then we could do this in person. I'd dropped a man a peg or five before with my words and I was sure I could summon the anger I'd just expelled to do the same to this one.

Yes. I could cut him down with a sharp tongue, but I wouldn't enjoy it. I wouldn't mean it. I'd do it though, if only to guard myself a little longer from the shit storm he had no doubt come to confess to.

I rounded my desk to find a takeaway coffee sitting just beside my keyboard. On instinct, I twirled it around looking for whatever note he'd written, oblivious to the fact that until now I'd come to look forward to whatever it was he had planned to write.

There was nothing there though, and I could feel his eyes burning a hole into my frontal lobes, so I raised my eyes to meet his.

"I waited too long didn't I?" His question was soft, almost like he was looking at me like an animal who could be easily spooked.

"Nathaniel, I don't care–."

"Of course, you care. You clearly think you care too much, that's why you made a comment about my sheets."

"Oh, very nice, mock me. I'm not the one who had another person *naked* in my bed–."

"What?"

"You need to stop cutting me off, it's incredibly–."

"What do you mean, another person naked in my bed?"

"Well if you'd just let me–."

"No, because you're not explaining the right thing."

I took a deep breath, "It's clear to me that you waited so long to message because you were…otherwise occupied."

He stared at me like I'd grown a third nipple between my eyes, and then he started laughing. Like a big, belly laugh that makes everyone else around you laugh too.

"Nathaniel," I hissed.

He just laughed louder.

"*Nathaniel,* this is a library," I whisper-yelled at him. Would he never learn?

I must have looked as serious as I was hoping because he tried to sober up as fast as possible. We just stared at each other for a while as he continued to attempt to compose himself.

"Great, so you came to laugh at me in person? You're really doing quite well. I wonder what you'll do next. Show me a photo?"

He frowned at that, like only now was he realising that I was quite serious. "You really think I'd do that?"

"Well, you've not denied it, and perhaps that was your end goal. Just to enjoy the chase of someone you couldn't initially have then–."

"No, Florence. There has been no one naked in my bed, besides me of course, since *you* were naked in my bed. There's actually been no one *but* you naked in my bed. You were the first person to ever be naked in my bed, besides me."

"Stop saying the word naked so much. And come *on,* you expect me to believe that I'm the *only one–.*"

"No. You're not the only person I've slept with. And if it's so important to you, I can give you a number. But I've never had anyone over. My space is my space and I don't share it like that."

"Girlfriends?"

"Sure, but always at theirs."

I frowned at that. "Didn't they think that was a bit weird?"

"A couple of them, maybe. But tell someone you prefer their bed and they're more than happy to go along with it."

"But you have a great bed." *Damn.*

The shit-eating grin plastered on his face made me roll my eyes. "I do." It was gone just as quickly though. "I waited too long to message. It was a fifty-fifty shot. Next time we'll avoid all of this."

"Next time?" I quirked an eyebrow at him.

"Or not, or just, you know, next time I see you."

I stared at him then, letting his words sink in a bit more,

before I nodded my head and he released a breath I hadn't realised he'd been holding.

"Can I take you out for lunch today?"

"Okay."

"Okay. I'll be back at twelve then?"

"Okay," I repeated.

He smiled and tapped the counter before giving me a couple of finger-guns and leaving the library.

It felt weird to go back to work now, unsettled.

My phone buzzed from my bag not long after I'd finally gotten into a rhythm of replying to emails.

Nathaniel Connors: Too soon?

I couldn't help the smile that spread across my lips.

Florence: Sooner than I thought.

Nathaniel Connors: So, too soon?

Florence: No, not too soon. Also, I'm not sold on the finger-guns.

Nathaniel Connors: You'll come around to them :)

29

Chapter 29

The rest of the week floated by the same way as the rest of my Monday did after Nathaniel showed up and convinced me of the cleanliness of his sheets, and his lack of devil horns.

Most mornings would start with a message of some sort. In classic Nate fashion, they weren't your standard greetings. Not a casual 'hello' or 'good morning'. Alright, maybe a couple of them started off that way, but his favourite was to enlighten me with random and incredibly useless facts.

On Wednesday morning my phone buzzed shortly after my first sip of coffee.

Nathaniel Connors: Florence, did you know that
    it's physically impossible for a pig to look
    up at the sky?

I didn't know that. Who knew that?

> **Florence:** I am actually unsure how I've
> gone so long without knowing that.

His reply was almost instant.

Nathaniel Connors: Worry not, milady. There is
plenty more where that came from, rest assured.

Smiling like an idiot if only because I knew the look his eyes
would have had, I sent back a last message before putting my
phone back in my bag to focus on work.

> **Florence:** I was fretting rather alarmingly.
> What a relief!

Without fault, Nate still showed up for his hour of unpaid
work, and every time I thought he might look to steal a kiss,
or maybe his hands would linger on mine a little longer as we
passed books to one another, it amounted to a whole lot of
nothing. *Sweet FA*. The man refused to touch me.

Okay, that's not entirely true. He'd insisted on dropping
me home a few times, his fingers entwined with mine as we
walked hand in hand to his car.

"You could have parked closer, you know." I chided mostly out of annoyance for his new found celibacy.

"Of course I know, Flossy."

"Well?"

"Well, what?"

"Why didn't you?"

He lifted our joined hands up and across my body so his arm rested across my shoulders and mine lifted up across my chest, our fingers still entwined, and planted a tender kiss on my temple.

"I wouldn't have been able to do that had I parked mere metres from the library door, would I?" His breath caressed my ear as he spoke the words quietly, causing a chill to rush down the length of my spine and my cheeks to go all tingly.

"No, I suppose not." His effect on me was clear in the breathlessness of my voice.

"Mmm." He placed another kiss on my temple but kept me tucked close to him. "You

smell lovely, Flossy."

I whacked the back of my hand to his chest in an effort to avoid a reply, because honestly, I was at a loss as to what to do with his compliments. I wanted to tell him to stop as much as I wanted to hear him say them again. It baffled me, to think that someone could be enjoying my presence as much as he did. If I thought about it too much, I'd ruin it for myself, so I thought about it only a little everyday in an effort to chip away at the nagging uncertainty that lingered at the back of my mind, that it was all in fact far too good to be true.

"Where'd you go, Florence?"

"Hmm?"

"Just now, where'd you go?"

His perspective eyes met mine intensely as we stopped outside of his truck, the pad of his thumb coming up to swipe at my bottom lip. I reached up to grab his hand, placing a gentle kiss on his knuckles. Half because I loved doing it, and half to stop him looking too deep into my own mind.

"Nowhere particularly important, I assure you." I offered him a small smile before climbing into his truck, pushing the whole moment far from my mind.

He dropped me home, his concern still clear, but called me later in the evening asking if perhaps dinner was on the cards at Dots for the following day as per usual (the last couple weeks being an exception).

When we both rolled up to her little yellow house, hand in hand, and he followed me straight to the kitchen to help get dinner ready, my chest filled with sparks of warmth at the fleeting thought that should Nathaniel Connors come to many more of these weekly Thursday night dinners at Dots, I might start forgetting what they were like before he ever had a seat at her table.

Chapter 30

The weekend was full of beautiful weather and perfectly balanced, home-made lemonade on Dot's porch.

I could feel the sweat trickle down my back as I pulled my hat from my head and fanned my face. That was exactly how I wanted to spend my weekends. It was exactly how I *did* spend my weekends. Saturday was all crisp, cold drinks, and dirt under my nails despite my gardening gloves. Topped with some sort of iced slushy drink that Dot had concocted in the blender and dancing around the living room. Sunday was exactly the same, except that Nathaniel had joined Dot and I.

And he was wearing shorts.

I watched him jump out of his truck still looking like himself for the most part, with a pair of all black high top Converse's on, but that's sort of where it ended. He was wearing a pair of black shorts and a black singlet with a baseball cap on backwards. I was in too much of a state of bewilderment to even think too long on just how utterly bedazzling he was.

He waved to Dot who was sitting on the porch out front as

he closed the little white gate behind him, walking right up to lift me into a hug. The toes of my own shoes barely scraped the grass below, before he planted a little kiss just behind my ear. Once he set me down and stepped back a little, I could lift my thoughts from the gutter where they had descended.

The absolute raw sex appeal of this man was going to kill me.

I cleared my throat, "Nathaniel."

"Nate. I thought we were past this now, Florence." His grin was still full of wicked amusement.

I waved him off. "Nathaniel," I pointed at his bottom half, "you're wearing shorts."

He looked down at himself as if the news caught him off guard. "It's warm outside," he shrugged, tucking his hands into the shorts in question.

"It's been warm for a while," I countered, knowing we were already halfway through the summer.

"That's true."

"I didn't even know you *owned* shorts." The disbelief in my voice was comical and I could see him trying to keep it together, to humour me through this conversation.

He reached out, placing a finger under my chin to close my gaping mouth. "Of course I own shorts, Florence." He tugged me closer to him by the gardening apron I was wearing. "You've already seen my legs so it doesn't matter now."

"What doesn't matter?" I could feel the frown form between my eyes a moment before Nate reached up to smooth his finger along the forming crease.

"If you see them again." He placed a chaste kiss on my brow before letting me go. He was always careful not to be too handsy around Dot, and though I knew she wouldn't care, I couldn't help but love him for it, just a little.

My stomach turned at my own choice of words.

It's just a phrase, Florence. Pipe down.

"Nate, that makes no sense." I reached out to hold onto the hem of his singlet, "I feel like shorts are something you have to work up to."

"That makes sense." It didn't really, but his face was thoughtful for a minute nonetheless before he continued on. "Well, I'm calling it. We're at shorts level now." His amusement became harder to hide. The idea of the entire situation was causing a bubble of laughter to form in my throat. It was bizarre that I could be at a 'shorts level' with someone. That implied ease, comfort, and casual hanging about. At least that's what it meant to me. The thought itself threw me off guard and a grin tore loose across my face.

I couldn't help the laugh that finally followed it after Nate mirrored my expression, flashing a smile that brought out both his dimples. It was the sort of laugh that got bigger the more air you breathed in and before I knew it, I'd snort-laughed. I don't think I'd ever moved as fast as I had to bring my hand up to clamp over my mouth.

"Flossy, did you—," Nate started, his eyes crinkling as his lips thinned, trying to hold in his own laugh. The hint of his hidden British accent flowing through. I dropped the hem of his shirt that I'd still been fiddling with, placing both arms at my sides. "No."

I stepped back, about to turn before he reached out for me again, hauling me up to his chest so my feet were once again not touching the ground.

"You did, I heard it." His grin was *massive,* dimples still very much on display.

"Yes, I heard it as well," Dot chimed in from her place on

211

the porch.

We both turned to look at her peering at us over the top of her glasses under her big sun hat. Nate beamed and I scowled. "Dot, that is entirely unhelpful."

"Happy to assist where I can, dear," she responded without missing a beat, then moving her attention back towards her crossword.

I turned back to face Nate and his shit-eating grin. "Shorts and snorts, I would say that's pretty even. A good level to be at." He nodded to himself before leaning in to place a kiss to the corner of my mouth.

"Fanny, would you mind taking Florence to begin in the back garden?" Dot called out to us without even raising her eyes. She could very well do this all herself but I think having a large, fit, and capable man around was making her lazy. That made me smile.

"Can do, Ditty," he called back, dropping me back down to my feet and blowing her a kiss. I fixed my own hat before I followed him through the house. "That was the weirdest conversation we've ever had," I mumbled after him.

"Yes, but you know exactly what I'm talking about, just like I knew what you meant. We've levelled up, Florence."

"I agree, yes, but you've decided to measure it with *shorts and snorts*." I loved it. But I still tried to suppress my grin even though his back was to me as he pushed through the screen door that headed out to the back garden.

"I think that's perfect though, don't you?" Nate cast one of his small, soft smiles over his shoulder, heading into the shed in the back corner to get all of the gardening things that Dot had bought him or that he had brought over himself and left here.

Before I could even open my mouth to reply, Dot had zipped out the door behind me and high-tailed it to where Nate was putting on his gardening apron and gloves. She pulled him right down into a hug, Nate's form was hulking beside my small, petite grandmother. Regardless of the dinner on Thursday, she was reprimanding him on how it'd been too long since she'd given him a squeeze.

They were fast friends. Besties, even. I knew that, had I not even been in the picture, I could still picture him here. Listening to her closely as he was now, about all the jobs she's had for him, including the things inside that she needed help with that were too far out of reach for her to bother about. That he'd still sit with her on Sundays and drink lemonade over a crossword, or prepare frozen lasagne, garlic bread, and salad for her on Thursday nights. The thought that there was someone who I knew loved Dot as much as I did settled something in me. Like placing your freezing hands in front of a roaring fire and feeling the heat melt away the ice.

I took a deep breath and basked in the weightlessness of it. The simple ease of being myself in this house, no matter who I had to be or how I acted beyond the white picket fence surrounding it. Hearing how Dot doted on Nathaniel the way she did to me also made sense, it felt natural. Much like our Thursday night weekly dinners, I could see that just as there was a place in her little garden shed for his gardening things, and a seat at her little dinner table that she now referred to as 'Nathaniel's place', we could both, Dot and I, begin to forget a time when it had only been the two of us.

So, as I had before, I shoved the little niggling thoughts to the back of my mind and walked down the rest of the steps off the back porch to where Dot was pulling Nate in for yet another hug in the same garden I had grown up in. The place that held some of my most favourite and loved memories, and relished in the knowledge of being confident in the answer I had for the question Nate had asked me. That yes, at least for right now, things were absolutely, unquestionably, perfect.

Chapter 31

I n the grossest, most cliché way ever, the weekend had left me lighter and happier than I had felt in a very long time, adding to the already incredible vibe I was riding on what was another beautiful Monday.

Nathaniel Connors:
There was a blue house, a red house and
a green house. What colour were the houses?

Nate had messaged me just as I was drying off from my post-run shower. A smile lighting my face in a way that made me want to roll my eyes at myself. *Eughhh.*

Florence: I thought your 'thing'
was useless facts, not riddles...

Nathaniel Connors: I'm sorry, did you just say 'useless'?

I barked a laugh and flicked him another quick message before throwing my phone onto my bed and making my way to the kitchen. As usual, I'd turned the coffee on to brew before heading out for my run so it was ready and waiting in the kitchen for me for this precise moment. It almost left like someone else had done it.

> **Florence:** Sorry my cat sat on my phone!
> Autocorrect. *face-palm*

I took my time with breakfast and, despite myself, I thought seriously about the riddle. The addition of Nate's presence in my life was made more constant by our continuous stream of conversation. If we weren't texting, he would call me, usually as I cooked or folded laundry, and we would just chat. It was easier to let my guard down when there was a phone between us, but I was absolutely kidding myself if I pretended that I wasn't coming to enjoy, or even *expect* my phone to light up with his name.

I swiped my phone off my bed as the last thing on my to-do before heading out the door.

Nathaniel Connors: You're the only person I know who
doesn't actually use emojis but rather
writes out the action. *heart eyes*

Nathaniel Connors: It doesn't have the same effect when I do it. Must just be a Florence thing.

Nathaniel Connors: Also I know you don't have a cat.
Don't think for a moment you've fooled me.
You haven't. (No offence to the cat should
it actually exist I just pegged you as more of
dog person.)

> **Florence:** Is Nathaniel Connors flustered
> and rambling?! And yes, very much
> a dog sort of gal.

His messages were never far behind my own.

Nathaniel Connors: You make me feel a great many things,
Florence Valentine. Flustered is just the
tip of the iceberg.

Well, how-dee-doo.

I dropped my phone into my bag without replying and busied myself with walking to the station near my house. There was nothing quite like a steamy scene being narrated to you in an audiobook to help you forget your worries. I waltzed into the library with the same, stupid smile on my face from this morning, and didn't so much as blink at my own exuberant wave to Melissa through the window of her office before sitting at my own desk. She looked less and less shocked every time I did that, so she just waved back with a small smile of her own.

Sitting right in front of my keyboard was a takeaway coffee, the sender clearly identified by the message written on a sticky note plastered to the lid of the cup, having been too long for any hospitality worker to worry about fitting it onto the side of a paper takeaway: *'Don't forget about my riddle Flossy, or the things you'll make me feel will not be the pleasant sort I'm used to.'*

I wasn't the sort to blush at the sight of relatively inappropriate things, but in reality it wasn't what he'd written, or even that someone had to write it out and someone else had to deliver it. It was simply that it made me remember everything that *he* had made *me* feel on a particular night not so long ago, and how I very much wanted to feel it all again.

* * *

The day moved on in the way most Monday's did. Relatively fast, considering the lack of work the weekend staff did, and always with the sort of headaches that you get from looking at a screen all day, regardless of my handy-dandy blue light glasses.

So, when I finally locked the doors to the library and turned on a deep breath to finish cleaning everything up, the very, *very* last thing I wanted was a tween knocking on the glass doors pleading to be let in for some book they needed ASAP. So when I was halfway to my desk and that knock came, I was about to combust. Turning around and gathering as much of my remaining strength to help whoever it was, my face already pulling half-way into a class-A 'work smile'. All my efforts fell away as my jaw went slack thanks to Nathaniel standing on the other side waving like an idiot.

For some reason I looked around to make sure it was me he was waving at (not sure why I still did that), the act was met with an eye roll from the man himself which made the side of my mouth lift up. I knew he'd picked up that particular little quirk from me.

"This is unexpected," I said as he shimmied in through the open door.

"Too soon?" His question was casual but I could tell he was genuinely unsure, and it made me smile remembering the very same question he'd asked me last time. How so much had seemed to have shifted since then.

"Unexpected, but not too soon." I locked the door and turned back to head into the library, still needing to get all the cleaning done. The thought made me want to hurl almost as much as putting my hand in baby boogers did.

"Did you solve the riddle?"

"Don't tell me that's why you came all this way?" I turned to look at him, standing halfway back to my desk now, eyebrows raised in serious accusation.

"Not the only reason." He made his way closer to me until we were standing toe-to-toe, and I had to crane my neck to look up at him.

"What are the other reasons then?" My face softened into a small smile laced with mischief.

"My reasons for being here are three-fold, Floss."

"Oh? That sounds serious." I frowned in mock concern, earning me a cheeky smile of his own making.

"Yes, quite. So?"

The little quip made the English undertones of his accent flare up which reminded me of the last time he'd reverted back to the lilt, and how there'd been much less clothing between us then.

I swallowed hard and Nate's eyes flicked to follow the action.

"Yes, I figured it out." I swallowed again and took a step back, conscious of the fact that we were in the library. The *public* library.

For crying out loud, Florence. Where is your dignity?

The answer was simple. At this moment, I had none.

"And?" He followed me back a step.

"Red, blue and transparent."

"Did you Google it?" His eyes were serious, but his mouth still held his grin that spelt *trouble.*

"Yep."

He barked a laugh, probably not anticipating I'd be so honest.

"We can't all frolic around at bars all day, Nate." I lifted an eyebrow at him in an effort to gain more of my composure, but really I was doing my best not to strip him of his clothes right freakin' then. "The next reason?" I asked, more for a distraction than anything.

"Do you really have a cat?"

It was my turn to laugh, not holding back on the little snort that followed which made him grin even more. "No, I don't have a cat. I'm allergic actually."

"Oh, that's good to know, I'm quite comfortable around pussy cats myself."

Pinching my lips I shoved at his chest. "I bet," scoffing as I rounded my desk with the purpose to do literally nothing.

My mind was all jumbled up. I needed to write a list

or something to remember what in the name of rushing hormones I needed to do so I could lock up and do what *really* needed to be done. Which was, of course, to move this man to a more secluded location and ravish the daylights out of him. I was pretty much done with waiting for him to make a move.

"There was one more thing." He moved right behind me so that when I straightened back up from my computer - which was blank and turned off, even though I'd been clicking the mouse like it wasn't - I could feel every inch of his hard body pressing into me. *Every inch.*

"What was that?" I rounded him so that I wasn't wedged between his body and the desk, but so I had the filing cabinet to my back. It wasn't much better, but there at least was a bit more space between us. I was *trying* to do the right thing here and he was making it incredibly difficult.

"I just wanted to see something." His hands were on my waist and the rattle of loose metal doors clanged as my back hit the filer.

"Nate." I wasn't sure if it was a plea or a warning. Probably both. *Definitely* both.

"Mmm?" His nose grazed up the side of my neck and my breath hitched.

Well there was no hiding that, Florence.

I'm not sure how, but I managed to hold onto my rational thoughts with my last breath of restraint, verbalising the reason why this shouldn't be happening right now. "We're in the library."

"Yes, I'm aware. I've actually been wanting to do this for a while."

Fuck it. I tried.

"Do what?" I breathed.

Please, for the love of God, say me.

He pulled back, which was the exact opposite of what I expected him to do, and I was damn proud that not a single whimper so much as left my lips.

"It's just back here." He reached down until my hand was in his and pulled me away into the stacks. I contemplated the reality that maybe he'd left something here. It was a very stupid thought, but I was spiralling and holding on by a thread. If I threw caution to the wind and this turned out *not* to be what I thought, I might never speak to him again.

"Did you forge—."

It was all very quick as we rounded the corner to the area we'd been working between last time he was here, and he hoisted me up against the shelves.

"Nathaniel!" I yelled, literally *yelled* within the library.

His face was full of mock shock that a bubble of laughter flitted out without permission. "Florence," he scolded me, brows furrowing, "this is a *library,* there are sound level rules here."

The laughter turned into a grin that I couldn't wipe off my face if I tried, especially when his expression turned into a mirror of my own and his hands started to slide up my body.

"You're lucky I know the librarian and can call in a few favours."

"Oh, is that right?"

"Mhmm."

I wrapped my legs around his waist to help him support my weight. "How did you know the shelf wouldn't fall?" I asked, getting increasingly more distracted as his hands worked to untuck my blouse from my skirt which was so hiked up it was practically a belt.

"I tested them last week."

I pulled back to stare at him. "You didn't."

"Of course I did, I told you I've been thinking of this for a long time." His lips finally met mine. His tongue swiped my bottom lip, earning a moan from me and giving him the perfect opportunity to push further into my mouth.

Sweet Aunt Josephine, I was going to burst into flames.

I collected myself enough to pull back just slightly. "Could have fooled me," I whispered against his lips.

"It's been one of my greatest trials keeping my hands to myself, Florence." Those very hands finally made their way under my shirt, wrapping around my ribs, fingers toying with the sides of my bra. I gasped and pulled back as a shiver wracked my body.

"Your hands are cold," I whispered to him, though the sound levels I'd worked so hard to enforce had nothing to do with it.

"I know." His eyes glinted with the same mischief I'd spotted before, right before he reached to tug the whole blouse off my body.

"And though this is something I would happily do all day, everyday, with you," he dropped the fabric to the floor, "I wanted you to know there was more to us than the physical."

"Okay." I was really trying to digest his words, but I was having a bit of a hard time, all things considered.

"Do you know there's more here, between us, than the physical, Florence?" His hands had moved to my back, and were toying with the clasp of my bra. I nodded my head and ran my hands down his chest, trying to figure out how to remove his *damn*–.

"Florence?" His voice cut through the lusty blanket of fog

that was dragging me down.

My eyes met his. "What?"

"Do you know there's more?" The look he gave me cleared the haze enough to give me a moment of clarity. I reached up and held his face between my hands, pushing all the truth I had into the words I spoke.

"I know," I said. He watched me for a moment longer before nodding. Satisfied with my answer and unhooking my bra so quickly he'd likely set a new record.

After that the clarity dissipated from existence entirely and I was once again on a mission. I was absolutely the sort of girl who went tit-for-tat, so my priority immediately became getting his shirt off, too. I pulled it up little by little from where my legs were keeping it pressed against his body until the thing came loose and I flung it somewhere far away from us, where it couldn't cover his body ever again. *Ever.*

"Don't lose that shirt, it would be weird to leave here without it." He glanced in the general direction I'd thrown the item long enough to give himself an idea of where to go looking for it later. I laughed as his hands moved to cup my ass through my skirt. I leaned in close, my lips a hair's breadth from his. "I wouldn't mind," I confessed, smiling against his kiss.

"*Florence,*" he tutted, "that's quite naughty."

I leaned in to whisper in his ear before pulling back again, "I'm not a saint, you know."

He hummed, "I know," sliding his nose against mine before nipping my bottom lip, "I like it."

We got caught in another kiss that was so consuming it was hard to remember where we were, or why it mattered so much that we kept quiet. He finally let me down, but only to reach behind me for the zipper of my skirt.

"I love it when you wear these skirts." His mouth was on mine again as he pulled the zipper all the way down and helped me shimmy out of the fabric.

"You never said." I reached down to undo the buckle of his belt and the button of his jeans, my hands so frantic that it probably took me more time than necessary. Nathaniel made good use of that time though, ridding me of my panties before kicking off his shoes and shucking out of his pants.

"This has been my first opportunity, really," he said, reaching down to the said discarded pants for the little foil pack that he'd tucked into one of the pockets. He didn't rip it open or put it on, instead he knelt before me, which had to be one of the most erotic things I'd ever witnessed with my own eyes, and reached for my leg to hook over his shoulder.

Oh my God.

He looked up at me, the corner of his mouth lifting ever so slightly, "You would've nailed my balls to the wall if I'd said it before."

And he was right, I would've, but I didn't get time to respond before his mouth was on the very place I'd been wanting him. My hand reached to grip his hair to steady myself. His tongue worked me until it was literally all I could think of, fingers digging into the insides of my thighs to the point where I knew I'd have bruises, and I couldn't find it in me to care in the slightest. His hands came up to cup my ass as he guided my other leg over his shoulder. "Sweet mother of Go-".

He stopped his fluid motions to look up at me, the immediate loss of him pulling a noise from me that sounded painfully like a sob. Nate's eyes met mine with my arousal glistening on his lips. "No. Say my name, Florence."

There was a ravenous glint in his eyes, entwined with the

lust that was weighing down his eyelids. "What?" My chest was rising and falling rapidly.

"My name, Florence. Not God, or His mother. *My* name." And so help me, his eyes didn't leave mine as he ran his tongue right up the centre of me.

A strangled mewl left my mouth involuntarily as I nodded rapidly, squeezing my eyes shut. My hand pulling at his hair so hard it had to have been hurting.

"I can't hear you." He purred, his breath casting over me, igniting flames all over my body.

"Nate." I breathed.

"Louder."

"Nate." I practically yelled just as he resumed his previous ministrations. I was thrust right over the edge of oblivion in a matter of moments, where riding the high of my climax was the only thing I wanted to do for the rest of my life. His tongue swiped the sensitive flesh until I'd ridden out every wave and I was eternally grateful the shelves behind me were secured to the floor. There was no way my legs would have held me up on my own.

The thought of folding in on myself into a boneless heap was becoming increasingly more appealing, but Nathaniel had other plans, and I still had a response to his last comment.

"I would have absolutely nailed your balls to the wall, but I wouldn't have meant it. It would have been more for self preservation than anything," I panted as he stood up to his full height before me, an arm circling my waist to keep me steady, and capturing my mouth with his in a kiss so fast and vicious I could taste every part of myself along his tongue.

He ripped the foil packet with his teeth and put it on, my eyes tracking every movement and my heart picking up pace until there was a small stallion galloping in my chest. He looked down at me then, his finger trailing up my inner leg, not hesitating at all as he plunged into my centre, a cry leaving my mouth.

This man was going to kill me.

The entire exchange was so different from the first time. Like he'd wanted to take his time then, to explore and learn my body, just as much as I'd to learn his. And now, now it was a whole different story and I was *living* for it.

He removed his fingers and lifted me up again like it was the easiest thing he'd ever done, positioning himself at my entrance.

"I know," he said, sinking into me inch by inch, until I knew that my nails would've drawn blood in the shapes of crescent moons along his shoulders. I didn't mind that one bit.

"Florence Valentine," he whispered against my lips, pulling out slowly before thrusting in again, making my eyes roll back into my head.

"Mmm?" It was hard to concentrate on anything, and the little conversation we were having really needed to come to an end in favour of much more important things.

"You look incredibly sexy right now." He pulled out to thrust back in again, even slower this time, and it took all my strength to fix my hooded gaze on his watching eyes.

And they were. Always watching, always seeing.

For fear of the moment growing heavier, and not trusting my own strength to hold it, I pulled his lips to mine in a silent command to give me *more*.

Needless to say, the sound level rule had gone right out the window, and I couldn't have cared less.

It was a good thing he knew the librarian.

32

Chapter 32

Since we'd levelled up in the 'shorts and snorts' way that Nate had so lovingly described, the pattern we fell into was so comfortable it was hard to think it hadn't always existed.

It had been many blissful weeks of dinners at Dot's on Thursday nights, mid-week stays at Nathaniel's, and weekends that were filled with the perfect mix of both time with Dot, time with Nate, and time with the three of us together. He still came in without question on his regular days to the library, and on the days where it was my shift to lock up - when he would come back to get me after the day was done - sometimes, he would lead me back into the stacks where rules about sitting on the tables and keeping your voice to a hushed whisper just didn't exist.

Or rather couldn't *exist, you saucy minx, Florence.*

Needless to say, the library had become a favourite place of mine for an entirely different reason than it had been before. Not to say that his presence didn't make it all the more wonderful on the days when that didn't happen. Where he would still spend his lunch hour with me putting books back, or some other random task I'd created just so he had something to do.

When he wasn't doing that, he would still find a stranger who wandered in, unaware, and ask them questions about the importance of recycling and using reusable bags when they went shopping.

He was still determined to bring me the opinions and answers of people, to show me their goodness, and although it wasn't nearly as much as when we first met, he still did it all the same.

Another of my favourite places to be was his house. His home.

God, it was just so, totally, utterly Nathaniel that the moment I stepped through his front door I could feel my worries melt away. Completely encased in the warm, safe glow I had come to realise was a telling sign that he was nearby.

It felt like I was spending more time there than at my own place, and we created a routine that almost always began together and almost always ended the same way.

A spot for my shoes had been made by the front door, right by where he kept his. It wasn't the sort of spot where I'd just placed my things there because he'd taken something off the shelf.

No.

No, he had *cleared* a spot, just for me. I'd noticed it after the fourth night I'd spent there with him.

I knew how long to wait for the water to even out in the shower, so that I didn't hop in when it was still blistering cold or flushed through with scorching hot water before the two found their balance. I knew where the cereal was kept and how many scoops to use of the coffee brand he favoured so that the pot wasn't too strong or too weak.

We'd bounced around a few different places before deciding that out the side of his house, on the little patio, was where we would eat our breakfast together. High enough so that you didn't really notice the houses around us, but rather focused on the hills in the distance and the way the clouds looked in the sky above them.

There was never a dry spell in our conversations, and the fact that he fed my mind as much as he fed (and tended to) my body made me obsess just a little bit more. It was a new topic every time we spoke, and every day I learnt more about him, and he about me. I realised that he made me feel alive in a way I'd never experienced before, and I wanted to drown in it.

Nathaniel was a master at board games, where I couldn't win if my life depended on it. He had an older sister who he didn't speak to much, and his parents lived a few hours away on a hobby farm. They were kind and simple, but he didn't see them often. The friends he had, he'd known since they were barely out of nappies, where I had no friends at all.

"Besides Dot," he'd said, not a question, but a statement.

"Besides Dot," I'd echoed.

Barbecuing was something he wanted to get better at, and he didn't drink when he was working the bar at all. "There's nothing wrong with my relationship with it," he explained in reference to the glass of wine in his hand as we sat on his couch one evening. "But it's what I do for work, you know?" He took a sip. "It just started to feel like a prerequisite of the job and very quickly didn't become fun at all."

"I can understand that." I sipped from my own glass.

"This though," he lifted up his glass in a sort of toast-gesture to me, "this is exactly how I like to enjoy a drink."

"On your couch, about to burst from over-consumption of my class-A pasta?"

"Yes, but you've missed a key criteria."

"Oh?" I took another sip.

"Your company, of course."

"Of course." I rolled my eyes. Sometimes I still found his honesty startling. He just said what he felt and he did it in a way that reflected his own feelings, but never invalidated mine or anyone else's. Never belittling anyone or any situation he was speaking about.

There was one word that came to mind every time I thought of Nathaniel Connors, and that was *kind.* But then that word led to others, like *selfless* and *thoughtful.* Words that I'd never associated with anyone other than Dot. And on nights when I was alone with my thoughts for too long, whether I was in my own bed by myself, or in his, feeling the even rise and fall of his chest as he slept beside me, I wondered when it would all come crashing down around me, and how bad it would hurt when it did.

His way with words was a skill, nonetheless. And his skills were not just confined to the art of speech. Oh, no. The man was good at *everything.*

One of his many wonderful ideas for a 'date night in' was that we should spend the entire evening trying to paint one another.

"I don't think this is a good idea," I mumbled whilst studying the canvas in front of me of what was *supposed* to be a likeness of Nate.

He looked like a meerkat.

"This is a great idea." He took a sip of his coffee (decaf), and I took a sip of mine (also decaf).

"You're probably very good at painting, that's why you're saying that."

"Absolutely."

I whined at his subtle reveal of abilities, and he laughed a little harder than the surface giggles we'd been volleying to one another all evening.

"Because you're making me do this by *force*, I should specify, you have to frame my final work and hang it up somewhere."

He peeked around his canvas from across the dining table where we sat, his face alight with the mischief that followed him almost everywhere he went.

"High stakes, Florence. What if it's shit?" The subtle flare of his English accent came to the surface.

"Oh, it's shit," I assured him, trying to figure out how to fix his hair in my painting into looking like actual hair, and not just a poopy blob on top of his head.

"Alright, those are odds I'll take." He sent a wink my way and at the end of the evening, when we revealed our masterpieces, I knew he regretted it.

When Nate turned his painting around, you could tell it was me. It was a beautiful painting, and there was no doubt in my mind that he had talent.

Mine, on the other hand...

"Florence," his voice truly sounded devastated, "that's awful." The devastation of his voice leaked into the expression on his face, and I knew that even though I'd told him point-blank, he didn't expect it to be so bad. I was a laugh-snort shy of pissing my pants, but after we'd both calmed down, and the tears of laughter dried from our eyes, we spent the rest of the evening looking for the perfect frame online that would suit the aesthetic of one of his bars.

33

Chapter 33

"I was wondering if you'd like to stay over at my house tonight?" I threw the query out into the space between Nate and I as we were putting books back on the shelf from the reading session that had happened that morning.

I'd certainly gotten his unwavering attention with that question. He didn't move his eyes from mine. Their quick, flickering movements told me he was looking, *really* looking, to make sure he'd heard me just fine.

"You're inviting me over?"

"I am." I nodded, giving him the extra confirmation and fortifying the question for myself. Not that I wanted to take it back at all.

He reached up to push his hair back. "We haven't stayed at your place yet." I knew he was still processing the invitation.

"I like your place more than mine," I admitted to him as I turned to continue sliding books on the shelf. I needed something to do with my hands. Nate didn't go back to what we were doing. I could feel his eyes tracing the side of my face, thinking about how to say what was on his mind. For him to need the minutes required to get his thoughts in order said a lot about the importance of what he wanted to say. He never said anything he didn't mean, and he always chose the words he spoke carefully.

"Are you sure that's the reason?" His voice was strong but quiet, and not because he was trying to respect the sound levels in the library. Closing hours was a different story, and I didn't care much for rules then. I knew the thought of why I'd never invited him over could have crossed his mind, but I never realised that he might be worried what that might mean, if he'd broken it apart and sifted through the layers. A pang of regret shot through my chest and settled in my stomach at the notion of being the person who'd caused that worry for him.

I'd never cared much for what others thought of me or the things I did. Up until Nate, it always seemed that no matter how hard I tried, people would always see me as not good enough in general, or simply just not good enough for them.

I cared what he thought. So, I looked him right in the face and gave him the only thing he'd ever asked of me; true and total honesty.

"There's no life in my little town house in the same way there's life in yours. It's not lived in, but really more of just a space to live. I like the way your house feels like a home. Plus, I've never had a guest besides Dot."

"Ever?"

I knew he was referring to the last part, because I was positive he already knew how I felt about his place.

"Ever," I confirmed.

We didn't move from our little face-off and I let him see

every bit of truth in that statement. That no, it wasn't about him at all. It was about me. Once he was satisfied that he'd read every thought and feeling that fluttered across my face, he nodded and turned back to stacking books, so I did too. The conversation was over for the most part, and even though he hadn't given me an answer, I was happy to leave the ball in his court.

Who even was I?

When his hand slipped behind the back of my neck and he slid himself between me and the shelf I was re-stacking, I wasn't expecting it. It made me jump like a spooked squirrel, but his grip held me in place.

"I would love to be your first, Florence," he said with a wink.

The grin that broke out across my face was one I wouldn't have ever wanted anyone to see. It would've been something that I suppressed into some kind of scowl, like I'd never smelt something so terrible in my life. But I didn't, because in a matter of a few simple words he'd made the whole situation perfect. So I told him just that.

"Perfect," I beamed, and then his lips were on mine. Slow and full of everything I knew he wanted me to know.

This was important, it *felt* important.

Still, despite my grin, despite feeling the absolute *rightness* of Nathaniel, the kernel of my fear that lingered too close to all the brave new things I was doing flashed in my mind, refusing to dissipate with the other fears I'd broken apart and watched drift away.

At that moment I knew that if I looked a little deeper and asked myself 'what if?', I would realise that I had already begun to hope for his presence everyday. That my ears were always straining for the buzz of my phone on my desk, or the coffee table at home, that told me Nate had messaged, or that he was calling just to chat about everything and nothing at the same time. That anytime the library doors opened I would look up and wish it was him, even when I knew it wouldn't be. That I'd stopped having more than a single cup of coffee on my way into work because I knew, *I knew* there would be one there on my desk with something witty, or cute, or dirty written on the side that would make me smile.

If I looked, then I'd see that this version of my life and the person I was becoming was far better than the version I'd been before.

But most of all, I knew that the moment he stepped foot into my house, it would begin to feel like a place that was lived in too, like a *home*, and somehow that made it all worth it.

Chapter 34

I felt Nathaniel watching me as I stared at the chessboard between us.

I'd never played chess before, and for whatever reason that I could no longer recall was good enough to place myself in *this* predicament, when he asked me if he should bring his travel chess board with him to his first stay over at my place, I said 'yes' with an absurd amount of enthusiasm.

I think mostly it was fuelled by the childish delight that Nate, this man who was a tall, dark haired wet dream had a *travel chess board.*

So, here we were; him, sat across from me, doing his best to keep his expression as serious as I was trying to keep mine, staring at me as I tried *not* to burst a blood vessel in my eye from the severe and strained staring match I was having with the board before me. I wondered if I stared at it for long enough, the ability to actually play chess would magically enter my mind.

I made a move that felt right to me in the moment, and then gestured to him make his move.

"Alright, your go."

He just stared at me, like he did after the last three moves I made.

"What is it?"

"Florence, have you ever played chess before?" His expression was amused, and it made me nervous.

"Why do you ask?" I picked up my wine glass to take a sip.

"Because you're playing checkers."

"I'm what?"

"You're playing checkers." He broke out this stupidly handsome grin and I wanted to choke him a little.

"They're not the same?"

That was the straw that broke the camel's back, apparently. An unrestrained belly laugh burst out of Nate and his wine glass was about a second away from spilling all over the floor.

"This isn't funny, Nathaniel." My cheeks had already begun to feel hot. My arms stretched out uselessly in front of me as if I could stop the wine should it depart from his keep.

He collected himself as best he could, "Florence, this is *very* funny."

"I'm not playing any more," I huffed.

"No, noo*ooo*," he whined the words, dragging out the last syllable. "No, I think it's charming." Nate latched onto the sleeve of my cardigan just as I got up, and tugged. He didn't anticipate that I would evade the move so expertly by letting the cosiest lounge wear I owned fall away. He only gathered it under his head as a pillow and smiled happily like it was his plan all along.

"This is going on our no-play list." I called over my shoulder to him, holding the scowl firm on my brow.

"What if I teach you to play?" The smile in his voice was

clear as a bell.

"You'd have to do it nicely."

"Of course, Florence. Aren't I always nice?"

"When it suits you." I teased him, knowing it would rile him up. The mock shock on his face drew a smile from my own.

"You don't mean that, do you Flossy?"

I glanced back at him, knowing he'd be able to read the mischief in my expression." "No, I don't." I brought over our dishes to the sink whilst Nate continued to lay on the couch with my cardigan as his pillow, happy and content to track my movements with his eyes. He continued to watch as I went about the tasks I always did after a meal.

I couldn't leave dirty dishes in the sink. The entire concept of leaving food on dishes to crust over made me want to gag. Let's place it right next to 'baby boogers on children's books' for reference.

The more I felt his eyes on me the more I felt a tension begin to creep into the space between us. Not necessarily bad, but maybe a little nervous with a touch of excitement. I decided not to entertain him by asking what answer he was trying to pull from my brain with only the sheer intention in his gaze, and instead finished up wiping the counter, snagging the bottle of wine we'd left there, half empty, and then returned to my spot across from him.

His eyes never left me, and he continued to stare as I finally met his eyes, the chessboard between us forgotten.

Thank sweet Lady Petunia.

"Would you like more wine?"

The corner of his mouth lifted like he knew I was playing the long game here. If there was one thing I'd learnt about Nathaniel Connors, it was that he didn't underestimate me.

Not one bit.

"I would." He didn't move from his spot to pass me his glass, letting me know he was playing too.

I topped us both up before setting back onto my spot on the floor where I'd made a nest of cosy pillows. Arranging them just so, to give me a bit more back support and smiling to myself as I settled back into them, knowing full well this was an influence of Nate's through and through. Just as I'd settled back, bringing the glass to my lips, he decided to hit me with his question.

"I wanted you to meet my friends."

I started choking immediately on the wine I had only just begun to swallow. I frantically tried to get up, forgoing grace entirely and ignoring the splash of wine on the carpet, and desperately trying to place the glass back on the coffee table and out of my hands, which I couldn't keep still, as my body was wracked with coughs.

Nate was up and next to me, hauling me to my feet and clapping me on the back to try and help the coughing fit. It felt like I had wine dribbling out of my nose, which after reaching up and swiping my hand under my nose was confirmed. With a groan I strode away from him to the bathroom. Nathaniel being Nathaniel, followed me closely and leaned on the door frame whilst I assessed the damage.

My eyes were red and watering, there was still a bit of wine dripping from my nose, and my face had gone blotchy. *Wonderful.*

"You have terrible timing," I croaked out, and although I knew he was amused at the entire ordeal, the most present emotion on his face was one of concern as he looked on from his spot near the open door.

"Sorry, Floss." He frowned at himself slightly.

I waved him off, bending down towards the sink to splash some water on my face. Once I was happy with the clean up, I grabbed Nate's hand and led us back to the living room. Motioning for him to take his place back on the couch, I resumed my place across from him, clearing my throat and gesturing to him to begin again.

"What?"

"You can start again."

"You mean you want me to say that I want you to meet my friends again?"

"Yes, exactly. I'm ready now."

"I just said it, Floss."

"Yes, but that was different." Scowling at him, I sighed, "Humour me."

He just grinned at me, running his hand through his hair and settling back into the couch.

"Florence." He paused dramatically.

"Yes, Nathaniel?" I fluttered my eyelashes at him.

"I want you to meet my friends."

"Mmm." I nodded my head thoughtfully.

"Mmm?"

"Mmm."

There were a few moments of silence between us whilst I held him in suspense of my answer, a bit of payback for the wine fiasco.

"I don't know, Nate."

"What?"

"I'm not sure it's a good idea."

"What do you mean Florence, you'll have to meet them eventually."

I hadn't thought of that, which seemed stupid. But it felt like Nathaniel was like me, in a circle of his own, even knowing about his past and the close circle of friends that he valued above so much else.

"I guess I didn't think of that." I felt a crease form between my eyes. Nate got up and walked around the coffee table to crouch next to me, reaching out to smooth the frown away. "You don't want to?"

"Honestly?"

"Of course."

"No."

He barked a laugh settling in behind me so he was reclined on the pillow mountain before drawing me back against him. "They're really great, Floss. I know you'd get along," he murmured against my hair.

"Don't you remember what it was like when *we* first met? I hated you."

"I don't think you did, but anyway, this is the final step of the challenge. You'll see that once we rock up and you meet them, you'll love them."

My heart sank, just a fraction. "You want me to meet them because of the challenge? I thought we weren't even doing that any more." Halfway through the sentence I tried to reign in the bite of bitter disappointment that spiked through my body, but I knew he would've picked up on it anyway.

"Of course we're doing it, we have to finish it. And no, that's not the only reason why. I want them to meet my girlfriend. Is that so bad?"

"Girlfriend?" My heart was racing and I was suddenly very glad to be facing away from him. "We haven't used that word before."

243

"It's what you are."

"Are you sure?" I turned to face him, needing to see his eyes.

"That you're my girlfriend?" His smile was blinding, "Quite sure, Florence."

"Alright, I accept the title." I nodded, trying to keep my expression neutral, but he still had that stupid blinding smile plastered on his face and it was seeping into my own expression.

"I'm glad to hear it." His eyes were bright, there wasn't a part of his face that his smile didn't reach, and it made my whole body shiver in delight. Knowing that I was the reason for it. I cleared my throat, turning around again to nestle into my previous position, getting back to business. "So it's half the challenge and half you want to get their take on me?"

He sighed heavily, silence coating us completely. It'd begun to turn just this side of uncomfortable when he manoeuvred me to look at him again.

"It's important you see the world isn't a scary place full of people who are chomping at the bit to simply let you down. My friends are a big part of my life, and so are you. Let's say that my reasons are threefold." He grinned, not quite as big as before, but enough for his dimples to still remain on show and the pressure in my chest lessened.

"Alright," I let my eyes roam his face, looking for any reason not to believe him, "list your reasons in priority, please."

His face moved into contemplative thought before nodding. "I think that's a fair request."

I moved back and sat facing him as he remained reclined in front of me, lifting his hands to tuck behind his head and making his shirt ride up a bit.

Good grief.

"Reason number one," he began as if he had no idea what he was doing to me with that sliver of skin on show, "I would like my girlfriend to meet and get to know my friends"

"You're going to start using that word a lot now, aren't you?"

"As well as its counterpart in reference to myself."

"Naturally." I rolled my eyes before motioning to continue.

"Reason number two, I would like my friends to meet and get to know my girlfriend. And my final reason, but no less important than reasons one and two, it will be the final event in Convincing Florence Valentine that people, in fact, don't suck."

I sat looking at him, digesting it all, and he gave me the time to do it. I sifted through his reasons and tried my best to ignore the snag on my heart as I thought of the last one, and how I'd wished the stupid challenge wasn't so important that he had to include it in his top three reasons to have me meet his friends.

Maybe I was being too sensitive about it, maybe I shouldn't really care at all and once it was done, it would be done.

I grabbed onto that thought like a buoy in rough seas. That's genuinely how it felt to agree to this. Anyone who wasn't a fan of meeting massive groups of new people, especially those who had a history and friendship with one another already, would know exactly what I was thinking about. But I would do this, I would meet them all and do my absolute best to like them, and have them like me back. If they were friends with Nate then I think we could strike a conversation.

We would have him in common, at least.

What a flimsy buoy to hold onto, Florence.

It would do, if only to force the words from my mouth.

"Okay."

"Okay?"

"Yes, I'll meet them." He practically tackled me then, a ripple of laughter erupting from me as he showed me just how glad he was I'd said yes.

When I woke up in the morning I didn't think too much about the wine stain on the carpet, but rather how it had looked with our clothes strewn across it instead.

Chapter 35

There was a parking spot right outside the bar, which I thought was quite lucky, but really it made sense. Nate owned the establishment after all, so naturally he should have a park so close.

"Great parking spot," I murmured as the sound of the parking brake broke the tension that had settled in the cabin of his truck as we drove.

"You think?"

"Oh, for sure. But then this is your bar, so, of course you'd have a great park."

"Florence."

"Mmm." I couldn't move my gaze from the window where I was staring at the entry to his bar.

"Florence," he slid his hand onto the back of my neck and began to knead gently, "you're nervous."

"How do you figure?" I turned to look at him. He was dressed in his classic black shirt, black jeans, black boots. His hair was still a bit damp from the shower we'd taken (yes, I said 'we', don't even get me started or we'll never make it inside) and he smelt divine.

"You're talking about my parking spot like it's the best thing in the world."

"Don't undervalue a quality park, Nathaniel." I tried to lift the corner of my mouth in a sassy smile but failed. Miserably.

His eyes flicked to the twitch but he made no comment. "Oh, I would never. I agree, it's a wonderful spot but surely it isn't the highlight of the evening?"

"It is to date," I countered with a smile that finally came easy, wiping my clammy hands on my jeans and grateful for our easy banter, knowing it was for my benefit alone.

"I can accept that as your answer." He nodded in confirmation and coupled it with a serious expression that did a great job of hiding his amusement and concern at the situation, but not so good that it hid them entirely.

I would be lying if I said I hadn't spent the week absolutely shitting myself about this exact moment. I threw myself into work, getting things done that hadn't even been on the agenda until next month. I even asked Mel to have lunch together a few times to avoid being in my own company, and simmering on the thoughts of meeting his friends and all the different versions I'd concocted in my own mind of how it would play out. She was shocked at first, but after the second invite we managed to fall into easy conversation. So much so that I was actually looking forward to going again.

I know, shocker.

I'd picked up my phone to cancel three times, but then I didn't, because I knew what this meant to Nate.

"Okay, I'm ready," I breathed, leaning over the centre console to steal a kiss. He kept me there for a moment longer with his hand still placed firmly on the back of my neck. My body began to flush with a heat that had quite literally *just* been subdued.

This man might kill me with sex. What a way to go.

"Okay?" he whispered the word against my lips.

"Okay."

* * *

I loved this bar. It was the only one of the three he owned that I'd actually been too, but I loved it nevertheless.

It was everything you could imagine it would be, from the wall hangings, the light fixtures, the bar, the stools, the menus. It all screamed 'Nate' with its outdoors-meets-industrial-meets-rock'n'roll and I loved it. So did dozens of other people, as it was fully packed with groups of friends, couples, singles, and a live band in the corner that was just setting up. In the background played a song from *Lady Luck* that had blown up from their recent release and the familiar tune immediately made me feel about 1% more at ease.

Nate was taller than your average person, and his apparel made him stand out, so as soon as we stepped into the bar, his hand firmly wrapped around mine as I tagged along behind him, a chorus of people called out to him, waved in his direction, or reached out to shake his hand.

I understood pretty quickly that all the people that were dotting our path towards the back of the bar were not part of the friend group he'd spoken so lovingly about.

After our little tussle on the carpet the week before, he'd told me all about his friends, adding onto the information he had shared with me before. I knew that the group that surrounded him now was the same group that surrounded him from the days where his age was still in single digits. I knew they'd been there for every birthday, holiday, good day, bad day, momentous event, and bitter downfall he may have experienced in his life. And respectively, he was there for all their moments of equal importance too. I knew before I even met them they were a family in their own right. My heart had tightened as he'd told me about them, feeling an overwhelming sense of gratefulness that this man that had come to mean so much to me had so many people around him to raise him up, but also feeling the desolate coldness that came with the knowledge that I'd never had that. I had Dot, but that was different.

Every person that called out to Nate, he called back a response to, and those that captured his attention for an exchange of sentences, he made sure to give them his full attention, but not before introducing me first.

"Hey, Roy." He clasped hands with a particularly barley man who had more hair on his face than on the top of his head.

"Nathan." He nodded in a gruff response. Not rude, just rugged.

"This is my girlfriend, Florence. Florence, this is Roy. We fish together sometimes. He has a cabin outside the city."

"Oh, how cool! I've never been fishing." I smiled at the man who was sizing me up against the term 'girlfriend'.

"Florence." He nodded at me in the same way he had to Nate. Or *Nathan.*

That's a new one.

"Speaking of, how's the fishing going lately? It's been a minute since I was up."

"Oh, they're bitin'." He nodded his head rather aggressively and I understood that Roy was a man of very few words, but there was definitely a southern twang in there. Diluted, but present nonetheless.

"We'll have a weekend soon." Nate shook his hand again and I waved a brief goodbye as he led me the last few steps to the group of people that resembled him in dress code more so than anyone else in here.

The moment they spotted us, they all let out a chorus of 'aahhh's' and 'there he is' as well as a few variations of his name that included 'Nat', 'Nate' and the new one, 'Nathan'.

I stood next to him as he hugged and shook the hands of his group of around twelve friends before things died down and everyone's gazes landed on me, all at once.

Fuck me I was going to pass out or piss myself.

Smile, Florence.

I smiled as Nate slipped his arm around my waist and pulled me to stand in front of him, resting his chin on the top of my head.

"Guys, this is Florence. Florence, this is Annabel, Jacob, Jess, Ryan, Lenny, Lauren, Austin, Rupert, Jen, Taylor, Frankie and Mike." He pointed to them as he went around the group, all of them waving and saying some sort of version of 'hello'.

"Hello, it's really great to meet you all. Nate has told me lots about you."

"Likewise, Florence," one of the girls he'd introduced from around the middle of the group called out with a warm smile that made me relax a little more.

His group moved around and I slid into the booth next to a guy who reintroduced himself as Mike, and Nate slid in after me. He turned to the bar and called out for a couple of beers before things dissolved into chaos.

Chaos, not in the bad sense of the word, but more like the overwhelming sense. We sat and spoke non-stop for what seemed like a very long time. I nursed my beer whilst everyone else at the table seemed to have gotten through three in the same space of time.

The conversation flowed easily though, and story after story of Nate through his younger years was passed around. They'd eagerly listened to our recount of how we'd met, and laughed without restraint at the different perspectives. The moment I mentioned his buckets of charm, there was a chorus of howling laughter as every single one of them could recall a number of occasions where said-charm got the man himself out of a pickle or too.

"You're all dickheads, you know that?" Nate picked up a handful of nuts from the basket in the middle of the table and threw them at his friends before leaning in to give me a kiss on the head.

I'd begun to wonder why I had been so worried as I nestled into his side and his friends began to strike up conversations with one another.

"Floss, I'm just going to grab another beer, there are a few people here I want to say hi to as well. Are you all good here?"

I nodded my head with an easy smile as he made his way to the bar through the thickening crowd, every second person almost stopping him to say hello.

"What do you think, Florence?" One of the guys who sat across from me asked.

"Sorry, about what?" I smiled in apology.

"The snow season that's just passed, we were saying it was probably one of the best yet. Did you get up to the mountains at all?"

"Oh! No, no I've never been, or done any snow sport stuff," I shrugged.

"Ever?!" The two other people he'd been talking to asked in unison. I couldn't be sure but I *think* I was speaking to Ryan, Lenny (short for Leonard I'd learnt) and Lauren.

"Ever. I was raised by my grandmother and she's more of a tropical weather lover. Lots of beach visits but not so much the mountains or the snow."

Lauren still looked shocked but recovered quickly, "You'll have to come up with us next time."

"That sounds great, I'd love to. I'll suck, but sure." I smiled and laughed into my beer. They laughed with me, which was nice of them, but I knew they were still surprised. Where things really started to stink was when they started to talk about their favourite hikes and camping spots, all of which were conversations I couldn't contribute too.

Eventually, they just kept talking amongst each other. A few peeled off to different people they knew in the bar, Annabel and Jacob, who were the only couple amongst the twelve, had bid farewell mentioning they had a three year old at home and a babysitter to relieve. They'd both bid adieu with a wave and a smile, and that encompassed my entire interaction with them.

I still held the same beer between my hands hours in and there was no sign of Nathaniel. That was okay though, he didn't need to babysit me, and I knew there were likely a plethora of people here he'd wanted to catch up with. I wouldn't be *that* girlfriend. The one who clung to his shirt all night. Instead I was the girlfriend who sat at a table alone, unable to relate to anything his friends spoke of or contribute to a conversation in any meaningful way.

"What do you do for work, Florence?" Frankie asked around Mike when he noticed I was, in fact, still sitting there.

"I'm a librarian." I smiled proudly. I loved my job, who wouldn't?

Finally something I can actually talk about.

Something that I wouldn't disappoint any of them by not knowing how to volley back a response.

"Wow, really?" Mike had asked, and I nodded enthusiastically.

"Oh yeah, it's honestly great. Nothing really better than spending my days surrounded by books." I grinned.

"I mean, I can think of a few things," Frankie laughed. Mike smacked him on the arm at the sight of my falling expression. I recovered quickly though, regardless of the pang in my chest.

Come on, Florence. You aren't this sensitive.

I never used to be. Or maybe I always was, but it was different when you expected the worst instead of the best. A lead balloon had been gradually inflating in my gut as the night progressed and was now full of thoughts and worries that had nothing to do with protecting myself from their disappointment, but rather the opposite. That I wouldn't measure up.

"He didn't mean that," Mike recovered for his friend.

"I did, I didn't even know you could be paid to be a librarian," Frankie countered, clearly oblivious to the glare he was getting from his friend.

"No, that's cool, it's not for everyone." I closed that down as fast as I could, my heart pounding in my chest at the absolute failure of that conversation.

Fuck.

Conversations continued on around me. From time to time I would catch the eye of one of his friends, and every time it was followed by a small smile from both parties, but that's where it ended. The hour that followed, no one tried to bring me into their conversation and hard as I tried, and I did seriously try hard, there wasn't a single conversation I overheard that I could contribute to. Anything that I would likely say, or any topic I would try to broach, I knew would end up in the same way as a piece of fruit determined to defy gravity. It would splatter, and implode, and cover everyone in gunk that would ruin their evening.

I was the gunk.

Oh god, I was the gunk?!

Nathaniel still hadn't come back. I'd cast my eyes over the bar a few times since he'd left, and caught the top of his dark hair above the majority. Every time I looked, he had moved to another part of the bar and was laughing with a different group of people. It made me smile, truly, because he was so in his element.

I was just completely out of mine, and worse, I knew that I was letting him down. The more I sat in that booth surrounded by people that loved Nate as much as I did, the more I realised not only did I have nothing in common with them, but I was an enigma. I was completely *other* to them to the point where they'd even thought of my job as a volunteer position.

A volunteer position?

I knew this would pop the bubble of happiness that so clearly encompassed his night. I knew that if I attempted to engage with any of his remaining friends that I would simply not meet their expectations. That was how life had always been for me, hadn't it?

The realisation hit me so hard it felt like I was winded. I suppose I'd always known to an extent that my aversion to people didn't really have anything to do with them, but more to do with me.

I was the disappointment.

The unfailing constant across all and every encounter. From my unplanned arrival into this world, to my inability to provide reason enough for my parents to stick around, to friends and one night stands that cast their eyes over me and always walked away with the disappointment clearly plastered across their features, thinking that there would be something *more* to me when there wasn't.

I could feel the pressure behind my eyes begin to intensify. I was concrete on the fact that I wouldn't cry at a bar in front of strangers, and desperately furious with myself for allowing my walls to drop so thoroughly that I'd let every thought I'd had in the last hour rush through my mind and bulldoze me over like it had.

There was no use trying to hide from the truth that I'd run from for so many years, but I needn't let it pummel me so publicly. I had enough self preservation left, at least, for that.

I drained the dregs of my beer and made to leave, aiming for an Irish goodbye, but that hope was shattered almost immediately.

"You're off, Florence?" Mike turned from his conversation with Lenny from across the table.

"Oh, yeah, just a bit of a headache. I'll send Nate a message later, all good. It was really nice to meet you all." Departing with a wave and a smile, a few called a 'goodbye' whilst the majority didn't notice at all, and I was left feeling a sinking sense of dread about the entire experience.

It was too late to safely consider the train, and I'd planned on going back to Nate's with a bag of my things already at his house, but all I wanted was my comfiest pyjamas and my own bed. I pulled up the Uber app on my phone, and by the time the clock had ticked its way through thirty minutes, I was unlocking the door to my house, and dumping everything at the threshold. Shoes, phone, bag included.

The time said it was 2 a.m. on the dot, and the sigh that left me was laced with so much defeat that even I cringed at the sound of it as it left my mouth.

Every moment of the entire evening ran through my head as I sat at my kitchen bench. I'd intended on having a shower and crawling under the covers, my body aching along with my head at the stress the entire night had caused, when someone pounded on my front door. The sound made me jump and my eyes shot to the clock which now showed almost an hour had passed since I'd been home. I was too defeated to even comprehend that.

I should've been confused and on edge at some random sound at my door, but I knew there were only two people it could really be, and only one of those two had any real reason to knock so thoroughly the door rattled on its hinges.

I pulled the remainder of my energy to the surface and walked to the door to open it up.

He was there. Right there as he had been so many times before, but this time was different. There was also no truck to be seen, which made me release a breath of concern. We'd been at the bar for a while, and though I knew Nate wasn't a big drinker, I knew he definitely shouldn't have driven here.

"You left," he breathed, his chest rising and falling a little too fast to be casual or calm.

"How did you get here?" My lame excuse at delaying the inevitable.

"Uber. Florence, you left."

"I did." I kept his gaze, realising that if he wanted to talk about this now, then we were going to have to talk about it now.

"Why?"

"Because Nathaniel, I didn't fit in." Not the whole truth, but a sliver of it.

"Florence, I wasn't even gone for that long. This was important to me and you left." His breathing was still coming fast, and I knew if it was anyone else their voice would have cracked on that last word. His didn't need to though, I felt his pain slice through me irrevocably.

What have you done, Florence?

"You were gone for a good couple hours there, actually. Which is fine, that's not the point. It was important to me too."

"Was it?" His voice was sharp and it tugged at the dread that already pooled in my chest, making it harder to breathe.

"Of course it was." My voice stayed even despite the racing of my heart.

"How could it have been if you left?"

I could see now, ever so slightly, the walls that I hadn't seen in a very long time begin to rise up around him as his gaze began to harden. I began to raise mine. I would not be out there on my own. Open, and vulnerable, and *hurt*. No matter that it was me who'd charged into battle first.

"Because I couldn't even speak to any of your friends. I sat there like a stunned mullet with a warm beer all night.

Everything they spoke of, I couldn't relate. There wasn't a single conversation going on that I could contribute to in a meaningful way, and anything I did say, I knew didn't meet the expectations they had of me, so I sat there. Smiling when someone looked my way, and saying goodbye as they peeled off one by one. The only conversation I was able to say more than two sentences in was when Frankie asked me about my work. Do you know what he said? He said he thought librarians were a volunteer position and then that was that conversation done and dusted."

He just shook his head, either not really hearing what I said or simply not finding it a good enough answer. For all the times he could read between the lines, this was not one of them. "You could've spoken about anything you were interested in. That's a cop out."

"You think they would've cared about gardening with Dot after what they thought of my volunteer position of a career?"

"How would you even know if you didn't bother to ask?"

"Oh, you mean in between the conversation on how great the swell was on the mountain last snow season or that literally anything was better than having a job as a librarian? I didn't need to ask, I knew they wouldn't have cared because–."

"Because people are all the same?"

Ouch.

That wasn't what I was going to say. I would have told him, I would have said because it's the pattern I figured out. That it's not me who was constantly disappointed, but rather it was *I* that constantly disappoints. I couldn't bear to see their faces in the same way I was seeing his right now. But I didn't correct him, I would rather he hate me than see that look on his face.

259

"Don't mock me, Nate."

"I'm not mocking you. That's what you were going to say though, wasn't it?"

No, it wasn't.

I just looked at him, not responding. Heart racing still.

"You can't assume things like that, Florence." His tone had caught up to the expression his face held, like I'd let him down.

Might as well go down with this ship. "It's not an assumption. It's an experience. I *know* people." What I should have said was I've learnt something *crucial* about myself. I wanted to ask him if he'd ever seen the thought cross my face in the way he'd seen every single other, about how the minutes of my life coincided with the bad minutes of everyone else's, and tell him I'd figured it out. That it wasn't them, but it seemed to be me, and *fuck* if that realisation didn't suck. If I had to let everyone else down for the rest of my life I would, if it meant never having to see him shut down the way he was now.

"You don't." It's the first time he ever said that, like he really thought I was full of shit.

"I do." My tone was final, and I felt the walls he'd worked so hard to break down continue to snap up with a clang that resonated through me, breaking my heart clean in half.

"You don't." His tone was certainly a match for mine, and all I wanted to do was end this now.

My heart was hammering now, my breaths coming sharp and fast, the words forming on my tongue. Words I didn't want to say. "So what, you're saying I don't know you either?" My nose was stinging from the pressure behind my eyes, and I absolutely did not expect the next words to tumble out of his mouth, but I knew they would. Because I *knew* Nathaniel Connors.

260

"You know what, Florence? Maybe you don't." He dropped his hands from where they were braced on the frame of my front door, and took a small step back.

No.

But I'd done this, hadn't I?

It was too late to back track, but I couldn't help myself. "I do know you, how could you even say that?"

"Did you know that every single second, or every minute, of every *hour* I've ever spent in your company was completely selfish of me? I couldn't keep away from you, Florence. I was there for my own benefit, because *I* wanted your company. You could say, arguably, that my being with you, really *was* all about me. Doesn't that sound exactly like what you were trying to run away from? People who were only ever in it for themselves? Does that *disappoint* you, Florence?"

But I knew he was lying, only Nathaniel Connors had never lied to me before, so how could I really know what one looked like now?

"I wasn't running away." Yes I was. I was running even now.

"Yes you were, and given the chance now you'd run for the hills." He didn't know I was already packed and halfway to those hills, fleeing like my arse was on fire. I hated myself for it.

I wanted to slam my door in his face. I wanted to scream at him, because he'd worked so hard to break me down, and now this moment was ruining everything. *Everything.* What was worse though? Divulging to him that he was fighting an uphill battle all this time? That although he might've been winning, he would lose this war? Or that it was bound to end sometime, but it was never him that was destined to fuck it up, it was me?

"This is ruining everything, Nate." I was being ripped to pieces, but still, I did nothing to stop it, and I swear I was breathing so fast I was sure to pass out at any moment.

"I'm being *honest,* Florence." His face changed, like he'd made a decision. I could see it too, I knew what he was going to say. "Florence–."

"Don't say it."

He looked defeated, like this wasn't ever how this was supposed to go, and yet exactly how it was always meant to happen. "It's true, you know it's true. I love you."

"You're lying, Nathaniel." I started to move back and close the front door, absolutely finished with this conversation, but he stopped it with his hand firmly on the wood. I stared at it there for a second, remembering how gentle his touches could be, and just *knowing* I wouldn't ever have them again. Not after this.

"I never lie."

I shook my head. "This was all a mistake, we should've never done this." I gestured frantically between us, "This version of a person you think I am? The one you thought to bring to your friends and have them see and love like you think you do? She doesn't exist in real life. The one you tried too hard to change. I'm *not* that person. You wanted to try so hard to convince me that people don't suck? That's how this all started, didn't it? Well, you lost the challenge, Nate. It's all over. There is no reason for you to stick around any more. You're free to go."

He just stared at me, like he knew the words would hurt when they left my mouth, but he hadn't anticipated just how much. *God,* I was going straight to hell for being the person that broke his heart.

"You think that's why I'm here?"

"Isn't it? Really?" I knew it wasn't.

"I never once tried to change you, Florence. Only to get you to stop showing the world the person you think you need to be, and to finally just be yourself. You refused to see beyond this tiny, little bubble that only ever had enough room in it for you and Dot. You're so set on thinking the world is against you that you *refuse* to live. And I mean *live.* But you did for a second, didn't you? You made enough room for me and a little more life and you liked it. I saw it, I felt it. You can tell me it's not true but I *know you,* Florence. You let me in for a second and it scared you, and that's why you're doing this. You only needed to just *try–.*"

His eyes, the ones that could always read every little thing I was feeling, and every word I didn't say, watched me as the final pieces of the wall I'd been steadily building back around my crumbled heart slid into place.

"You know what, Florence? You're right. Maybe we should've never done this at all."

And then he turned, and he left. And just so I didn't have to watch him leave, I slammed the door as hard as I could and held in the scream that was clawing at my throat.

Chapter 36

Nathaniel

I walked and walked. I walked because if I didn't, I knew I would turn back, I'd go right back to her and I wouldn't stop knocking until she let me in.

My phone buzzed in my pocket and for a second I thought it was her, calling me to say the same thing.

Come back, come back, come back.

But I'd seen the look in her eyes. The moment she closed herself off from me, I'd seen it.

The screen showed that it was Rupert. I sent him right to voicemail, promising myself I'd call one of them later, knowing that if I spoke to anyone right now, words wouldn't come out of my mouth.

I wanted to scream, rip out my hair, and yell at everyone and everything. I was angry, because she'd left. She'd given up and shut me out, despite it all.

Because she'd only just started to let me in, just to lock me out again. Because I'd *seen* the fire in her eyes, and knew there was something to peel back and uncover, that whatever she'd held so close to her beneath the layers, and layers, and *layers* of shit she used as a reason to blame the world, was someone who I wanted to spend every second of every day with.

Didn't she know that? How could she not?

Someone who'd gotten under my skin, and into my veins.

I was angry because maybe I pushed her too hard, maybe all at once was too much.

I was angry because she didn't even try. she'd given up and run away.

I was angry because I knew this was some feeble attempt to stanch the bleeding. To fill in the cracks that were forming and threatening to cause it all to fall to rubble around her. 'It' being whatever she was so scared of letting go, or letting out. Of showing me.

Florence Valentine had walked right into my life with purpose in a pencil skirt that did things to me I couldn't rightly put into words, and I was undone. Completely and totally undone.

If there was one thing I'd never wanted, it was to change her, only to show her everything she refused to see.

How could this woman, this smart, and beautiful woman with such a fire in her eyes, hate the world as she did? How could she see herself as someone only worth the bad minutes that other people had to give, none of the good?

My phone buzzed again, this time showing Jess's name. I sent it to voicemail and walked, and walked, and walked.

I walked because if I stopped moving, I'd fall apart.

37

Chapter 37

<u>Florence</u>

I'd never called in sick before.

Not ever, not once. Not even when I *was* sick. But there was nothing in the world that would get me off Dot's couch today.

I'd fallen asleep curled up on my own couch, only to wake up at the butt crack of dawn and hightail it to Dot's house. I'd called Melissa on the way to let her know I wouldn't be able to make it in today.

I didn't need to say a single thing. Dot took one look at my face and led me to the bathroom with instructions to have a hot shower and wash my face. When I managed to tear myself away from the relief of the hot water, Dot had already placed some clothes near the sink. I shuffled from the bathroom, my hair still wet and dripping, and curled up in my childhood bed, in my childhood room.

I'd give myself a day. Just one day. To sleep, to cry, to *hurt*. To convince myself that I was right to call it off, that I was right on how his friends would have responded to the things I would've said. That I was right about the fact that the person he'd said he loved wasn't me at all.

If I hadn't called it off, then he would have.

Once the challenge was done, and there was no longer a mystery to solve on who exactly Florence Valentine was without all the walls around her heart, he'd have left. It started with a bet after all, didn't it? What did that say about him?

Low blow, Florence.

What did that say about me? About how far I'd fallen just to be in the arms of a man who I didn't really know at all. Just like he'd said.

He'd been right, hadn't he? That I'd never known him at all. That I'd misread so completely the time we had spent together, and it was only for his sake, and never mine. That it was completely selfish. I knew he'd said those words in an effort to make me categorise him with everyone else, but that group of people no longer existed. It was no longer me against the world. No longer *his* actions would disappoint me, but rather the other way around now.

I closed my eyes against the light pouring into my room, trying hard not to think about the last time I was in this house, and who had been here with me.

Nathaniel Connors had made his mark on every single part of my life. He'd left his mark on the house I grew up in, the kitchen I learnt to cook in, the room that had seen every monumental moment of my young adult life.

He'd left a mark on the gardens that surrounded Dot's little yellow house, on the gate that kept the world out that never swung straight, and now does, thanks to him.

I slept until it evaded me completely, my hair completely

dry and sticking out in so many different directions it gave the real meaning to 'bird's nest'.

The garden looked beautiful in the light of the afternoon, and I soon found myself with dirt under my nails, and my fresh pyjamas dirty and ruined. Dot would be furious whenever she found me out here, destroying her garden. But I'd plant her new flowers. I'd give us both a beautiful new garden, with beautiful new flowers that didn't remind me of Nathaniel Connors.

38

Chapter 38

There was order in working your nine to five job.
There was structure, and structure was important.
Routine was important. Rules and reasons for doing things were important.

How were these things established, you might ask? By learning. By doing it wrong and figuring out a way to ensure the task was never done wrong again. Fool me once, and all the jazz.

The unfortunate thing here was that my routine had been flipped. Completely and utterly obliterated. In fact, I doubt I'd even know my past routine if it sat on my face and began to shimmy. What was worse, was that I couldn't very well tear down the library and build it anew, the way I did with Dot's flowers.

She was furious, by the way. She had loved the flowers Nathaniel had picked, and in the colours he'd chosen. I knew that he'd thought about it a lot, and had been nervous amongst his confidence on what she would think. If she'd love them.

Rubbing my chest, I ignored the pang that shot through me,

bringing with it a rolling nausea.

At least the library was quiet, whoever was looking down on me was doing me that solid. I knew it was out of pity, but a win was a win.

I couldn't stop myself from looking at the clock on the wall and then to the door. We were well within the hour of the day that *he* would've already strolled in here, calling out something about needing to tend to his 'leather bound babies' before marching onward and tucking himself away somewhere in the stacks. A task that didn't need doing at all, that I'd made up just for him, just to keep him around.

If Nathaniel had been selfish, then so had I.

That was precisely the thing I'd claimed to hate most about people. Their selfishness and how it led to disappointment. It was the inherit foundation for the system I had built and then let crumble all those months ago.

I hadn't expected him to come, but there was still a bud of hope that tried to bloom inside the cracked fissures of my heart. He didn't, of course. And I was glad of it in the end. It would only make things worse. There was nothing left to salvage in a relationship that was rocky at best, fuelled by the selfishness of two polar opposite people, and then blown to smithereens by my revelation that it was me who was rotten, not the world around me.

If I thought about it enough, and picked it apart, I could imagine that his presence had, truthfully, been so minimal in this part of my life.

It had been a nuisance at the start, hadn't it? He'd filled me with anger so hot it sometimes felt it was burning me from the inside out. I wished for it now.

I had begun to curl in on myself as I sat at my desk, thinking through every thought that acted like another stone being added to my pockets, pulling me deeper down to the murky depths below in the pool of sorrow I'd flung myself into. I was practically a living, breathing, letter 'C'.

I shook myself out, not too dissimilar to what a dog would do after receiving a bath they didn't ask for. I would learn from this. I would, and I would not make the same mistake twice. I would pull out the blueprints to my last system, burn them all, and start fresh. The rules *and* the structure. I would reinforce it with everything I'd come to know, and be better because of it.

I'd always been efficient, and so the days stopped feeling so sluggish, and eventually they turned into weeks on weeks, and then, faster than it ought to have happened, I was sitting at the dinner table with Dot, getting ready to blow out candles on a carrot cake for my twenty-eighth birthday.

I spent the day like I'd spent every single one that had come before it, with Dot, in the comfort of her presence, and in the comfort of my own. Forcing myself to believe it was enough, that it was the life I was meant to have.

My birthday sat in the stunning transition between autumn and winter. My favourite thing to do was sit on the front porch of Dot's house and admire the colours of the trees in her front yard. They were beautiful and bright and what I spent most of my time cleaning up after now.

Along with the days and the weeks, the summer months that consisted of Nathaniel Connors turned cold without him, coating his memory completely in warm days and bright flowers. I had done my best to maintain his philosophy of never lying, even to myself, so I could admit that I spent a good deal of my time trying not to think about him, and all the things I would have said, if given the chance to do it all again.

That new things are fucking scary, and sometimes it's easier to run away. So what? I'm human aren't I? That maybe he'd expected too much from me, and maybe I'd expected too little from myself. And maybe it was all fucking doomed to begin with because I had lied to him right from the start, even though I didn't really know it then. I'd told him it was people that were the problem, forgetting the common denominator between them all was yours truly.

Cue world's smallest violin.

A sigh fell from my mouth that was filled with the weight of everything I seemed to now carry with me everywhere I went. Ripping the birthday hat from my head, I placed it on the table next to the cake.

"Make a wish, Flossy." My grandmother smiled at me from her place next to mine, her hand clutching mine.

"Dot, we don't need to do this every year, you know." I looked at her with pleading eyes. She dropped my hand and ripped the candles from my cake, waving them around haphazardly to extinguish the little flames.

"Florence, I know the sort of woman I raised you to be, and someone who walks around feeling like the world owes her something is not it."

"Wha—."

"Oh, I'm not finished."

I snapped my mouth shut. *Uh-oh.*

"You're a force to be reckoned with, Florence, and when you put your mind to it, you're unstoppable. But you can also be kind, generous, and giving when you let people in. Behind this system you created, whatever that means I still don't really know. We all have our own ways to cope, but you've seen the grass on the other side and you've spent far too much time in this garden to not know it's far greener."

Dot put the candles back into my cake, grabbed the lighter from the kitchen counter and came to sit back next to me.

"You must learn to know when you're wrong, Florence. The world doesn't owe you a single thing. If you want something to happen, you make it happen. If you sit and wait for it to come to you, it never will. If, for some reason, something is dropped on your lap by the grace of the universe, you have a responsibility to see it through, to do better. *Be* better."

Dot lit the candles again and gestured for me to make a wish. I was still looking at her though. "Aren't you supposed to take my side?"

"Absolutely not. What sort of grandmother would I be if I did that?"

I reached out to take her hand before turning back to my cake and making a wish. We moved about the kitchen getting a couple plates, making teas, and sitting down for a slice each.

"You never did say what happened," Dot began, and it only took me off guard because she was never one to pry.

"I didn't think it mattered." I shrugged, shovelling some cake into my mouth. It was awesome, as always. A Dot speciality.

"You know, you never were very good at trusting. Even as a little girl you were never willing to part with your thoughts, even those that weren't secret."

"Do you want to know what happened?"

"Not if you don't want to tell me, Florence."

I didn't, not really. Because the more I talked about it, the more I wanted to change about the whole thing.

We ate our cake in comfortable silence until Dot dropped

a question that I never thought I'd hear her say. "I was wondering, if maybe you'd like to know about your parents?"

"My what?"

"Your parents, Florence."

"I know what I need to know. They had me young, and then they gave me to you." *When I turned out to be everything they didn't want.*

"That's not all there is to it. You're still twisting those words and the only person they're hurting now is you."

My heart was hammering, and I suddenly never wanted to eat carrot cake again. I'd resigned myself to never wanting to know about my parents, namely for self-preservation. Dot had told me to come and ask her when I was ready for answers, and then they just seemed to matter less and less. Or was it more and more? That to have everything I already knew reaffirmed, even if it was delivered in Dot's kindest, most vague of ways, I would be ruined.

I cupped my tea in both hands and sipped it lightly, feeling her eyes on me. I realise that in my refusal to learn about them, I'd also stopped Dot from being able to talk about them. I knew that she was my mothers mother, but that's all.

What if I learnt about them and I didn't like what I learnt? I guess my philosophy had always been to expect the worst and that way I'd never really needed to know and did my best not to care.

"Alright, Dot. You can tell me about them if you'd like." My stomach hollowed out and what was coming was only what I deserved. Punishment for what I'd done to Nate. Making him fall in love with someone who didn't deserve him.

Something in my grandmother's eyes lit ever so slightly, and it made me want to do better, like she said. *Be* better.

"Your mother was very young when she had you, Flossy. Only eighteen, and she was so bright, so colourful. Your father was a couple years older than her and a real go-getter too."

"She sounds like you." I smiled, looking at my grandmother and feeling just so much love, I fought the sting behind my eyes. It was entwined with fear though, because it sounded nothing like me. Maybe that's what had disappointed her first.

"Oh yes, Maisie and I were very close."

That was the first time I'd heard her name in years and it settled over us feeling both familiar and foreign at the same time.

I swallowed. "And my dad?"

"Charlie Valentine was a real life-chaser. He was an academic but also a musician and he was always on the road. Quiet, just like you. When Maisie fell pregnant she was devastated at not being able to head out on tour with him."

Ouch number one. I frowned a little, feeling the truth in how I felt about my presence in their lives. "It sounds like I held her back."

"Oh, not at all, your parents were thrilled about the news of your arrival, Florence. I was a little nervous, given their age. Maisie was still just a girl to me, but they were certain they were ready. Your mother had you just after she finished high school, and loved you as best she could."

"But?"

There was always a but.

"But we were meant for each other right from the start, you and I. As soon as I held you in my arms I knew we'd always be together, that I'd always be there for you."

"Dot." I reached for her hand, my eyes welling up a bit.

We were quiet as we sat there together and I wanted to tell

her but I was worried that I'd throw up before the words got out. She waited, holding my hand tightly as her eyes stayed on me intently, giving me the space to get my words right.

"Sometimes," *all the time*, "it feels as though I was born in a pocket of time that was filled with bad luck." I kept my eyes on our hands, not brave enough to look at her. "An unexpected poor excuse for a gift in the form of a teenage pregnancy. That somehow, though they'd made peace with it, I wasn't what they'd expected, that I disappointed them to the point where they preferred to be apart from me than have me with them. If I wasn't good enough for them, the people biologically programmed to want me, then how could I be for anyone else? And it's followed me around Dot, everywhere I go, everyone I meet.

For a long time I thought it was the world, or maybe I knew it was me but thought if I could shift the blame I could shift the issue, but after Nate," my voice broke on his name and I winced, "I realised that it's me. I'm the jinx, and I let him down. I disappointed him too, beyond anything I've ever done before, and I even tried not to in the end. I really did. You could see that too, couldn't you? But it happened anyway." I felt the tears drip off my chin, fighting the urge to wipe them away. Clinging to the hot trail they left behind to remind myself that I'd finally said the words out loud. Put a voice to my biggest fears.

"I won't tell you that how you feel is wrong, or silly, Florence. I won't pretend that I didn't think there was always something more, and that when you were ready you'd speak about it, and all I could do was watch you closely and hold you tightly 'til you did. But I will ask you one question."

I looked up at my grandmother and nodded my head, feeling

my eyes well with more tears already.

"What do you think of me?"

The question took me off guard, because I told Dot all the time. "I think you're everything, Dot. I think you're kind, strong, and badass." She smiled at that because she thought so too. "I think you were probably a goddess in another life and there is no one better than you."

"You think all that about me?" she asked.

"Every word," I confirmed.

"Florence, there has never been a day that has passed where I haven't thanked my lucky stars for you. Where I haven't looked at you in awe and wondered if I was good enough for you."

"Dot–." I was shaking my head.

"No, you listen here," she cut me off, "I see your beauty in every flower planted in my garden, I see your strength in the trees that help anchor this home to the ground. Proud, and tall and immovable. I see your freedom in the way you dance in that very living room," she nodded behind me, "the way you have almost every week of every year since you were able to walk. First steps that you were brave enough to take with your eyes set on me with so much trust that you knew I'd catch you if you didn't make it all the way. That look is what has driven me every day, of every week, of every month, of every year. To be someone that deserved that look in your little eyes." My bottom lip quivered as I saw the truth of every word she spoke reflect in her face. "If I am what you say I am, if you believe it all Florence, it's only because you made me into the person I am."

I lurched for my grandmother, sobs wracking through me in the ugly sort of way that made you forget about the snot that was dribbling out of your nose. We held each other like that for a long time. Dot rocking us back and forth, humming to another of her favourite songs she couldn't remember the name of. When we finally pulled apart, my cheek peeled off hers, the salty tears having all but fused us together, it sent us into a fit of laughter and I could already feel a shift. The weight seemed to lessen. The pain seemed to dull.

She reached into the pocket of her dress and pulled out a photo of a couple and a little girl. The girl had long wild hair and bright yellow gumboots matched with a pink dress covered in mud. They were standing just out front of Dot's little yellow house.

I knew those gumboots.

"You were three in this photo, and it was just before they headed out on tour again."

I took the photo from Dot and stared at it.

"They loved you very much, Florence, but they were young. Maybe too young to do it on their own. Too young to know what it would take to earn that look in your little eyes, but they did their best because you were worth it all to them."

"I look like her." Flicking my eyes up to Dot, only to find her looking at me already. It wasn't the first time I'd seen a photo of my mother, but it was the first time since I'd settled into my bones as an adult. Since I'd grown out of the weird hairstyles, the baby-fat that didn't shift out of my face when the rest shifted from my body, transforming into the dips and curves of a woman.

"You look exactly like her," she said fondly, if not a little sadly. "One of the band members had fallen asleep through their shift to drive and the van had gone off a bridge into a lake." Dot's hand squeezed mine a little harder.

I looked at my grandmother then and said with everything I could muster, "I'm sorry you had to go through losing them on your own, Dot. That I wasn't able to keep them alive with you."

"I wasn't alone Florence," she lifted my hand up and kissed the back of my hand, "I always had you." And I knew she meant it, I knew that even if I hadn't really known what happened, it was what forged our bond so thoroughly.

"It's okay to open up dear, it's okay to be hurt, to be let down and disappointed or to even be the one doing the disappointing. That's how we learn in life. If things were always peachy you'd never have a chance to learn, and grow. To find out who you really are, and what you really want. It's better to have loved and lost, than to have never loved at all."

My tear ducts were really getting a workout today as a fresh set of big, hot drops practically poured from my eyes. Dot reached out to wipe them away.

"That's a quote from Alfred Lord Tennyson," I laughed and reached out to wipe the tears that had escaped her eyes too. I could count on one hand the amount of times she cried over the course of my life. If you wanted someone who had a firm grasp on their emotions, look no further than my grandmother.

"Well, I'm sure I said it first." She winked and wrapped her arms around me, holding me close. "Happy Birthday, my sweet Florence."

With a kiss on the forehead, Dot left me at the dinner table with only the picture of my parents and my thoughts.

I stayed up staring at it for hours, well into the night. Taking in my little three year old form and her wide, bright smile. A little arm wrapped tightly around each parent.

I felt something I never thought I would. I felt at peace. I didn't see a little girl who'd only disappointed. I saw a young family, happy in each other's arms, and no doubt stumbling through life together, with plans of a big, bright future, of birthday parties already planned in advance, and systems of their own on how they'd navigate the inevitable teenage years that were still so far away, but terrifying nonetheless. Maybe if they'd been given the chance, they wouldn't have left forever without so much as a goodbye, they would've eventually brought me with them, and I'd have been belting out the words to every song my father sung held tight in the arms of my mother as she did the same. That even if my grand entrance into the world hadn't been planned, it wasn't inconvenient. It simply *was,* and that was okay too.

The minutes captured forever in the photo I held tightly didn't seem like they'd been bad, or hard, or unwanted. And all the minutes I had with Dot could never be described as anything but absolutely perfect.

I think they might have wanted the chance to get to know me, and I would have given them the chance too, even knowing there would be bumps and bruises along the way. Knowing that from time to time, I would have disappointed them, and they would have disappointed me.

It would've been worth it. And If I would've given them the chance, then why not anyone else?

39

Chapter 39

I was going to ask Melissa if she wanted to grab a drink. Colour me shocked, surprised, and absolutely shitting myself, but I was going to do it. You know that little saying 'to assume makes an ass out of you and me'? Yes, well I was doing my best to stop assuming things about people, the first being Melissa, who I'd assumed a great many things about and was trying very hard to forget all the opinions I had made up without any reasonable grounds.

I'd been thinking about doing it in the week that had passed since my birthday. Before even considering I had the know-how to apologise to Nathaniel, I needed a friend. A real friend who wasn't related to me.

Just one. Or at the very least an acquaintance.

Forgoing my early end of week knock off, I ended up staying late anyway, needing to keep busy. It was now or never. "Knock knock," I said in lieu of actually knocking on her door.

Stupid start Florence.

"Florence, I thought you were leaving early. Are we still on for Monday?"

She'd asked me to open on Monday and for once, having looked at it through my new lens of life, I didn't mind saying yes at all.

"Oh, yeah," I waved her off. "Monday's all good, I just didn't really have anywhere to be."

"Oh." She gave me a soft smile that I would have usually thought was belittling, but to be honest, it was just a nice smile. It was rather liberating not thinking the worst of literally everyone. Who'd have thought?

"So, I was wondering if you might want to grab a drink after we close up." I definitely said that sentence too fast but it was either all at once or not at all.

"A drink?" She was shocked, I couldn't blame her. Her mouth was hanging open so far I feared she'd catch a fly. It would make sense that my first ever task as her new friend would be to perform the Heimlich to dislodge a *fly*.

"Yes." I smiled genuinely because I knew it was bizarre.

"With you?" She was still, clearly, very shocked, "I mean, I'd love to Florence, but I didn't think you did stuff like that."

"Well I don't. Or, I didn't. I'm trying this new thing where I don't assume things." I shrugged and Melissa laughed lightly, standing from her desk.

"Well, I think that's great. First our lunches and now a drink? I like this new side to Florence, and I have just the place." She winked, grabbed her stuff and towed me out of the library.

Melissa had picked some cocktail bar that was well known for Friday night drinks amongst the younger professionals, and I did my best not to let it show on my face just how far my heart plummeted when we pulled into a park on the same street as one of Nathaniel's bars. The very one we'd actually gone to.

Swell.

Melissa unclicked her seatbelt and started to get her things ready but I couldn't really move.

Deep breaths, Florence.

I wasn't being a bit ridiculous thinking it was a little too close to home, was I?

"Florence, what's wrong with you?" She didn't sound pissed off, even though her question was phrased a little abruptly. I think she was just concerned I was going to go all bitch-supreme on her at any moment and maybe throw up in her car.

"I just need a second," I breathed.

"We can go somewhere–."

"No. No, this is good. Your suggestion sounds awesome. Sorry, I just had a big week."

"Okay, if you're sure." She nodded at me in what I took as just a really nice show of support. It was funny, the moment I stopped assuming the worst from her, everything she did was sort of sweet.

The cold weather grounded me as we walked by the bar. It was bustling, and though I allowed myself to look for him for just the few seconds it took us to walk by the open front doors, I didn't see him.

I let myself wallow in my puddle of self pity for about half a second before pulling up the Dotty-Wisdom she'd bestowed upon me. The world didn't owe me anything. Just do better than what you've done before, and be better than you've been.

No biggy, I can do that.

I poured my energy into Melissa for the rest of the night.

We ended up being out for a few hours, which was impressive even for me. I couldn't get a word in edgewise, but it didn't matter because I really didn't have much to say.

She spoke of her book club, their current read and exploration of indie authors, and her plans for the weekend. Her family loved to do winter barbecues which I thought was nice, and it was her father's birthday on Sunday. She'd just started at a new gym and couldn't get over all the 'super hot dudes' that went to said gym, though she was adamant that it wasn't why she had joined.

I was content to nod along and listen to her share parts of her life that weren't overly exciting, but interesting to learn about all the same. What surprised me most was when she asked me if I wanted to join her book club, that it was just her and five of her girlfriends who all loved books, chatting, and wine.

And what surprised me even more, was that I said yes.

40

Chapter 40

I was nervous, and I'd been nervous over the weekend and the days that followed because it was now Wednesday night and it was also bookclub night.

Bookclub.

It was actually Mel's turn to host which worked out great for me, seeing as we'd gotten lunch together everyday so far this week and that she would give me a lift to hers for bookclub if I wanted to work late.

I fully intended on using the time I had to get things done, but I'd spent pretty much all of it learning about the work of all the indie authors they were loving, and the shifter romance which was going to be the topic of this week's meet up.

Mel had whispered conspiratorially to me over our cocktails last Friday that the contents of this book were well beyond any spicy scene I'd likely ever read. *Ever.* Naturally I was all in and my attention was very much captured.

We locked up the library and walked the block to her car. She couldn't stop chatting about this book, but she was also trying to be broad because I'd ordered them on Amazon and she didn't want to ruin it for me.

"Ruin away, really, I don't mind knowing what happened. The fun is in the detail, isn't it?" I grinned at her.

"Florence!" She swatted at my arm before digging for her car keys, "You're so into the spice, I knew you would be!"

I wagged my eyebrows at her, "I'm just sad I didn't know more about them sooner."

It was freezing, so as soon as we got into the car, Mel wasted no time getting the key in the ignition and blasting the heater.

"Once you give indie a real, serious go, you'll literally never want to read anything else. Oh, that reminds me, I have to stop and get wine."

"Oh, and that reminds me," I reached into my tote and pulled out three bottles of wine I'd wrapped in tea towels and brought from home, "No need!"

"Florence, you're already *such* a bookclub girl you have no idea, the girls are going to love you. I'm so excited I could die." She squealed mid shoulder check as she weaved between the traffic. And they were all incredibly excited to meet me. They arrived together and passed me around for a hug whilst introducing themselves. Sarah, Penelope, Tash, Olivia and Megan. Now, which face belonged to which name I was hard pressed on remembering, but I was getting there.

"Florence is an indie book virgin ladies," Melissa announced from the kitchen, tasked with opening up the wine and pouring everyone a glass. I wasn't, but I couldn't really correct them as they all gasped and squealed with varying amounts of delight, and a plethora of offers of series and book titles were hurled my way in the space of five seconds.

I went with it, because I had read some, but not much. "It's true, but I'm ready to pop that cherry. Bring it on," I announced back in what might have once been a very un-Florence thing to do in front of a group of people I'd only just met. But as soon as the words left my mouth, a glass of wine was thrust into my hand and a toast was being raised in my name.

Before the book chat started, everyone spoke a bit about themselves and I learnt they'd all found each other a few years ago after meeting online, in some corner of Instagram they kept referring to as 'bookstagram'.

It turned out Melissa was a closet book blogger, and it suited her down to the ground. Everyone asked questions about me and I had also had the courage to ask things back, to put myself out there, and every question was easier to get out than the last. Melissa was shocked, and I mean *shocked* to find out I was an only child, and when I mentioned Dot, she couldn't say enough wonderful things which made me beam with pride and happiness.

I'll be honest, I felt shit a total of six times through the evening at all the different moments I hadn't had a too pleasant thought about Melissa, especially having not known her from a bar of soap. I was glad I gave myself the chance to get to know her because it turned out she was pretty great.

When they asked me to come back next week, and the week after, I wasn't surprised in the slightest when I said yes.

41

Chapter 41

I'd spent the last few weekends cleaning up Dots garden. We were firmly planted in winter now, and most of the trees had lost their leaves. The flowers had all either come to the end of their cycle or were dormant, so most of our garden work was prepping for spring.

After the shock of seeing her garden initially destroyed, Dot hadn't been as angry as I'd first assumed. I wasn't sure who cut the cord of their friendship, but I didn't have the ovaries to ask, and Dot never brought it up.

I felt sad for her regardless. I knew she'd enjoyed the time she'd spent with Nathaniel. I'd enjoyed seeing them bond, too. It had been the two of us for a really long time and then all of a sudden, there were three.

I was sitting on the porch looking into the front yard and I still saw him everywhere. It'd been almost two and a half months since he fell off the face of my world and still, everywhere I looked, there were bits and pieces of him.

The chair creaked beside me as Dot settled in with a mug of earl grey tea for herself and peppermint for me. I whispered my thanks as I clutched the mug between both hands. Anything louder felt like it would disturb the peace of the late afternoon.

For a while the steam from our tea was the only real movement between us, and I knew that she was waiting for me to talk. Specifically, I knew she was waiting for me to talk about Nathaniel. Two and a half months was a long time to go without uttering his name out loud.

Dot had done this a few times; sat with me from time to time, always coming with an offering of tea, or cake, or leftover lasagne, and giving me the option to speak. Providing the space, time, and safety to air out my thoughts, no matter what they might be. But I really didn't think I had anything of value to say. Nothing that I thought could really change anything, and if I wasn't moving forward, I might as well be heading the other way.

"I wonder," my grandmother started, earning my attention, "if this is really how it ought to be." I knew what she was talking about. It was Nate, of course.

"I think it's a version of the way it could be." I looked back across the front yard as the sun set everything ablaze with golden light.

"You know," I started after a few breaths, "when I first met Nate, he asked me what it was about him that I didn't like so much. I told him that it wasn't really him at all, but rather people as a whole. I said that they sucked, there was no convincing me otherwise. Do you know what he did?"

Dot smiled, "I can guess."

"He looked me right in the eyes and said 'Challenge accepted.'" Looking back on the memory now it made me smile. Thinking about the dimple in his cheek and the mischief in his eyes. The flair of that subdued British accent of his youth. My smile faltered a bit. "Sometimes I wonder if it was just a game to him, if that's why he hung around as long as he did."

"I don't think that's true for one second Floss, and neither do you." Dot had a crease in her brow, confirming just how much she really didn't think that was true. In a very Nathaniel gesture, I reached out to smooth the crease away and it tugged at my heart.

"No, I don't really believe it, but it felt like that sometimes."

"Trust, Florence," Dot reminded me. "He was the closest that ever got to your heart, and still, I think you mightn't have trusted him as much as you could have. As much as he deserved."

"That's true." I nodded, having learnt in the last couple of months that knowing when you're at fault isn't only helpful to move forward, but to heal. "You've never really been in the business of telling me what to think though, Dot." I quirked an eyebrow at her in mock accusation.

"This is a different thought, isn't it?"

I just nodded and sipped my tea, it was cool enough now that I didn't have to worry about my tongue singeing off. I kept my eyes on my mug as I spoke. "I think there were things on both ends that meant we were both at fault, but he was right when he said I would run away given the chance. I'm a coward."

"You're not." She set her tea down and reached out for my hand, "You're learning, and it's a brave thing to do, to open yourself up to change, especially later in life after your habits are all but set in stone."

"He just left, Dot. Up and left, and disappeared from every part of my life. That's not the actions of a person who wants to be spoken to."

"Yes, but haven't you disappeared for him as well?" She looked at me pointedly.

"Well, I—I guess so." I hadn't really thought about it that way. That he might be waiting for me to make the move.

"Seeing as I'm breaking all the rules tonight, I'll tell you one more thing about what you should do. I think, if you do decide to do anything, that you need to let go of whatever you're holding onto, Florence. It will curdle in your stomach, those feelings and emotions. They fester and they take you down with it. I'm proud of you, of the friends you've made, of how you're more open, and honest and showing the world the woman I've been lucky enough to be privy to these last twenty eight years. I see how you're trying, and I don't want you to just settle for 'okay' or 'good enough'. I know that you know what you want, and I want you to grab onto it with both hands and take it."

42

Chapter 42

I stared at my phone forever.

Gently sipping on the glass of wine I'd poured myself as I sat on the floor of my living room surrounded by a nest of pillows.

I'd begun typing a dozen different things to Nathaniel. The first thing I'd thought of was a request to meet for a coffee. I deleted that one pretty quick, thinking that it might've been too much pressure.

I also had started just trying to explain *why*.

Why I said what I said, did what I did. *Why* I haven't reached out to him at all in almost three months now. The message had surpassed the word count you're allowed to send for a text. Did you even know that was a thing? Well, it was. So I scratched that entirely.

I'd begun another with an apology, and a really clear, and thorough understanding that I knew he'd never want to see me again, but I was sorry for my part in the downfall.

It all felt cowardly to just text him. Nate deserved more than that, and I wanted to give him more than that.

I thought about calling. The silence that would've stretched between us would've been too much to bear. To not be able to speak to him the way I'd learnt how to speak with him.

Show up at his house? Sure, I'd thought about that too. But what if he had a girl over? My stomach dropped at that, even though I had no right to feel that way at all.

I knew I hadn't reached out to him, but he hadn't reached out to me either. I fucked up, for sure. There was no debating that. But he'd fucked up a little too. I could totally stop by his work. But that felt like crossing a line, even though he all but made the library his new address. I drained my wine and rinsed the glass out in the sink, trudging upstairs to my room without taking my eyes from the phone. I wouldn't do any of the things I'd thought of. I wasn't even brave enough to do the cowardly thing and just *text* him.

The best thing, after all, might be to let his life continue on as it had been, without me in it.

43

Chapter 43

I t was still dimly lit in the morning as I walked from the station to the library.

During the winter it was harder to start my days, always a little touch and go with the early wakes. The time was the same, but the sun obviously rose later and it always set me on edge.

I fumbled with the keys to try and get inside as fast as possible. My gloved hands (mittens, not even finger gloves) made it especially hard to hold onto the keys. I could barely breathe with my scarf so tightly wrapped around my neck and face, and I was breathing so hard that I could literally *feel* the condensation forming on my face. It was all so overwhelming that I ended up dropping the keys.

"Crap," I mumbled

The thought of bearing my fingers to the frigid winter morning was about as appealing as having an ice bath, or belly flopping naked into arctic waters, so I was determined to get this done with my mittens in place. Reaching down to grab my keys from the ground, I celebrated with a triumphant

"Yes!" holding up the little metal bastard in a momentary blaze of glory. It was so quiet around me that I noticed when a car door closed behind me. It jarred me enough that I was back to standing and turned around so fast I was 78% sure I'd given myself whiplash, but I wouldn't know until I got this scarf off. The thing was practically a neck brace.

I wished I could've felt something other than my heart falling out of my ass and rolling into oncoming traffic, but that's exactly what happened. I wanted to sob and throw up all at the same time, and then promptly lose consciousness. Hope (that stupid thing with feathers, just like that poem said) burst free in my chest, cascading wave after wave of heat to envelop my entire body, and I wished for a few fleeting moments that it would sweep me up in an inferno and I'd wink from existence.

"Oh." There he was. I was looking at him, and I wanted to laugh and scream all at the same time. "Nathaniel."

He seemed taller. He had a beanie on and a black hoodie paired with his black jeans and boots. He looked the same, but different. I wanted to step towards him, but it left like approaching a wild animal, that if I made any sudden movements, *poof*, he'd disappear all over again.

"Why haven't you called?" His hands were in the pockets of his hoodie while he leaned against his truck.

"What?"

"With your phone, you haven't even called. Not a text or so much as a letter in the mail." He didn't sound mad or angry, he sounded hurt. Broken. Unsure. Like coming here had taken a lot for him to do. He sounded tired and I hated myself more than I did before, because I knew it was me. I was the reason why.

295

"I don't think people really send letters in that capacity any more." I offered him a small smile but he just stared at me.

Alright. I get it.

"Did you even think of calling?" his voice was soft, like he both did and didn't want to know the answer.

"I did." I saw his shoulders ease a fraction.

"And?"

"I had a lot to figure out before I called you."

"And?" he prompted again.

"And what?" If there was something specific he wanted me to say, I wanted to know what it was if only so I could just *say it.*

"Did you figure it out?"

The heat had dissipated as quickly as it came on, now being forced with that question. God, I was fucking *freezing* and we were standing here like it was a spring day with a light breeze.

"I think I've figured some stuff out." I nodded.

He lifted his arms out on either side of him before shoving them back into his pockets. "Enlighten me then, Florence."

"You can't just come out of nowhere and demand that sort of thing like a madman on the street." I gave him a pointed look.

"I think I can." He returned my pointed look.

"Why?"

"Why? Because I think I deserve that much from you."

Okay.

It was silent for a bit and I moved to loosen my scarf. If I was going to do this, I wasn't going to do it with a scarf in front of my face.

"Alright, I think so too." I gave him my full attention. His eyes widened a fraction before he schooled his expression again. Maybe he thought he'd be stepping in front of the Florence he first met.

"I figured out that I wanted to do this in some sort of grand way. In a way that was the apology you deserved, or an explanation that made some sort of sense to a sane person. In a way that we could sit down after, and I could tell you what you did hurt me too, and though I'm sorry, I think you should be sorry too. But I realised after a while that I'd disappeared from your life the same way you disappeared from mine. Well, actually, Dot pointed that part out. She misses you by the way." I was staring at my hands now because *fuck* this was hard.

"Anyway, so I thought maybe that it was for the best. It couldn't have been that enjoyable, trying to convince me of the opposite of something that I'd believed so thoroughly, in all its lying glory. I realised a lot of things after meeting your friends, and after sitting down and realising that no matter how hard I was going to try and fit in with their conversations, everything I would've said to them, would've been a let down. To them. To you." I cast my eyes up to him quickly. His face was unreadable and I hated it.

"It was a hard pill to swallow, realising that the fear that was so deeply rooted in me had nothing to do with anyone else, and everything to do with me. My parents—." I let that trail off, not needing to dig up all that dirt after the grave of those buried emotions had only just begun to sprout a covering of delicate, green grass.

I offered him another small smile. A real one too as I finally lift my chin up to meet his still unreadable gaze. "But I've been trying. I'm friends with Mel now." I smiled wider at that, thinking of the girls in the bookclub and how much I looked forward to seeing them all every week.

"I mean, a few things still irk me but whatever, I know I annoy the daylights out of her from time to time. I'm in a bookclub, and I catch up with friends on the weekends now sometimes too. I know that probably doesn't mean a lot, but I was looking for something that I think I only just now realised."

I looked up to see Nate had stepped forward. The guarded look in his eyes had slipped like he had truly listened to every word I said.

"What did you realise?" His eyes bore into mine and I'd all but forgotten about the cold now.

"That I needed to convince *myself*, Nate. That the world doesn't owe me anything, and it isn't such a bad place. People can be good, yes. But I can also be good for people too. I can be relied on to not let someone down, and even if I do, that's okay. That's how we grow, isn't it? I wanted to convince *myself*. Because then I'd know how I feel is real."

Another step forward, and my heart picked up pace again. "How do you feel?"

He stood unmoving now, his face open but his emotions still held on a tight leash, regardless of how I was handing him my own battered heart.

I gave him a small smile again, turning to slide the key into the door of the library before looking back to him. "I don't know that it matters much any more, does it?"

I waited, I did.

I waited for him to say something. To move, to see a flash of anything across his face that this was what he'd been waiting for, like it had been what I'd been hoping for.

But there was nothing, and I couldn't stand it. It almost broke me right there, but I held it together. Determined to only lose my cool when I was alone, with a locked door between me and the outside world.

Things could've gone a number of different ways, but this was the way I had feared the most. Regardless, I was determined to let go of everything that was eating away at me, because I knew it would fester, just like Dot said.

I nodded and pushed the door open slightly, the warm air of the library seemed too hot now. "That I love you. I wanted to convince myself, so I'd know that even if it's all done now, at least that was real." I tried to give him my best smile even though my lower lip wobbled. The smile that said 'I'm sorry, and have a good life' all in one go.

Pushing into the library I did feel lighter, but also a whole lot worse. I was resolute to keep looking forward and fight every urge in my body to turn around. I wouldn't. So, I walked to my desk like I did every morning, shucking off my jacket, and hanging it over the back of my chair, followed by the scarf and my hat. My heart was still beating wildly, and I fought the catch in my throat that threatened to turn into tears if I let it, but I wouldn't.

Tipping my hair upside down, I ran my fingers through the wavy length to give it back some of the life the beanie had stolen from it (I'd taken to wearing it down more often) and made my way into Mel's office to turn up the heating just a little. After taking off my layers; it wasn't as hot as I'd thought when pressing against the chill from outside. I walked back out into the main reception space just as the front door to the library was pushed open.

My breathing sped up, an echo of every single step he took until I had to tilt my head all the way back to see him. His eyes were searching, looking for whatever he was trying to find. He'd find no walls here. No guarded hearts or systems to keep the world out. Keep *him* out.

He looked at me the way he'd looked at me many times before, and I couldn't help the sheen my eyes took on as I fought the emotions that were going absolutely nuts inside my body.

"I love you too." He sounded breathless, and perfect, and like everything I'd ever need.

I swallowed thickly. "You're only saying that because I said it though, aren't you? How do I know you mean it?" My voice sounded rough with emotion but I didn't care. Let him see every crack and bruise and healing scar.

"Because, Flossy," he reached out to tuck a strand of hair behind my ear, my body erupting in goosebumps and involuntarily moving into his touch, "I never lie."

I was in his arms within the same breath. My hands moved into his hair, and across his shoulders, and just anywhere they could roam.

This was *home*. It was the place I'd longed for since I had the realisation that night after the bar that he'd never hold me the way he had before. This was something I hadn't ever thought I'd get back. That I'd had my once in a lifetime with him, and no one was ever lucky to get that twice.

But I was.

His lips claimed mine and a small, broken noise was pulled from the back of my throat as the tears that fell from me blended with the ones that had made tracks down Nate's own face. I pulled back to reach up and swipe them away, barely holding back a sob as I looked into his eyes, and seeing nothing but clear and unrelenting emotion staring back at me. Open and freely given.

"Nate," I whispered his name into the quiet of the library, scared that if I said it too loud he might disappear.

"Florence," he said back, just as quiet but with no trace of fear. It was filled with absolute calming certainty that he'd never have to be without me again. So, he took my hand and led me back into the stacks of the library that had started off as my haven, and turned into a place we now shared, and I'd never been so happy to be on the opening shift.

44

Epilogue

I t was particularly warm, and I was glad to be housed under the shade of the front porch, sipping on my glass of fresh, home-made lemonade with my favourite floppy hat in place.

A sigh of pure contentment escaped my lips, my eyelids ever so slightly beginning to flutter closed as a yelp of either fear, surprise, or delight snapped me out of my little peace bubble.

"For the love of all that's holy," I mumbled. It was with no semblance of ease that I managed to hoist myself from the chair on the front porch and waddle my way back through the house to the back porch.

"Dot, this is getting out of hand. I *insist* you put the hose down. I don't want things to esc—." Another surprised yelp pierced the air as Nate was being chased around the backyard by Dot who held a hose and wore a wicked grin.

"Ditty, I am *serious*, I have a bucket of water and I won't hesitate to— Florence! Flossy please, help me—," Nate began to whine toward the end, his face crumping in frustrated helplessness.

"No, you don't, you little bugger. I told you 'Ditty' was off the table as a nickname." Dot scowled at him all whilst mumbling to herself that she couldn't believe it had taken her so long to figure out that he'd placed such a loving nickname upon her purely because it rhymed with 'titty'.

Nate had lost it at that, and the look on his face was pure elation as he howled his laughter at the blue sky above us. He was never going to see Dot coming as she finally got him with another spray right to his face, and then they were in hysterics together. I mean that Dot was bent over, clutching her stomach and practically wheezing with joy.

A single moment didn't go to waste as Nathaniel bound across the yard, swooped in to capture the hand of the bucket filled with water, only to launch it directly into my grandmother's face, effectively cutting off her diabolical laughter, and soaking her from head to toe. I was grinning from ear to ear, staring at the pair of them and wondering if they were going to get any of the work done they'd planned to do today.

"You both have the maturity levels of an infant." I attempted to scold them, but all it did was earn me Nate's precious dimples and mischievous grin.

"I've missed you, Florence, can I have a hug?"

"No. No no *nonono.*" I turned as fast as I could, but a fast waddle was about as quick as it sounded. I couldn't risk looking behind me as I made strides for the back door.

"Nathaniel Connors if you put so much as a—." A scream tore from me as Nate pressed his cold, sopping, wet front to my back, soaking the back of my sundress in a way that wasn't entirely unpleasant, but I knew the material would stick to my ass.

303

"Don't upset the pregnant woman!" Dot called out from behind us.

"Yes, exactly. Thank you, Dot." I attempted to release myself from his waterlogged grip but only found myself being turned around and held in place as Nate held us front to front. My rounded belly was now covered in a sopping sundress along with my ass.

"Well, you're going to upset her if you're not careful." I looked down and pointed at the bump between us.

"We can't have that, can we Mrs. Connors?" Nate leaned down to place a kiss behind my ear.

"I'd imagine it would be in your best interest to keep the pregnant lady happy, as well as your daughter. She's due any day now and you don't want to put *her* off."

"So wise. You must get your advice-giving abilities from your grandmother." Nate moved down to place both hands onto my stomach., "And you will probably have all the very best parts of them both. Don't keep us waiting too long, sweetheart." Then he leaned in closer and whispered, "Sorry about the cold water, but you can blame your great-grandmother for that one."

I pretended I didn't hear as I often did, letting him have his private conversation with our little girl. He kissed just above my belly button before leading me back inside and through to my childhood room for something dry to wear. A room that he had spent almost every day of the last nine months fitting out with everything my heart desired, and everything he'd had time to build to make it ready for our newest addition.

"Arms up," he said, as he lifted the dress and dropped it on the floor with a thud beside me. Nate pulled another dress from the closet that was pretty much the exact same as the one

I'd just had on but in a baby blue. It was by far my favourite of
them all. We'd realised very quickly it was best to keep a good
stash of clothes here seeing as we were here most weekends,
and it wasn't so easy to rush home for a quick outfit change,
especially when you were twice the size as everyone else and
moved at half the speed.

"Better?"

"Better. Maybe next time you can save yourself the trouble
and just keep the pregnant lady dry," I muttered, moving to
knead my back to alleviate the pressure that'd been growing
there the last week or so.

"I could, but where's the fun in that?" He grinned at me in
the infectious way of his, leading me back to my spot on the
front porch and popping himself beside me. "How are you
feeling?" he asked, stealing a sip of my lemonade.

"Same as yesterday and the day before, just a little cramping
and my back *hurts*."

"I'll leave you to relax, and I promise we'll keep it down."
Nate got up, leaning down to give me a kiss before leaving
with my glass of lemonade in hand and a cheeky grin on his
face.

We had tied the knot the year before and it wasn't long after
we found out we were expecting. It was terrifying at the start,
the prospect of growing and raising a child, but the look on
Nate's face when I told him was one of the top five moments
of my entire life, and I already knew she'd be his carbon copy.
I hoped for it every single day.

It was with that thought that I fell into a sleep, lulled away
by the breeze that cooled my flushed skin and the rustling of
the leaves in the trees.

I was jolted awake and realised I must've dozed off with

my drink in my hand. My face scrunched, feeling it spill all down the front of me, through my dress, and onto the chair. I groaned knowing I'd have to change *again* and it was a mission to even breathe at this stage.

But then I realised that Nate had taken my drink with him, and I hadn't been holding it when I fell asleep.

"Oh, shit," I said. "Oh, shit. Oh, shit. Nate! Nate! *Nathaniel. Oh, shit.*" Bless his soul, he flew out the door so fast there should've been skid marks on the porch beneath his feet. He looked from me to my dress to the little growing puddle on the floor beneath me.

"Oh, my god." He was breathless, and flushed, and so excited. "Is it time? It's time, right? Oh, my god, it's time! Dot! It's time!"

I heard Dot yell something incoherent from the other side of the house but all I could do was focus on Nate. "It's time," I reached for him to help me up, holding his hand firmly, and not letting go.

He pulled me to my feet. "It's really time." He grinned at me and I craned my neck to ask for a kiss which he kindly obliged.

"Alright, my love." I let him lead me back through the house before he ran to get Dot. "Let's go have our girl."

About the Author

Celine L. A. Simpson is an Australian romance and fantasy author, a dog mum, Punk Rock enthusiast, and owns at least 6 dungarees that she consistently pairs with Converse.

Most commonly known for her Romance publication Music to my Ears (2021), she was raised on the Mid-North Coast of Australia and graduated from La Trobe University with a Bachelors Degree in Creative Arts, majoring in Creative and Professional Writing. Growing up with a passion for reading, she began writing at an early age, moving into content creation as a career path before writing and publishing her own novels.

Also by Celine L. A. Simpson

Music To My Ears

"He had one of those side, half smiles that you read about...I always thought that was absolute nonsense - no single smile could make you want to cry out for mercy, but there you have it.

I did manage to, however, maintain enough of my dignity to cry on the inside."

Allie could sum up her entire life in two whole minutes. She lived walking distance to everything; work, her best friend's place and perhaps most importantly, the 24-hour corner store that was only a 1-minute walk away. Allie frequently sought comfort from the bottom of premixed brownie boxes at all times of the evening when she perused the baking aisle alone, until one night...

Wyatt Smith was the frontman of the most popular modern rock band to date. Lady Luck travelled the world, their look and their music was recognized by everyone, everywhere. That was until he found himself the midnight errand boy for a runaway baking ingredient where he met Allie. And she had absolutely no idea who he was...

It's true that when someone catches your eye you start to see them everywhere.

But what happens when you do see them again?

Sometimes it's easier to put feelings in boxes, and sometimes it's easier to run away when the going gets tough. But sometimes you find someone to help you unpack, someone who will stand beside you, feel the fear, and take that leap of faith with you.

Terraleise (The Lost Child of the Crown #1)

Terraleise turns 18, only to discover she is now gifted with the elemental power of Earth. The thing about elemental gifts is that only those with royal blood possess them.

Terraleise is thrown into a life she never dreamed to be a part of, discovering all of the secrets entwined with her past, and her future. The heir to a kingdom overthrown by a corrupt branch of her own bloodline, Terra will see what it means to have courage and be brave, learning that the fate of the four kingdoms of Vaashaa rests on her shoulders.

Finding a life to fight for only to be faced with sacrificing it all, Terraleise will have to risk her love and her life to keep the world from falling into darkness. Will the Lost Child of the Crown find her rightful place?

Heir of Vaashaa (The Lost Child of the Crown #2)

The land is dying and the promise of war is thick in the air. With Terraleise still held captive by the enemy, Silas is forced out of his grief to move forward, to march on and ensure Terra's sacrifice, her life for his, doesn't go to waste.

The threat to the World of Vaashaa is more horrific than anyone could have ever anticipated. A long-forgotten darkness has crept back into the hands of the wrong person and time is running out to stop it. The Kingdoms of Vaashaa will have to come together to save their world from the bleak future it is heading towards, all while hoping for aid to come from the truths laced within myths and legends.

There is only one who stands to be a force between the darkness and the light, only one who can save them all. Will the Heir of Vaashaa rise from the ashes?

www.ingramcontent.com/pod-product-compliance
Lightning Source LLC
Chambersburg PA
CBHW030529120726
47904CB00005B/1685